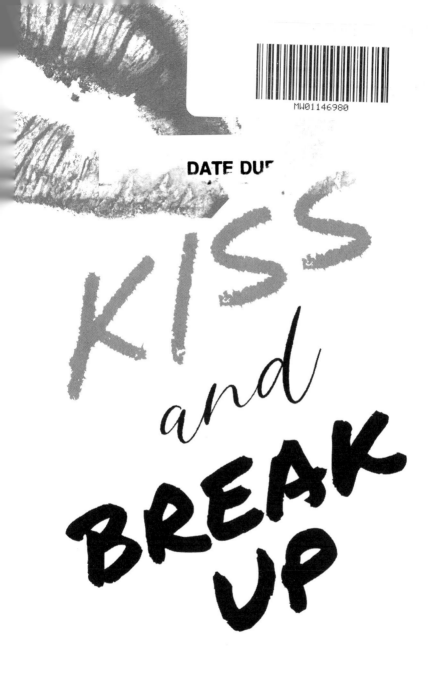

DATE DUE

KISS *and* BREAK UP

ELLA FIELDS

For Taryn
Who knows my heart and seems to like it anyway

There's no knife sharper than that of betrayal

ONE

Peggy

My tongue skated across my teeth for the millionth time since yesterday, feeling the smooth enamel, the freedom that had become my mouth.

"You keep staring at them, poking and prodding the way you're doing, and soon enough, you're not going to have any teeth left to lust over."

My lips smacked closed, and I spun around, glaring at my mother. "Two years, Mom. Almost two whole freaking years of tasting metal. Let me lust a little."

"Another day, then I want to see you doing something more productive with the last few weeks of summer break." She adjusted her hold of the laundry basket on her hip, then scowled. "And watch your damn mouth." I smirked as she walked away, then groaned when she called out, "Meet me in the car; our appointments are in fifteen minutes."

"We've barely been home an hour. I haven't even had time to check my updates yet."

"Updates smupdates. Your hair needs a trim, and my grays are showing."

She had about five gray hairs, but if Phil, Mom's boyfriend, or I tried to remind her of that, she'd give us the hairiest eyeball known to mankind. The truth was, she enjoyed going to the salon every month. As much as our lives had changed over the past eight years, certain things from our previous life, like pampering oneself, never would.

My phone beeped for the second time as I was stuffing my feet back into my boots. I plucked it from my waistband, moving the layers of puffy material to reach it. Not very practical, but a lot of my skirts didn't have pockets, and I wasn't a big fan of purses.

I kept any change I had in my bra. While I unlocked my phone, I gave my chest a pat, checking I had a twenty in there.

Dash the Demon: What gives?

Dash the Demon: Freckles, this isn't funny. You said twelve. It's now one o'clock, in case you can't tell the time.

Dash the Demon: … but you can. Which means you're actually ignoring your pledge to the cause.

With a huff, I blew some curls from my face and responded.

Me: Going to salon. Need a trim, Jim.

Dash the Demon: Who the fuck is Jim?

Dash the Demon: Never mind. You're the worst kind of person. I hope they cut off all your hair and leave you bald.

Laughing, I locked my phone and barreled down the hall as Mom's car started up.

Checking the door was locked, I pulled it shut behind me, then jumped down the three steps off our porch, and bounded over to her Honda CRV.

My phone beeped again in my lap, but I ignored it.

"Dash isn't happy?" Mom asked as she backed out onto the street.

I pulled down the visor, checking my teeth again. "When is Dash ever happy?"

She laughed as she straightened the wheel, tires crunching over the pebbles that'd escaped the newly lined driveway next door. "True."

Dashiell Thane had been my best friend for as long as I could remember. He wouldn't have been my first choice, but then again, since he learned how to talk and use his words and that scowl as a weapon, I never really had a choice.

One of the earliest memories I had of him was from preschool. He'd tipped ice-cold water from the water station over my head, then said I'd formally been initiated as his best friend. I hadn't wanted to be his best friend, but whenever I'd screamed that at him over the following years, he'd give one of those infuriating smiles and simply say, "Like I care, Freckles."

And that had been that.

I had no say, and if I was being honest, sometimes it still bothered me. But as the years swung on, I'd somehow grown to care about the asshole. He was the brother I never ever wanted.

"I'm dying to know if that boy has caused May to go gray yet," Mom said with a dry lilt to her voice.

Once upon a time, our mothers, May and Peony, had been best friends. They'd met in college, and before they graduated, they'd made a pact. Marry rich and never settle for love. The crazy idea had worked, though my mother married a man almost twice her age, my dad, while May had scored a guy ten years her senior with the looks to go with it.

May didn't care about her husband's affairs with any woman wearing a skirt or blouse too tight at his company because she'd been smart and hadn't fallen in love.

However, she was rather fond of their gardener, Emanuel, a man eight years her junior, though she'd never admit it or leave Mikael, her husband, for him. That would mean giving up everything she loved.

Money.

"Probably," I said through a yawn, eyeing the small row of shops up ahead. "But it's not like anyone will ever see it."

Mom's lips pursed and what sounded like a sigh slipped out as they parted.

Mom met her boyfriend, Phil, when I was ten. Phil taught English at the public high school, treated her like a queen, and drove a secondhand white truck with a dent in the bumper he still hadn't fixed all these years later.

We'd moved out of my father's mansion by the bay a month later, and even though she did seem to love Phil, we hadn't moved in with him. He didn't live with us either, though he was often at our place. Somewhere along the way, I guess my mother had grown tired of being a kept woman, and that was when the rift between her and May had formed.

She'd gotten a job.

Working at the local library four days a week didn't pay much, but it was enough for her to be able to put aside a nest egg, thank my father for everything he'd done for her, then high-tail it out of there as soon as the moving truck had arrived.

From mansions to three-bedroom cottages and ball gowns to Chucks and worn denim, when I was ten, my life changed overnight, and even though I'd been petrified, it didn't take me long to realize we'd be just fine.

Dad had offered for me to stay with him, and although it would've been convenient to keep living close to Dash, who remained one of my few friends, I'd declined. If Dashiell wanted to see me, he'd find a way.

And find a way he did. Though it took him longer than I'd have liked to quit griping about slumming it in the 'burbs, and he still complained about the mildew scent that drifted off the creek and seeped into our windows.

I loved that creek. It ran right along the edge of our back-yard, and while the amount of mosquito repellent I needed to wear out there left me smelling like a walking chemical, listening to the water gurgling downstream through my cracked open window was the best lullaby I'd ever been sung.

Hair Repair was a tiny salon smothered in purple. Purple chairs, purple sinks, purple countertop, purple dryers … and you get the point.

Suella smiled as I walked in, twisting a chair she'd just wiped down with a towel. I marched over and slumped into it, grinning into the mirror.

She gasped, slapping my shoulder and spinning me around to grab my chin. "It's about time, girlfriend. Just in time for senior year." She gasped again, her glittery acrylic nails digging into my skin as the overbearing scent of Chanel hit my sinuses. "Homecoming. Oh, tell me you're already hunting for a dress."

Pulling out my phone, I lost her harsh grip on my chin as I spun around and rearranged my skirt, getting comfortable. "I already know which dress I'm wearing."

Mom groaned, taking a seat in a chair beside me as her hairdresser and close friend, Bev, finished up with a call at the front counter. "She found this god-awful thing in the thrift store a month ago. Her father said he'd buy her any dress she wanted, but no, of course she picks something that costs fifteen dollars and reeks of mothballs."

I unlocked the screen of my phone.

Dash the Demon: Are you bald yet?

As Suella spritzed water over my hair, I tapped out a message while Mom described the bubblegum pink eighties gown and its layers upon layers of tulle and ruffles.

Me: Negative.

Dash the Demon: Hmm. One-word response. You're mad?

Me: No.

I laughed as he no doubt overanalyzed every facet of my second one-word response. I'd cop an earful later, but I didn't care.

"You can't wear that dress," Suella said, dragging a comb through my hair.

I tucked my phone in my lap, wincing as the comb snagged on a knot. "I can and I will."

Mom sighed, opening a magazine.

Suella pinched her lips together as I met her stare in the mirror. "So what are we doing? Trim?"

About to nod, I studied the long curls that fell into a frizzy mess around my face and down my back. *Hagrid hair* had been how the fantastic people I'd attended school with described it.

Dash's texts came to mind. I smiled, seeing the pearly, straight whites of my teeth, and exhilaration coursed through me.

"Let's cut it all off."

Mom sucked in a shocked breath, the magazine slipping and almost falling to the purple painted concrete floor.

Suella grinned, then immediately got to work.

As blonde curls tumbled, splashing onto the ground around Suella's knee-high black boots, my slick hands slowly unclenched, relinquishing the grip on my phone.

While Mom was waiting for her color to be rinsed, I decided to head to the newsstand to find the latest issue of *Scrapbook & Cards Today.*

The breeze kissed my legs as I stepped outside, my new hair bouncing around my shoulders. Suella had dried the curls into soft waves, and the absence of the heaviness that typically fell over my back and shoulders had my lips curving.

Outside the poster smeared shop, I waited for two guys I recognized from school to pass, who barely paid me any notice, nothing unusual there, then quickly took a selfie.

Inside, the scent of magazines caused my chest to flutter, and I waved to Rich behind the counter before scurrying over to the craft section.

With a magazine in one hand and my phone in the other, I paused as soon as I heard the latter beep.

Willa: I'm sorry, I think you have the wrong number.
Daphne: Right?! Talk about a lame case of *who the hell are you and what have you done with my friend?*

I texted back, trying to contain my smile as someone crept behind me in the otherwise empty aisle.

Me: CRAZY! I feel like a brand-new person.

"Hey. Peggy, right?" a deep voice asked.

I almost dropped my phone, pivoting slightly to discover a broad, hard chest. My eyes zoomed up, and the face of Byron Woods stared down at me.

"Uh, yeah." I laughed the type of nervous laugh that made me want to smack myself. "That's me."

What did he want, and why was he smiling at me?

His bright whites held my attention. So much so, it took me too long to notice the smooth lips around them moving.

"I'm sorry, what?"

He chuckled. "I said, I just passed you outside, but you must not have seen me."

"Oh, my bad."

"I didn't want to go all stalker on you, but …" He seemed to be flushing a little. "There's a party this weekend at Wade's house. Ah, so I just thought I'd see if you knew about it."

I lowered my lashes, shifting. "I do now."

"Right." He ran a hand over his close-cropped hair, huffing out a laugh. "I guess what I meant to say is, it'd be pretty cool if I saw you there."

My stomach dipped, and my hand grew clammy around the glossy cover of the magazine. *He was asking me out?* Maybe? I didn't know. All I knew was that Byron was cute in that boy-next-door kind of way. Okay, cute was probably an understatement. He was tall, muscular in all kinds of lovely places thanks to being on the lacrosse team, and had deep brown hair and biting green eyes.

And, as far as I knew when school had let out, not single.

"Don't you have a girlfriend?" I blurted, immediately cringing.

"Not anymore." He eyed my phone, which was hanging precariously between my slippery fingers, as if he was contemplating asking for my number. "So I'll see you Friday?"

All I could do was nod and watch him swagger outside to where his friend Danny was waiting.

Not anymore.

What did that even mean?

Panic mixed with excitement, and unable to pinpoint which one was winning, I fired off another text.

Me: Emergency meeting required. Meet me at my place tomorrow.

TWO

Peggy

"He and Kayla apparently broke up like two weeks ago after she was caught making out with some college guy at a party." Willa took a sip of soda. "Pictures everywhere." Setting her can down, she flipped some of her long, wavy brown hair over her shoulder and started fiddling with the box of lace.

Mom was at work, which was why I'd waited to hold this little gathering until today even though I'd been desperate.

It was hard enough to deal with Dash, who'd persistently said I was acting weird when I'd gotten home yesterday and logged on to play *Blitz*.

I'd brushed him off, but he wouldn't be kept in the dark long.

The way he had to pry into every facet of my life infuriated me. Nothing was sacred. But when it came to him, he'd look at me like I was crazy if I ever dared to ask about what he was doing or who he'd slept with.

"That's gotta suck." I spun the glue gun around on the table, resting my chin on my fist.

Daphne was the only one of us actually scrapbooking. Today, she'd brought along some vintage stamps she'd purchased for a huge sum on eBay, and she was using them to make a border in the album she'd been working on.

Though she didn't seem to care, Daphne was the most popular out of the three of us. Her green eyes glowed in a way that snatched anyone's attention. Paired with her silky straight dark brown hair, she was damn near mesmerizing to look at. Her confidence was another striking quality. It was the ease in which she held herself and the way she didn't care about anyone else's opinions of her that drew me to her.

"I'm done with Kayla's shit," she said, a long finger smoothing over her page. "She's the worst kind of bitch."

"Does that mean you'll sit with us at school now?" Willa asked.

Daphne's brows furrowed, and she sat back in the dining chair. "I do sit with you." When we said nothing, she looked at me. "Pegs?"

"Well," I hemmed. "I mean … sometimes?"

Her lips pursed as she sat with that a moment. "As I said, done. So sometimes will now be all the time."

Willa and I remained quiet.

It wasn't that Daphne was ashamed to hang out with us. We weren't exactly losers. It was that she'd befriended us over our mutual love for crafting early last year in art class, but she'd been with the *it* crowd all through high school. Elementary too.

"Back to Byron." I shifted a little. "Was he asking me out?"

"He was so asking you out," Willa said.

Daphne raked her hands through her hair. "He didn't ask you out. It's not a date, but he does want to hang with you. That, my friend, was the least formal, official way of asking you to."

Willa and I glanced at one another, then I nodded. "And I should?"

Daphne made a sound of frustration. "Do you need a slap to the face?"

"Uh …"

She continued, "You're freaking gorgeous. He wants you,

just as a lot of guys at school probably secretly do. So quit acting like you're so shocked."

My tongue dried thanks to my mouth hanging wide open. "But, um, I *am* shocked."

Willa's eyes ping-ponged between us with her soda can poised at her lips.

Daphne's expression smoothed, and her voice gentled. "Look, guys have always noticed you. Dash just doesn't let them notice too long."

"Dash?"

Willa coughed.

"Yes, dummy. He's stamping out fires before they even start." She paused, green eyes narrowing on me. "You so already know that."

"I guess, yeah." I wasn't lying. I knew he was protective of me in his own weird, asshole-ish way, but I wasn't sure it happened as much as Daphne was implying.

Daphne and Willa shared similar smiles as Daphne murmured, "Well, I guess they are, or at least Byron is, done giving a crap what Dash Thane thinks."

After they left, I cleaned up and took my unopened album to my room.

This non-date thing was confusing. Maybe Byron did just want to hang with me, and maybe that was okay. Or maybe not. Was *hang* code for something? I made a mental note to ask Daphne about it later.

I would've screamed at the sight of the body splayed over my bed, the combat boots and leather jacket in a heap on the floor, but it was too common an occurrence to startle me.

"You're not bald."

I smirked, dodging last night's pajamas on my bedroom floor. "Never said I was."

"You never said you weren't either." Dash set down the book he'd brought with him and pulled his thick, black framed reading glasses off.

I put the album on my desk, then traipsed over to the bed and crawled over his legs, clad in their usual black denim, to sit against the wall by the window he'd crawled through.

"It would've looked good on you."

I raised a brow at him. "Shut up."

He chewed on the arm of his glasses, narrowing his sea blue eyes on my face. "You look different."

Yawning, I mumbled, "Haircut, remember?"

His golden blond hair was perfectly coiffed, pushed back one too many times and therefore permanently styled to stay off his face.

That hair, his angular cheekbones, and the dimple that appeared when he smirked had many foolish girls looking past his vulgar actions and nasty vocabulary, intent on trying to tame the untamable.

"Who would've thought getting that metal off your teeth would make you so brave?"

"Don't even start."

"Oh, I haven't." He sat up on his elbows and let his gaze travel over me. "I liked your long hair."

"And I like being able to walk into my bedroom naked after a shower, but I haven't been able to do that for years."

He didn't even crack a smile. "I've seen you naked."

"Before I had boobs, Dash." I picked at the chipped pink polish on my nails.

"I wouldn't give a shit."

That deep, velvet-singed voice and those words grated. "I would."

He hung his glasses from the V of his white shirt. "What's eating at you?"

"Nothing." I coughed, realizing too late I'd managed to mess up saying one word.

"My, my," he drawled. "You're turning as pink as that ugly ass polish on your nails."

I said nothing and went to climb off the bed. Maybe if I got the vacuum out, he'd take that as his cue to leave. Though he never had before. Dash came and went when he wanted, living on no one else's timeline but his own.

"If you're done with the insults for today …"

"Sit down."

"What?" I almost yelled.

He grabbed my wrist, pulling me back down onto the bed. "You've been acting weird since yesterday. Speak."

"Speak?" An incredulous laugh burst free. "I'm not a freaking dog."

A thick brow rose. "I didn't say you were. But I feel I do need to encourage you to use your words, which is fucking frustrating to say the least."

"Let's play *Blitz*."

"Fuck *Blitz*."

Oh, shit. If that couldn't even sway his attention, then there'd be no swaying at all.

I slouched, shoving his feet away. "I ran into Byron from school yesterday after getting my hair done."

"In the physical sense? Elaborate."

"At the newsstand. He, um …" I blew out a breath that pushed some of my rogue curls aside. "He asked me to go to Wade's party this weekend."

Silence blanketed the room; the buzzing insects outside the only sound.

I looked over at Dash, my stomach flip flopping. We didn't talk about boys. *Ever.* There usually wasn't any need. Any crushes I'd had, I kept to myself or told Willa and Daphne.

"How sweet," he finally said, tone mocking. "And are you going to go to this party?"

"I'm considering it," I admitted, relieved he'd finally said something. "Daphne and Willa might come too."

"Good. They might be able to keep the filthy animal from trying to get into your pants."

Shocked, I swallowed a hard inhalation. "Filthy animal?"

Dash sat up, his white shirt shifting over his tanned stomach, flashing a glimpse of the dark hair above his jeans. I looked away. Whenever I caught myself looking at him, a creeping feeling a lot like shame washed over me. Not only was he not my type—because he was horrible—but he was also like a brother to me.

"Woods only wants one thing from you, Freckles. He's on the rebound. So don't get too ahead of yourself."

My shoulders slumped, and I bit my lip to curb the disappointment I felt threading inside.

"Let's play." Dash switched my small TV on, then the Xbox, and returned to his spot on the bed, tossing me the second controller.

I stared at it a moment while he logged on since he knew all my passwords and then picked it up.

I didn't want to play. I wanted to ask why boys were so confusing, but that would've been weird. "Don't shoot me this time."

"It was an accident."

I tutted. "Sure, sure."

THREE

Dash

"My heels are getting stuck in the dirt," Mila whined.

Jackson cranked his bike beside me, the sound thankfully drowning her out.

He gave me a look that said, *what was she even doing here?*

I shrugged, then jabbed a finger over my shoulder at Lars, who was sucking back a cigarette and fiddling with my two-stroke's spokes after hitting a boulder the size of Mila's melon-esque head.

Lars was too poor to buy his own bike, so whenever we got the urge to ride, he used mine.

He once had his own, a Honda older than my mom, but admitted he'd sold it to pay for school uniforms two years ago.

Regardless, that didn't mean I wouldn't rip his shirt from his back if he fucked those wheels. They were worth more than the bike itself. Kind of stupid, but whatever.

"Lars, did you invite the melon?"

Lars flicked his ash to the packed dirt, looking back over the grass speckled hills to where Mila was stumbling.

You could see my house through the trees if you squinted. Three acres of undeveloped land was all mine for the taking. Dad purchased it with the house, and he never failed to remind me that I should be outside riding the bikes that cost him a small fortune instead of playing video games. I didn't take suggestions or reminders too well. So I guess you could say I didn't take them at all. I rode when I wanted to and never when he pointed out that I should.

"Shit." Lars spat on the ground, then stubbed out his cigarette.

I frowned, adjusting my gloves as he smashed down his helmet and threw his leg over the seat. A second later, he was tearing off into the orange smeared sunset.

Jackson shook his head, his eyes laughing before he did the same.

Halting some feet away, Mila watched them go, then looked at me with clear dismay. I shrugged, slapped my goggles on, then sprayed her with dirt as I raced off after them.

We thundered over the jumps, clefts, and ditches we'd created after hours of patting, shoveling, and using the bulldozer Dad had bought me last Christmas.

Twenty minutes later, near the edge of our property, we stopped by the small stream hidden behind a smattering of rocks and weeds.

Lars pulled off his helmet, swiping back his sweat-soaked hair. "Do you think she's gone?"

"She's probably still hobbling back to her car." I set my helmet on my lap, then plucked out my pack of cigarettes from my pants. They were squashed, as expected, but they'd do.

Jackson leaned over his handle bars, his cheeks mottled as he pushed a loud burst of air past his lips. "What was she doing here?"

We were in as good a shape as we could be for a bunch of idiots who drank, smoked, and took the odd drug here and there. But I didn't care. I'd quit racing when I was fifteen and found more interesting things to do with my time. Things which, of course, involved my dick.

Jackson still raced from time to time. Lars never did. Too

costly to upkeep.

Lars looked a little chagrined. "I might have said I was riding here today when she called me."

"You actually answered?" I scoffed. "Dipshit."

"I was half asleep when my phone rang." He looked through the trees. "I thought she'd given up."

Jackson tutted. "You thought wrong. How long has it been since you dipped in that anyway?"

"Right before school let out. At that huge bay party."

I laughed.

Lars's worn boots kicked at a sharp looking rock. "She wanted to meet up, and I said I'd be too busy riding to hang. Guess she didn't take the hint."

I'd be concerned that she knew where I lived, but everyone knew where most people lived in this hellish town.

Jackson pushed his hair back, sliding his helmet on. "The word no doesn't exist in Mila Groove's vocabulary."

"You'd know, you savage." I drew in a deep inhale, coughing laughter as he flipped me off.

"I never fucked her. That was Rave."

I pondered that, then decided I didn't give a fuck.

"Enough vag talk," Lars said. "Wade's having another party Friday. We in?"

I felt my body pull taut as I remembered Peggy mentioning that Byron Woods had asked her to go. Though the guy had some nerve, I wasn't worried. Peggy probably wouldn't even go.

I'd texted her this morning, telling her she should come over for a ride. It wasn't something she did very often, but she usually made a point to during the summer. We were a few weeks shy of returning to school, and she'd yet to take me up on the offer. She couldn't ride well, but she liked riding with me. At least, I thought she did.

I wasn't privy to what she was doing instead, and I didn't really care to be. Probably scrapbooking, Instagramming, or thrift shopping. Maybe staring at her metal-free teeth in the mirror for hours on end.

"Get up."

Peggy moaned and rolled over, peeling an eye open.

"Freckles. You promised me."

"Promised what?" she said, but it came out slightly mumbled.

"That you'd come riding with me." My brows cinched. "What's wrong with you?"

Her tongue snuck out to glide between her lips, and she winced, then grabbed a pillow and shoved it over her face. "It kind of hurts, Dash."

Shit. I'd forgotten today was the day she was fixing some of the gaps between her teeth. I wasn't even sure why she was bothering; her teeth were pretty much perfect as they were. But she'd been wanting them since sophomore year after seeing Daphne's teeth slowly change into perfect pearls. Her words, not mine.

I hadn't needed them. Thank fuck. But even if I had, fuck that. No metal was getting near my mouth unless it was in the form of some chick's piercing.

She'd mentioned her dad was taking her, but time had either flown, or I was a forgetful ass. I was thinking a combination of both.

"What'd they do? Saw your gums open?" I tried to make light of it to see if she'd laugh. I failed.

She threw her middle finger up, making some grunting sound. "Go riding without me."

"I told the guys to scram because I know you don't like them giving you shit."

She was cool with me giving her shit but not so much the rest of my friends.

"In case you didn't hear me the first time, the answer is no." Her purple pillow muffled her voice.

I walked over, climbed onto the edge of the bed, and snatched it off her face. "Show me."

Her gray eyes rounded. "No."

"Come on. Unless you're going to have a change of heart and ply the suckers off, I'm going to see them eventually. Open up."

Her nose twitched, then she sighed and cringed as she opened her mouth, forcing a wide smile.

The braces were an assortment of colors, ranging from blue, green, purple, and pink. "Huh," I said. "Not as bad as I thought."

She tossed a pillow at me. "Get lost."

Grabbing it, I laughed and flopped down beside her. "What do they feel like?"

She took a minute to think about it. "Like something's constantly pulling at my teeth."

I snorted. "Duh."

She reached over and slapped me. I squeezed her hand before propping myself up on my elbow to grab the TV remote. "It shouldn't feel weird for too long, right?"

"It's not supposed to, no."

I flicked through Netflix. "We'll go riding this weekend, then. No ditching this time."

Peggy was silent for a moment. "What are you doing?"

I settled back into the pillow, folding my arms behind my head. "Watching Inglorious Bastards.*" It was one of our favorite movies.*

When I glanced over, I found her smiling. Her lips were shut, but she was still smiling. "Thanks."

I smirked, giving my attention back to the TV. "Shut up, metal mouth."

"... guess I'll let you know," Jackson said, pulling me out of my musings as he kick-started his bike. He'd yet to upgrade. He said it didn't feel like a dirt bike when you could switch it on with a push of a button.

I'd agreed until I tried it for myself. His loss was all I had to say.

Lars scratched his head. "Dash?"

Shoving my goggles and helmet back on, I pretended to ponder it. Even if Peggy didn't, I needed to go. Byron needed a friendly little reminder not to play rebound with my best friend. "Sure, why not."

It wasn't personal.

I was sure Peggy would meet a nice guy someday, and I'd be happy for her, but it wouldn't be any of the assholes from Magnolia Cove Prep. So, until then, it was my job to make sure none of them fucked with her.

FOUR

Peggy

The day before the party, I woke from an afternoon nap with my headphones and cords tangled around my face and half a dozen messages from Dash on the TV screen.

I ignored them, untangled myself, then switched everything off.

My new hair was a mess, an actual bird's nest hanging every which way atop my head, so I decided to wash it for the first time since having it cut.

Afterward, I cracked open the bathroom door, steam billowing out into the hall that smelled of Phil's award-winning spaghetti.

I wasn't even joking. He often reminded us that when he was in college, working as a chef four nights a week, he'd entered the dish in a local contest and placed runner-up.

My stomach grumbled. I toweled off my hair, tossed the towel into the hamper, missed and cursed as I went to pick it up so Mom didn't have a fit, and then hustled to the kitchen.

"Hey, Pegs." Phil smiled, stirring the delicious scent in the pot on the small olive green stovetop.

"Hi." I glanced around, looking for Mom, then saw her head over the back of the couch in the living room. "How long until it's ready?"

"About ten." His head tilted, and he scratched his short beard. "You get a haircut?"

"Sure did." I fluffed my wet locks.

He chuckled. "Well, when you look less drowned, I'm sure it's fantastic."

"Gee thanks." I headed to the living room and parked my behind next to Mom, who was reading on her Kindle.

"What's happening?"

"Hmm?" She didn't remove her eyes from the screen.

I tapped my hands over my bare legs, trying to figure out a way to tell her about the party tomorrow night. I'd been to a few before, but they were more like small gatherings and never with alcohol.

Out with it, I told myself. Then I channeled Dash. *Speak.* "So, ah, there's this party at Wade Eldin's tomorrow night."

That did it.

Her head snapped up, her lashes fluttering around gray-blue eyes so much like my own. "Wade Eldin?"

"Yep."

"A party?"

I nodded. "Yeah, you know, those shindigs where people make out, take drugs, and get drunk?"

Her caramel hair fell over her shoulder as she laughed. "Well, sure. What time shall I take you? We can stop at the liquor store on the way."

I laughed too but then sobered. "I'm sure it's not that bad. I do want to go, and you trust me, right?"

She heaved out a breath and set her Kindle aside before hiking a leg up and curling toward me. "I trust you. It's the other misfits who attend these things who I don't trust." Her eyes widened. "Not that long ago, I was young and attended these things."

Moving my foot to the couch, I shoved my knee beneath my chin. "I'll take one of the girls with me."

"Willa? I feel like she's less likely to get you into any trouble."

I grinned. "Daphne isn't some deviant."

"No, but she's certainly more used to that crowd than you are."

"All the more reason to have her with me. She'll know the score. What to do. What not to do." I wasn't sure if my argument would get me anything but a resounding no.

So I was shocked when she said, "I need to work Saturday morning. I can't be up late picking you up. And you are *not* getting a ride home from some random person."

"Okay." I was about to suggest that Dash could pick me up, or that I could take her car and not drink, but she was already shaking her head.

"There's no way Dash would go to a party and not smoke or drink something, and you're not taking my car. I don't want you driving that late."

"Does some random person mean no Uber?" I sighed, feeling as if her reasons would be never ending. At that moment, I wished I was more rebellious. The type to sneak out windows and call an Uber, then sneak back in before anyone knew. I could've kicked myself. But Mom didn't fall asleep until around ten most nights, and half the fun would be over by then.

Plus, we had the kind of relationship where I'd always felt I could go to her for anything. To talk about anything. I didn't want to ruin that.

"Call your dad." My entire body pulled upright. "If he agrees and is willing to send Alfie out to pick you up and bring you home." She raised a finger when she saw the beginning of my smile. "Before eleven thirty. Then yes, you can go."

I dived over the couch, wrapping my arms around her.

Laughing, she squeezed me. "Quit growing up."

"Love you too."

She pushed me back, then stood to leave the room. "Ugh, now you've scrunched my cashmere top."

I laughed as I picked up her phone to call Dad. You could take the woman out of the castle, but you couldn't take the princess out of the woman.

The phone rang twice before he picked up. "Hey, Daddy."

"Peggy Sue. How're those pearly whites looking?"

I smiled, feeling kind of bad that I hadn't called him afterward or even gone over there to show him. "Good. I got a haircut too."

"Yeah?" I heard him take a sip of something, likely brandy. "You'll need to send me a photo."

My ears and nose pricked as I heard Phil serving up dinner. "Have you worked out how to view the photos yet?"

"I run a multi-million-dollar business, Pegs. I can find my way around a damn phone."

"Uh-huh." He'd only just started texting and used to say it was for chumps who couldn't be bothered to pick up the phone and give someone their proper attention. "How about I come over on Sunday? Will you be in town?"

"I'm here until next week, then I'm in Dubai for the better part of next month."

Dubai was one of the countries that manufactured his medical equipment.

"I'll come see you on Sunday, then. But I wanted to ask you something."

"So," he said, "ask."

"I'm heading out tomorrow night with some friends. Do you think Alfie could pick me up?"

"Out? Like a party, out?"

I closed my eyes, then reopened them and said as firmly as possible, "Yeah, a party. Wade Eldin is hosting one. The big blue mansion a few streets from your place, closest to the bay."

He whistled. "That family's a bunch of idiots." After a tor-turous thirty seconds, he sighed. "Okay, I'll have him pick you up and take you home."

"Thanks, Daddy."

His tone firmed. "You should have Dashiell go with you."

"Yeah," I lied. "I think I will."

There was no way I was letting Dash accompany me tomor-row night.

"This jacket is bomb," Daphne breathed, running her hand over the worn leather covering my arm.

"Thrift store find. I'm worried I'll get hot." I dipped my mascara brush back inside the tube, then brushed it over my lashes one more time.

"You won't get hot," Willa said, lacing up her heeled boots. "He'll have the A/C on all night."

We were getting ready at Daphne's place, a French provin-cial-styled home near the woods on the other side of the creek that sat behind my house.

I loved going to her place. Not because it was huge and filled with amenities—I could get all the amenities I wanted by visiting my dad—but because it was renovated tastefully. A lot of the patterned molding remained in the ceilings, the brass fixtures on the fans, and the lamps in the hall. The wooden floors were original, polished, and lovingly maintained. Her mother was a lingerie model, and her father was a doctor at the local hospital.

"Okay, selfie before we go."

I scrunched my nose, capping the mascara and tossing it in-side the tiny purse I never typically used, but I'd need for tonight.

"Where are you posting it?"

"Who cares?" Willa said. "We look great. We need proof we can look this good again."

I snorted but moved in beside Willa while Daphne took photo after photo. "How many is that? Twenty?"

"It takes that many to get at least three photos worth sharing."

"Sure."

She smacked me, then got to work posting on Instagram as we filed outside and down the hall. Wade's house was a five-minute drive from hers, and we spent it staring at our Instagram accounts while her driver sat stone faced up front.

"I look constipated."

"You are smiling a little too hard," Daphne agreed. "You'll get used to the no braces thing in a few weeks." The ones she'd worn were mostly invisible, and she hadn't had them for longer than the duration of our sophomore year.

Willa zoomed in. "You look stunning. Like a sexier version of Marilyn Monroe sans mole. I, on the other hand, look like someone slapped me in both cheeks." She dropped her phone and started rubbing at her blush coated cheeks.

Daphne grabbed her hands. "Quit." She laughed. "It looks good on you."

The car stopped.

Willa looked panicked as the driver got out and opened the back doors, exposing us to the partygoers who were lingering on the sprawling front lawn. "I really think I need to fix my face."

"Your face looks amazing. Let's do this," I said, pumping my shoulders.

Daphne muttered what sounded like, "Oh, Jesus."

Together, we sauntered over the grass. Some kids from school smiled or waved, mostly at Daphne, but I smiled anyway.

I was wearing my signature floral Doc Martens, a bright purple skirt that looked more like a tutu, and a ripped black T-shirt featuring Stevie Nicks. My curls bounced around my face with each step I took, and Willa's straightened hair stuck to her lips. She pushed it away, her eyes still veiled with uncertainty as we reached the door.

Leon Franklin, who was in my trig class last year, slouched against the door. "Tickets, ladies."

"Ticket this, Franklin." Daphne flipped him off, and we headed inside.

"Badass," Willa said, stealing an unopened beer as soon as we neared the ice box in the living room.

"Don't drink beer," Daphne said. "You'll bloat. Here." She grabbed some fruity looking drinks, handing one to Willa, then grabbed another for me. "Drink this."

Shrugging, I removed the cap and sniffed it.

"Did you just sniff it?" Willa asked.

"Smells like apples." I took a careful sip. "Hey, yum."

Daphne popped open her own, and Willa and I watched as she drained half of it in a few pulls. She dragged a finger over her red lips, inspecting it, then nodded. "Right. Let's mingle."

Mingling wasn't so fun, and sick of feeling awkward standing off to the side with Willa while Daphne chatted with some girls I'd rather not talk to, I decided to grab another drink.

Three drinks later, I was feeling fuzzy around the edges, my limbs limber, and my smile a permanent fixture on my face as we danced around to the little jukebox we'd found in the upstairs living room.

That was, until we went to the bathroom and found a bunch of guys inside smoking pot.

"Dash?"

A slow grin shaped his lips, and he flicked ash from his blunt into the sink he was sitting next to. "Freckles."

Heat infused my cheeks. "Don't call me that."

"Embarrassed?" he asked.

I rolled my eyes as Daphne pushed the door open, then walked right over to Lars. She plucked the blunt from between his lips and stuck it between hers.

I turned to leave. I couldn't believe he was here.

"Aw." I heard his boots thud to the tiles. "Not happy to see me? What am I, your dirty little secret?"

"I don't care. You can do what you want." I just hoped he'd leave me alone to do the same. I grabbed Willa, who was looking around the confined space as if she was trying to find something. Probably alcohol, I mused. "Let's go."

"Not so fast, Cotton Candy," Lars said when Daphne turned to leave with the remains of his joint. "You owe me."

Daphne opened her purse, fished out a twenty, and tossed it at his feet.

Lars blinked down at it, then at her, tilting his head. "I don't need your money."

"And I don't need to be nicknamed after a pointless sweet."

"You're still mad?"

Mad? I looked back and forth between them.

"Mad would require me to actually care about you, and I don't, so …" She tipped a shoulder, her coral, fluttery dress skimming her tanned thighs as she left him sitting there, scowling after her.

Willa turned to me. "I'm so lost right now."

"Me too." I sighed, then pulled Willa with me outside, thankful for the clean air in the hallway. Screw Dash. I should've known he'd show up anywhere there was booze, pot, and willing girls. I looked around, wondering where Byron was, and if he was looking for me.

We tried to find Daphne but that proved impossible. The bass thudded harder, and the rooms filled up so much, I figured half the town had to be here.

We got another drink and stood in the hall, people watching as couples drifted off, searching for privacy, and others outright groped each other where they stood or sat.

Dennis Bradley, who I had three classes with last year, strode by, and I moved my hand to wave, but it fell as he stumbled to a huge ceramic vase and threw his head inside, puking.

Willa and I both looked at him, then at what remained of our drinks. Taking stock of our lightheadedness, we ditched them and wandered away before the area started to smell.

A hand grabbed mine outside the kitchen, and I got ready to growl at Dash until I realized it wasn't him. It was Byron.

A very drunk, very smiley Byron. "Hey, been looking all over for you."

I smiled back, nodding at Willa when she gestured that she'd be hanging in the kitchen. "You have?"

He took a swig of beer, his head bobbing. "Oh, yeah. Wild party, right?"

"Yeah," I said, hardly hearing myself over the music. I was getting tired of half-shouting. "Wild."

As if he could sense it, he pulled me toward the glass windows and doors that overlooked the bay beyond Wade's house. I let him, knowing I was safe when I saw shadows of partygoers out by the Olympic-sized pool.

There were no seats available on the deck or around the pool, so we ventured down the lawn to the bay. Not wanting to get sand in my boots, I took a seat on the small grassy edge that divided Wade's property from the sand, and after finishing his beer and tossing the bottle toward the water, Byron did the same.

"Pretty loud in there, huh?"

He reeked of beer as he leaned back on his hands while stretching out his long legs. "Sure is. You get used to it after a while."

I tried not to let his comment irritate me, but it kind of did. "At least the weather is nice." The weather? *Someone slap me.*

"Yeah, it's nice out, and now I can see you better. You look great," he said, leaning a little closer. "You've always been this cute thing, waltzing around school in your black boots instead of heels or those ballet things, like the rest of them."

"Oh, thanks." Cute. He thought I was cute.

"Yeah, but now?" He reached out, startling me as he grabbed a strand of my hair. "You're like this sexy minx."

"Minx?" I asked, trying not to laugh.

He chuckled. "My ability to flirt is severely hindered right now. You'll need to cut me some slack."

"I guess I can." The way his finger wound around my hair felt nice.

"You should come out more," he murmured. "Give me a reason to smile."

"You smile plenty."

"Not in the way you make me smile."

I laughed, turning to face him. "I don't think anything's wrong with your ability to flirt."

"No?" he whispered, lashes lowering as he stared at my mouth.

Was he about to kiss me?

His hand moved from my hair to the back of my head, pulling our faces even closer. He was going to kiss me.

Shit. Oh, shit.

I'd never been kissed by anyone other than Dash, and even then, he'd only done it in the sixth grade so he could claim my first kiss. I told him that one-second pecks didn't count, and he said he'd better kiss me again then before I shoved him away.

The scent of beer mingled with the sweet spice of his cologne, and I tried to stop it, but as his lips neared mine, I sneezed, pulling back just in time to avoid spraying his face.

Byron's eyes were wide as he wiped at his shoulder and neck.

And oh, how I wanted to run down to the bay and throw myself under water until he disappeared.

"I'm sorry," I said, then sneezed again. *Sweet holy shit.* "Something's up with my sinuses."

He chuckled, and then someone called out to him from the pool behind us.

I kept staring at the bay, my face a wildfire of embarrassment, but out of the corner of my eye, I saw him get up. "I'll be back."

I knew he wouldn't. I shut my eyes, mortification pricking at them. One of the most popular guys in school tried to kiss me, and I'd sneezed my germs all over him.

A slow clap started, and then a plonk beside me had my eyes opening.

I groaned when I saw Dash grinning like the devil he was, teeth and all. "Nice, Freckles. Real smooth."

"You were watching?"

"Duh. Someone had to make sure that shmuck didn't take advantage of you."

I exhaled a tremulous breath. "You didn't need to worry about that."

"I don't now, so thanks."

"Asshole."

He bumped my shoulder with his. "Could be worse. Kissing him would be like licking the inside of a toilet bowl, he's hooked up with so many people lately."

"Not helping, and like you can talk." Dash was notorious for leaving girls hanging.

"Hey, I didn't scare anyone off by spraying them with spit and phlegm."

My stomach shook. Tears threatened. I stood, wanting to head inside and find the fastest route out of here. I pulled my phone out of my purse, firing off a text to Alfie.

"Freckles?" Dash said, poking me in the cheek. "Don't be sad. That's stupid. He's a bastard anyway."

"It's ... whatever. I'm going home." I brushed some sand from my butt, then swerved through the crowds outside, keeping my head down.

Willa was where I left her in the kitchen, her chin on her fist, looking fascinated as she watched a couple of guys make out against the refrigerator. Daphne appeared, looking flushed as she ran her hands over her hair. "There you are."

Willa turned, blinking out of her trance as she saw us. "Where's Byron?"

"God knows, probably halfway to Mexico by now."

Daphne's hands paused, and she crept closer. "Huh? What happened?"

"What happened with Lars?"

"Touché." She sighed. "Let's trade in the car. Alfie's coming soon, right?"

"Just asked him to come earlier. Let's wait out front."

"Freckles," Dash said, latching onto my hand and spinning me around. "Where're you going?"

"Home."

"Over some lousy kiss?" He pulled a cigarette from behind his ear, then lit it, not caring that he was inside. "You can hang with me."

"And get laughed at some more?" I shook my head, turning away to join the girls. "No thanks."

FIVE

Dash

P eggy Newland had been a permanent fixture in my life since the dawn of my existence. In fact, I remember our mothers laughing about it when they were still friends, telling anyone who'd listen how I'd learned to write Peggy's name before I wrote my own.

In my defense, what kind of assholes named their kid Dashiell? My asshole parents, that was who.

So it was a given, if you asked me, that I wasn't going to bother trying with that shit until I had to.

She was the one constant in my life. A pillar of light among the ever-gray bullshit that stalked from one day to the next. But lately, she'd started to change.

I couldn't tell if it was the removal of her braces, the haircut, or the way her tall body had curved more around her chest and ass. Either way, I didn't fucking like it. I was a needy bastard, a taker, and she wasn't as available to me as she'd always been.

And let's not even talk about that almost kiss. I'd never been more grateful for an attack of sinus in my life, and I'd spent the past few days stewing over why.

Yes, she was gorgeous. She always had been. But she was like a sister to me, which probably explained the sickening twist in my gut.

Only I wasn't sure if that feeling was due to her sudden interest in dating stuck-up idiots, or because I could feel her shifting, swaying away from reach.

"You keep scowling all the time, and you're going to age faster than me."

"Not likely with all those Botox injections."

Mother Dearest didn't even gasp; she knew better than to poke at me.

I still blamed her for Peggy moving away. Though I knew it wasn't technically her fault, I didn't like the way she constantly tutted whenever I went to Peggy's place or said her name.

Resentment had burrowed deep inside her veins, and I sometimes wondered if she'd ever slice herself open, admit she was being a rabies-infested hyena, and let it bleed out.

Not everyone had the courage to stay in a loveless marriage, and not everyone had the courage to leave one either.

In my mother's eyes, her ex-best friend had betrayed her by leaving her to rot in this world of money all alone. Not only that, but she now felt as if she couldn't even associate with her due to how far down the social ladder Peony had jumped.

No one had pushed her. She had well and truly jumped and of her own accord. I couldn't lie, I loved the luxury I'd been born into, but that didn't keep me from respecting the amount of balls that'd take.

"For your information, I haven't seen Dr. Bryant in four months."

I dodged left, but it was too late, and some asshat shot me. "Probably because you spend too much time with Emanuel in the pool house. And would you get out? I'm fucking dying here." Literally. Her fucking perfume was smothering the life from me.

"Watch your mouth."

"Why? Not my fault you've never been a fan of honesty."

Her hands flew into the air, the books and jeans she'd been collecting from my bedroom floor falling back to the floor in a heap. "I don't even know where you came from."

"Let's not talk about such nasty shit before dinner, thanks."
With a growl, she stomped out of the room.

Grabbing the basketball from beside my bed, I tossed it at the door hard enough to make it close.

"Slam dunk, motherfucker." I restarted the game and waited to be teleported back to the lobby. "Finally," I said, seeing Peggy's username pop up.

I started a chat and typed out a message.

F*ckoffandie666: Yo, yo, Frecks. Where you been??

Her character wandered around in circles, sword bared, then stopped as she responded.

PegSue12: napping

She didn't even ask how I was, so far up her own curvaceous ass she was.

I frowned, scratching my face for a beat. She liked to nap, sure, but that was her answer for everything these past four days. Since the party.

F*ckoffandie666: sounds positively riveting

She didn't respond, and we played a few rounds before her silence finally got the better of me and I shut the game off.

She was upset, and though I knew it had everything to do with her feeling embarrassed about what'd happened with Byron, I was sick of it. She'd never stayed upset about anything this long before. Even when her grandparents had died, she'd at least spoken to me.

I got up, combed my fingers through my hair, checked my

teeth, and threw on a clean shirt and my leather jacket before grabbing the keys to my Rover.

I parked in the narrow dirt lane near the creek that sat behind her tiny house, spinning my keys around my finger as I strolled past her neighbor's fence to their unfenced yard.

I pocketed my keys and slid the window open, then I jumped up and dived onto her bed.

"Oh my God, watch it!"

My eyes popped out of my head when I tried to find purchase and felt something large, soft, and … shit. Her tit.

Christ.

She started whacking at my chest, and my dick stiffened. I froze, then quickly pulled my hand away and rolled over. "My bad. Jesus. Calm down."

SIX

Peggy

"A little warning would've been nice," I said.

"Warnings make life boring. But hey, your tits are kind of nice."

I got up and stomped out of the room to put on the bra that had been hanging over my desk chair.

When I returned, Dash was studying me, running a finger over his brow with his other arm tucked behind his head. "So I'm done with this weird-ass mopey behavior."

"I'm not being mopey," I said, righting my shirt. "I'm mortified. There's a difference."

And in just over a week's time, we'd be back at school, where I'd be forced to live this embarrassment down. To be honest, I wished it'd hurry up so we could get it over with.

"Come on. You've been embarrassed plenty of times before. Remember that time in seventh grade gym?"

It'd replayed vividly in my head for months afterward whenever I'd gotten my period. "This isn't the same as getting your first period and having your best friend shout, *Dear God, who left the beetroot on the fucking chair?*"

He spun his hand. "You're welcome."

"Beetroot? In the gym? Beetroot is purple."

"Like they even noticed. They were too busy laughing."

I groaned. "Yeah, at me."

"For thinking you'd sat in beetroot, not bled all over your gym shorts."

"Ugh, be quiet."

He mimicked me, then laughed when I tossed a sneaker at his head. It missed and bounced off the wall. "You're a psycho, Freckles." He patted the bed. "Come, tell me all your girl-tastic problems. Let's get this shit aired so we can go back to being the gun-slinging duo everyone loves to fear."

I raised a brow. "Girl-tastic?"

"You are a girl, last I saw." He waggled those thick brows. "And felt."

My eyes went wide. "Ew."

"Is the thought of me seeing you naked really so bad?"

"It ranks high on the bad scale, for sure." Though, thankfully, it'd been some time since that'd accidentally happened.

He mock gasped. "I'm deeply offended."

"Pegs, have you taken my push-up bra?" Mom called, halting in the doorway with her fluffy purple dressing gown on. "Oh, hey Dash. How's your mom?"

"Still a superficial bitch, thanks for asking."

I could feel my cheeks tinge as Mom looked at me, waiting. Dash snorted.

"Uh, yeah. I wore it last weekend to the party." I started digging through my hamper, which was only half full due to hanging at home since the sneeze that'd dampened my spirits and ruined a chance at, I don't know, something.

"It's dirty?" Mom made a whining sound. "Never mind. I'll buy another one with my next paycheck." She stabbed a finger at me when I straightened, her lace yellow bra dangling from my finger. "Keep it. But don't touch this new one."

Then she was gone, the pipes groaning as she shut the bathroom door and turned on the shower.

"That would drive me insane."

"What, sharing a bra with your mom?"

He pursed his lips. "That too. But I was referring to the old pipes."

"Used to it," I said, dropping the bra and dumping myself on the bed.

"This party, the kiss that almost happened, it's really gotten to you, huh?"

His tone wasn't mocking, and for that reason alone, I nodded, staring at the yellow paint on my toenails. "Yeah."

"But why?" He seemed genuinely perplexed.

"It's just …"

"Speak, Freckles."

I swallowed down my pride. He'd seen me far worse and had heard far worse than what I was about to admit. "I feel so inexperienced. I'll be eighteen next month, and I don't care that I'm still a virgin. But I thought …" My cheeks billowed with a loud exhale.

He prodded. "You thought?"

My shoulders drooped. "That I would've had some other, um, well, encounters by now."

"What, like covering the other bases?"

I nodded, unable to look at him. "I came so close," I whispered. "So close to finally feeling like I could have what everyone else seems to have, or is doing, and then—"

"You sneezed your boogers all over him." I slapped his thigh, and he groaned through a burst of laughter. "Just messing with you. Fuck."

"For once in your life, can you not be a dick and be serious with me for a moment?" I was as shocked as he was at the half-shouted words and tried to calm my erratic breathing. "Sorry, I—"

"You're not sorry, and there's nothing wrong with that." He sat up, scooting close until the scent of his aftershave reached me, calming some of my frayed emotions. "You're worried, but you shouldn't be."

"Why?" I said, noticing his lashes were really kind of long.

"Because most guys aren't going to care how inexperienced you are. Especially not the right one." He coughed, and I watched his lips roll together.

I sniffed, sighing.

"But you know, if you really want to boost your confidence, you can always practice."

"Don't you dare bring up the Nick Jonas poster."

He raised his hands. "Didn't even have to."

I went to get up because I needed some chocolate stat, but he caught my wrist and tugged me back down. "You should practice with someone."

My brows shot high. "What, kissing?" His lip slid between his teeth as he nodded. I scoffed. "Right, and with who? The one chance I had ran away from me."

"With me."

"What?" The buzzing outside my window ceased, and the shower shut off, drenching the world in silence. I searched his deep blue gaze. "You're telling me I should make out with you?"

"Who better?" He spread his hands. "I won't judge, and even if I do, it stays with us. It's safe, and we both know I'll be a good teacher."

I couldn't contain my shock any longer, and so I got up, laughing as a cloud of confusion followed me out of my room. "Very funny."

SEVEN

Dash

Very funny.

I didn't think so.

Those words, the nonchalant way she'd let them roll off her tongue with her wind-chime laughter, had ripped through me like an unseen serrated knife.

"Back up," Lars said. "No, no, *no*. You fuckhead." He tossed his controller, falling back against the couch as Raven snickered, leveling up.

Church, my black Scottish Fold, had somehow crept inside the pool house and was rubbing up against my ankles. "Who let Church in?"

Lars lit a blunt, exhaling a plume of smoke while eyeing my cat. "Fuck if I know."

"Who cares?" Raven, or Rave, as we called him, said.

"I fucking care." I stabbed out my cigarette, waving the smoke away from Church's direction, then bent forward to pick him up and set him beside me on the recliner. "No smoking around the cat. His lungs aren't as heavy duty as ours."

"Aw, you big fucking sweetheart." Lars ashed into an empty bowl beside him.

"Pussy-whipped." Rave laughed, reaching for his drink while he had a lull.

I threw my boot at him, and it hit the can in his hand. Beer sprayed over his face and rained down the leather chair, leaving a puddle on the floor beside the dented can.

"Seriously?" Rave raised a brow, his empty hand still poised at his mouth.

I didn't bother responding, satisfied when I saw someone shoot his ass dead on the screen.

"Mother of fuck." He scrambled for the controller.

Lars chuckled, staring off into space.

Very funny.

Two words had never bothered me so damn much. She'd rejected me. Her best friend. The only guy she was comfortable around enough to be wholly herself.

And she'd fucking rejected me.

Laughed at me.

Then walked away from me.

I was so pissed, so unexpectedly thrown by her response and the weird stabbing sensation that cut at the insides of my chest, that I'd climbed out her bedroom window and gone home before she even came back to her room.

Then I'd texted Ruthie Brooks, which was a bad fucking idea. The chick was apparently on the rebound something fierce, but I needed my cock in someone's mouth. I needed to numb the waves of rejection that wouldn't quit crashing into me.

And most of all, I needed to remember who I damn well was.

Which was reinforced when Ruthie had called and told me to meet her at her place after eleven when her parents had passed out. I came home feeling better. Offing a load always makes one feel better, but I still wasn't feeling like myself.

And I still didn't want to talk to Peggy.

I was mad, and I knew I was acting like some petulant chick, but come on. If you can't kiss your best friend with no strings attached, who else can you kiss? Besides, I didn't think I imagined the way her long brown lashes dipped over the faint freckles beneath her eyes, eyes that were curious, staring at my fucking mouth.

She'd considered it, I knew that much. I mean, what hot-blooded female wouldn't? But then she'd laughed it off like I was crazy.

And yeah, maybe I was. Maybe we'd have kissed, made out, fondled a little, and I'd have to fight back the memories of seeing her wet her pants in kindergarten and the farting competitions we'd had in the third grade. Maybe my stomach would have roiled, or maybe I'd be unable to quit laughing, to block out who was touching her lips to mine.

But god damn it, I guess we'd never know.

"What time are we meeting Cad at the skate park?"

"He's working until four," Lars told Raven.

I pulled my phone out, checking the time, and saw I had a message.

Huh. I wasn't high, at least, not yet. Later, maybe. I wasn't like Lars. The amount of times I'd almost broken my damn neck riding my bike due to smoking some weed was fucking embarrassing.

Freckles: Hey, so I kind of need you.

The message was sent a half hour ago, and something stirred in my stomach.

Church rolled over, nuzzling his head into my thigh. I stroked his belly, taking my sweet-ass time to type three simple letters.

Me: Why

Her response came instantly.

Freckles: Byron asked me out. Like, on a real date.

My hands tensed as I read her message again and again.

Me: When?

Freckles: DM'd me on Insta.

Fucking fuck. Of course, he did. He probably saw the latest photo she'd uploaded, one of her long ass legs and freshly painted mint green toenails, and thought to hell with sneezing on someone's face, I need me some of that.

All the scumbags at school knew to stay away from her. It rarely even needed to be said.

I'd have to kill him.

All in good time.

"Are you even here? Or are you sexting Lizzie again?"

Ignoring Rave, I texted back.

Me: What do you need me for then?

"Earth to fucking Dash? Are we getting more beer before we hit the skate park or not?"

It took her a solid minute, bubbles dancing and disappearing, but she finally found the courage.

Freckles: I need to practice.

A twitch shook my lips, and that stabbing feeling in my chest dissipated. I pocketed my phone, then grabbed Church to take him back to the house.

"You fucks work it out. I've got plans."

They didn't bother asking where I was going, seeing as I'd never bother telling.

EIGHT

Peggy

Nerves ignited the second I'd sent that message, catching fire when I realized he wasn't going to respond.

With a sour stomach, I switched back to Instagram, rereading Byron's message for the eighth time since he'd sent it almost an hour ago.

Hey! You took off the other night? I don't have your number, so I thought I'd find you here. I'm sorry for ditching you. Wade almost got into a fight, and then I got so wasted, I passed out by the pool.

Let me make it up to you with a real date? How's this Friday sound?

And my response?

I was still dying over it, wishing I'd had some chill and waited.

Of course! Totally fine. What time?

Totally fine? Ugh, what was I? Some kind of pushover? It was *not* totally fine. Far from it. The embarrassment that'd been tearing at everything I did this past week, further hurling the feelings of inadequacy I'd always struggled with at Magnolia Cove Prep, made it so far from fine, it was sometimes hard to breathe.

I'd never had a problem with feeling as though I didn't

belong. I'd found my people, few as they were, and I didn't need anything more than that.

Mom once told me that trying to fit into someplace you didn't belong was like wearing a pair of jeans two sizes too small. It'd slowly strangle and squeeze every last drop of life from you. Eventually, you'd find yourself stuck, all alone with nothing but the unrecognizable scraps of who you once were.

I didn't need cheap friendships that would only fall apart the second we left this town and went our separate ways. But what I wanted, what tormented my insecurities, was to know what it was like to fall for someone. No matter how much that fall hurt on the way down, I was sick and tired of wondering if I was doomed to finish high school without having been on one date. Without experiencing the butterflies, the late-night phone calls, and the stolen kisses in the school halls.

Because I hadn't. The last time I thought I was getting close to scoring a boyfriend, it was when Simon Rogers had asked me out in biology in the eighth grade. He wasn't the best-looking guy, but he was cute with his wire-rimmed glasses, and he smelled nice. Like the lemon-scented spray Dad's cleaner used. He said he'd have his mom pick me up at seven and take us to the movies.

But he never showed, and he never even spared me a glance in class the following week at school.

A message came through from Byron.

You're seriously the best. Wish all girls were as understanding as you. I'll pick you up at eight?

I locked my phone and set it down.

He could wait a while longer after that comment and my ridiculous mistake.

I fell to the bed just as a thump hit the exterior of the house, and Dash launched himself through the window.

"Can you ever land gracefully?" Or you know, use the front door. For as long as we'd lived here, he'd snuck in. At first, it was due to being unsure whether my mom would still want us hanging out, but it didn't take her long to figure out what he was doing.

She didn't care. When I'd shaken like a mouse cornered in a kitchen, she'd smiled and told me she'd never stop us from being friends. Yet the window always remained unlocked.

Dash kicked off his boots, and they hit the aging floor with two bangs. "I'm all man, baby. Not a fucking cat."

Hearing him say that reminded me of why he was here. I sprang to my feet, hurtling out into the hall and into the bathroom.

"What are you doing?"

Too busy gargling mouthwash, I didn't answer and spat it into the sink as he appeared in the weathered mirror behind me.

"Seriously?" he asked. "You burp in my face after eating garlic pizza, so this is just fucking dumb."

"You burped in my face first." I put the cap back on the bottle, not meeting his gaze. I couldn't. I headed back inside the safety of my room.

But I had to wonder, as I heard Dash gargling mouthwash too, if it would be considered safe again after this. Would this ruin everything by making it awkward?

"Dash," I said, wringing my hands as I paced the floor of my room. "We probably shouldn't be doing this. What if—"

"What if it's awesome and you fall madly in love with me? Well, we already know I don't do commitment."

A tiny laugh skittered out. "No, what if it gets awkward? I don't want anything to change."

He took me by the shoulders in the middle of my rainbow knitted rug and leveled me with his vibrant eyes. "We've done some pretty awkward shit, so what's a little mouth to mouth going to change?"

I nodded, exhaling slowly, then I frowned. "Why are you doing this? I mean, I know why I want to, but you? What do you even get out of it?"

He grinned. "You might be my best friend, but I've always wondered what it'd be like to stick my tongue down your throat." He tipped a muscled shoulder. "Let's just say you'll be killing that curiosity."

"You've always wondered?"

"I've got eyes, Freckles. And I don't need my glasses to appreciate the sight of something beautiful."

I blinked. "Wow. That was actually really swe—"

"Shut your inexperienced mouth and kiss me."

I was still laughing when he grabbed my face, and then I squeaked as the world changed color, and his lips lowered over mine.

My heart became a trumpet, blaring in my ears at the first touch of his lips.

I pulled away, startled and still laughing. "Oh, my God."

Dash's hands were warm on my face. "That good? They barely even touched."

"No," I choked out, pushing his hands away. "It's just ... a little weird."

"Weird?" His brows scrunched. "We've barely even begun."

I blew out a shaky breath, unable to look at him as my hands flapped at my sides. I stared at his white shirt, looking at where the cotton met his tanned skin. "I don't know, Dash."

"Wanna try again?"

I looked at him then, at the eager glint in his blue eyes. "It's not weird for you?"

He chewed his bottom lip which was a little fatter than the top. And it'd just been touching mine. Oh, how crazy. "Maybe a smidgen. I can just picture Margot Robbie, and I'll be good."

I froze. "Margot Robbie?"

He gestured to my hair. "The blonde hair helps."

"Jesus." I swiped my hands down my face. "This is dumb. Let's just forget it."

He stood there a moment, glancing around my room. "Why don't you imagine someone? That guy from the *Thor* movie. You like him."

"Chris Hemsworth?"

"Yeah. Imagine him." Then he grinned, waggling his brows. "Pucker up, baby."

"You didn't just say that." I laughed, plopping down on the edge of my bed.

"Whatever. Are we trying again or what?"

The thought of Byron and that mischievous twinkle in his green eyes, the way he'd wasted no time moving in to kiss me … yeah. I needed to do this.

"Okay." I shook out my hands, bouncing a little on the bed. "Okay, let's do this."

Dash's lips thinned. "This isn't a cross meet. We're only swapping germs."

"You just had to say that, didn't you?" My pep had officially vanished.

Dash tugged me off the bed. "Close your eyes and relax."

I tried, but I was as stiff as a board when his mouth met mine again. He tasted like spearmint and cigarettes, but his hands were gentle as one held my chin and the other glided through my hair to the back of my head. Slowly, with the soft press of his lips on mine and the gentle exploration of their shape, my limbs loosened.

"Open," he whispered, his voice threaded, rougher.

I did, expecting the invasion of his tongue, but the velvet feel of it only traced the inner edges of my mouth.

Out of all the things I'd expected to feel when he'd suggested this crazy idea, it wasn't relaxed, and it certainly wasn't the buzzing sensation currently warming my insides.

"This isn't so bad," I said when he pulled back, my voice a low exhalation.

"Good. Now repeat the same to me." My eyes were about to spring open, but he growled. "Keep them closed. Don't think, just do and feel."

Drawing in a quick breath through my nose, I found his stubble-coated cheeks with my hands and lifted myself on my toes. I tried to do the same thing he did to me, but my tongue plunged deeper, meeting the warm softness of his. I licked it, stroking cautiously until I heard him hum, the sound vibrating up his throat and causing our lips to mash together.

His hands became firmer around my head, his tongue greedier, sweeping inside my mouth before my teeth found purchase on his plump bottom lip, and pulled.

He groaned, and it had me staggering back, my heart racing and my breath an unsteady, embarrassing sound.

Dash swallowed, then cleared his throat as he shifted on his feet. His eyes met mine, and I looked away, down to where my mint green toes were curling over the abrasive fabric of my rug.

Awkward. This was so awkward, and I prayed we hadn't just made a huge mistake.

"So that's how it's done." He grabbed the TV remote and plopped onto my bed. "Got any popcorn?"

I shook my head. "Wait, that's um, it?"

He started flicking through Netflix. "Well, yeah. Not much else to it. We can practice again before your date if you want, but I'm fucking starving, and we need to re-watch the last season of *GoT* before the new one is out."

"Oh, yeah," I said, remembering I'd promised him that weeks ago. Hungry myself, I stepped outside, then scowled at him from the doorway. "Don't put your socks near my pillow."

He grumbled but shifted and moved over to the other side of the bed.

NINE

Peggy

"Wear the blue dress. I haven't seen you in a dress in so long."

I flicked through my hangers, my finger traipsing over the rainbow kaleidoscope of tulle, satin, denim, and frills. My skirts. My favorites. My true loves.

"No offense, Mom, but when did you even get in here?" She must have snuck in while I was distracted.

"Oh, just a minute ago."

"She's right," Daphne said. "You're always in skirts and those god-awful boots."

My hands landed on my hips, and I spun around to glare at her. "They're not awful. Mind your manners."

She licked her teeth, inspecting her nails. "Just saying. You have great ankles. You should show them off."

"I can't walk in heels. I'll fall flat on my face." Forgetting my mom was there, I tacked on, "I've already embarrassed myself enough in front of this guy."

"What? When?"

"Shit."

"Manners," Daphne said with a curl to her glossed lips.

I flipped her off, then tugged the stupid royal blue dress off the hanger.

"At the party," I said when Mom's eyes kept bouncing back and forth between us.

"What happened?" She paused. "Oh, God. You came home

early." Panic struck her features, pinching at the fine lines around her eyes. "Why didn't you talk to me?"

I pulled my extra-long men's T-shirt off, then struggled into the constricting fabric of the dress. "It's fine, really."

Daphne laughed. "Really, it's classic. She freaking sneezed in his face when he went to kiss her."

"It wasn't in his face," I said, huffing.

Mom snorted, waving her hands in front of her eyes as she tried to keep from laughing. She failed, and I glared at her when she finally gave in and set it free.

"Sorry," she wheezed, wiping beneath her eyes. "That's terrible, Pegs, but it's not the end of the world. I've heard worse."

"Like what?" I didn't believe her, but I was desperate to.

Her lips pursed and so did Daphne's as they both tried to think of something.

"Ugh." I pulled at the skintight bodice that fanned into a flowing skirt at my hips. "I hate you both."

"Is this sneeze why you've been moping around?" Mom asked. "I thought you had your period."

"I did. Double whammy." I moved to the mirror, inspecting my hair which I'd blown out, then grabbed some vanilla lip balm and smeared an extra layer on.

"Lord." Mom fussed with the books on my nightstand, most of them Dash's, and wound up the cords dangling from the controllers Dash and I had left out yesterday.

There'd been no more practice since earlier this week, and I was glad. I wasn't exactly confident that I was an awesome kisser, but I did feel better knowing what to expect. Warmth. Lots of warmth. A little wetness and loss of breath. Remembering caused my cheeks to burn, so I snuffed the memory.

Things had been relatively normal between us. Well, as normal as normal could be with Dash's mood swings.

"It's going to be just fine, Pegs. He's asked you out again."

"I'm not worried." Lying was easy after they'd made fun of me.

Daphne snatched the lip balm from my hand, then plucked a tissue from the box and started dotting my lips. "Tell that to your lying, over balmed lips."

My shoulders deflated. "Okay, so I'm a little nervous. This could be my last shot."

"If he doesn't want to take you out again after this, that's his loss, Pegs." Mom stabbed a finger at me.

"You're my mom. It's your job to say that."

Daphne tossed the tissue. "It's the truth. He's a bit daft, but he was sweet to Kayla. If he can be sweet with that girl, he's going to find he's hit the jackpot with you."

Kayla was a piece of work at times, but I'd chalked it up to her being captain of the cheerleading team, head of the prom committee, and the daughter of a movie director.

"I can see that look in your eyes," Daphne said.

"What if she's still upset over their breakup?"

"Her mom's a bitch, so I'm guessing she is too," Mom interjected. "Don't sweat it."

"What?" I shot my eyes at her, and she shrugged.

"You already know she's a bitch." Daphne dragged my gaze back. "One who should've thought about that before cheating on him."

That was true.

A knock on the door had us all freezing, then Mom was off the bed and racing out of my room. Daphne spritzed some perfume all over me, and I coughed.

Mom ran back into my room with a pair of white strappy sandals, then started shoving my feet into them.

"I feel like I'm being sent on stage."

"Shush. Here." Daphne handed me my one and only clutch. "There's a stick of gum inside. Use it after dinner but ditch it as soon as you can. Even if you have to swallow it."

Mom tutted. "Don't swallow gum. Seven years in your intestines, Pegs."

Thoroughly whiplashed, I wobbled to the door, shaking my head as I drew in deep breaths.

Byron was wearing crisp blue jeans, a deep blue polo shirt, and a dimpled smile. "Well, hey."

"Hey." I instantly regretted my choice of dress. "Look, we match."

He chuckled. "Your mom home? Thought I'd better say hello before we leave."

Mom yanked open the door behind me, and I almost jumped out of my skin. "Hey. Byron, yes?" She gently pushed me aside with her hand outstretched. "I'm Peony."

Byron winked. "Peony. Wow, you guys have great genes."

Mom clapped her hand over her chest with a giggle. "Oh, stop."

"Okay, let's go. See you later, Mom. Bye," I rushed out, pushing past her and heading down the steps to Byron's tricked-out truck.

I opened the door before he had the chance, then closed it as he climbed in the driver's side.

"I'm so sorry. God."

He started the truck, turning to me as we fastened our seat belts. "For what?"

I waved a hand at the house where Mom was still smiling in the doorway.

"Oh." He chuckled once more. "Don't sweat it. Your mom seems cool."

I pursed my lips, unsure if I believed him.

"Seriously. I wish my mom greeted people like that. She'd rather hide away upstairs and remain self-medicated while watching daytime TV. All hours of the day."

I winced. "I'm sorry."

He backed out, his arm looping behind my chair, bringing with it the scent of that nose-tingling cologne. "It's fine. She's been going through a rough patch."

"How long?"

He shifted into drive, his arm falling away. "About five years."

Well, shit sundaes on Thursdays. "That's, um …"

"A bit heavy for first date material?" He scrubbed a large hand down his face. "Yeah. Sorry, I'm out of practice."

The word practice jolted me. "It's okay. I'd rather talk about real things than the weather."

Briefly, he glanced over at me, eyes bright and smiling. "Right."

He remembered, so maybe he wasn't that drunk. That didn't bode well for the sneeze thing. "I'm still sorry about, um, sneezing on you."

He laughed. "Not gonna lie, it was unexpected."

"It was gross. You can say it."

We crossed the small bridge that divided the mansions from the average homes of Magnolia Cove, the lights from town flickering bright up ahead.

"Okay, yeah. It was gross. But honestly?" He shot me a smile. "More funny than gross."

I bit my lips, staring at his profile. "It's your cologne."

"What?"

"It made me sneeze. In fact, I can feel my nose itching right now."

He let out a huff of air, turning to me at the lights. "For real?"

I sniffed for emphasis, my nose twitching as I tried not to sneeze.

"No way," he said, laughter tinging his voice. "Well, I'll be sure not to wear it next time. I've got some others I wanna try out anyway."

I smiled at him, and he smiled back before facing forward when the light turned green.

Ten minutes later, a server at the steak house directed us to a booth in the back, away from the squealing children who were pounding on the jukebox by the bar.

"What are you having?"

I ran my nail down the menu, stopping when I saw the spicy chicken tenders Dash always ordered. I couldn't stand hot food, but the sight of them made me pause and wonder how long it'd been since we'd eaten here. We used to grab dinner here after or before every movie we saw, but I was sure the last time I'd seen him eat them was earlier that summer.

I shook my thoughts away and shut the menu. "I think I'll go with the salad wraps. You?"

His lashes crested the tops of his cheeks as he studied the menu. "I think the T-bone."

He flagged the waitress and we ordered, and then the awkward arrived again.

"So," I started.

"What's with you and Dash?"

Startled, I sat back in the seat, the wood biting into my back. "What do you mean?"

He seemed to pick his words carefully, his green eyes bobbing over my face. "It's like this unspoken thing that no one touches you. But I'd always wondered why. Especially when he won't date you."

Whoa. "Excuse me?"

"Wait a second." His brows furrowed. "You didn't know?"

I'd thought Daphne had been exaggerating. I never thought it was an actual *thing*.

I was going to kick Dash square in the junk, then go to his house and empty his Pokémon card collection, mess them all up, and put them back in the folders in the wrong order, and, and ... and *so much* more.

"I'll take that shocked look on your face as a no." A harsh breath puffed his cheeks. "Shit, look, I didn't mean—"

"No, it's okay." I had to set him straight. "He's been my best friend since we were in diapers." I forced out a dry laugh. "Not even joking, we were potty trained together." I cringed. "God, um, just ignore that last comment."

Byron was grinning. "No, please." He leaned forward, fingers steepled beneath his strong, smooth chin. "Tell me more."

I laughed, despite feeling like I was close to screaming, and then I did. "Our moms were best friends in college, and they met our fathers at the same time, not long before graduating. They don't talk anymore, but Dash and me, well, we're still close." Though after this, I wasn't so sure.

All this time, I'd thought if I just got my braces off, wore a little more mascara, maybe a push-up bra for my b-cups, then someone would notice me. I knew I wasn't hideous, but for so long, I'd wondered if maybe I was missing something.

What an idiot. I clearly had.

Fucking Dash.

"I was surprised, you know," Byron said, ripping the wrapper off a straw and dumping it inside my Coke when the waitress set our drinks down.

I thanked her as she left. "Surprised?"

"To learn that he's seriously best friends with you. You're just so different."

"Maybe personality wise," I said. "But we have some things in common, I guess."

"Like what?"

I groaned. "Can we skip the Dash talk? I'm not exactly happy with him after finding this out."

He nodded. "You're going to tell him, aren't you?"

"What did he do exactly? Warn people off me?"

Byron bobbed his head side to side. "Sometimes. Mostly, it's just this widely known fact. Don't fuck with Peggy Newland or Dash will fuck with you."

Mother trucker.

My hand curled too tight around my glass, slipping and almost losing purchase as I dragged it closer and took a long sip. "Yet you still asked me out."

His grin had the straw plopping out of my mouth. Green eyes danced over my lips. "I got done with giving a shit. Let him try."

Our food arrived, and thankfully, the subject changed to less frustrating topics. Such as movies, *Game of Thrones*, and the return to school the following week.

"What about Kayla?" I felt comfortable enough to ask, especially since he'd pried about Dash.

He twisted his lips, then sighed. "That got complicated for a bit, which is why I didn't get in touch right after the party."

What did that even mean? Judging by the sour pinch to his lips, I'd hit a nerve. "Sorry."

"Don't worry about it. It's done now. For good."

"You had a fight?" While I didn't mean to pry, I was here. On a date. With him.

He pushed his plate away, then stretched his arms up and over his head. If he was doing it to distract me, it was working. Muscles gathered and contracted in his arms as his fists opened and closed. He yawned, dropping his hands to his lap. "She'd heard about the party, came over to my place, and tried to start some shit."

"Oh damn."

Jerking his head, he grimaced. "She can get a little crazy. I wanted to make sure there was no blowback."

"Blowback?"

He reached over the table, grasping my hand with his. Fingers warm and rough sent flutters pouncing around in my stomach. "I want to keep seeing you."

"You do?"

His teeth grazed his lip. "Yeah, so I needed to make sure she knew we were done. Which meant fighting some more, and all that fun *this is a real breakup* stuff."

I wouldn't know, but I didn't want or need to say that.

A warm smile nudged his lips. "Can I show you something?"

"Sure."

He studied me a moment, and I sat enraptured by the curl of his lashes and the specks of gold in his eyes. "Come on, let's get out of here."

He paid the bill, left a tip, and led me by the hand outside to the parking lot.

Opening my door, I went to climb up when I felt his hands land on my waist, and then I was in the air before my butt hit the seat with a puff.

I laughed, dazed as I tried to right my dress and keep the color of my panties a secret.

My laughter died when he carefully moved me to face where he was still standing in the door, and I saw the intent in his eyes a half second before he tipped my face up. "Is this what you wanted to show me?"

A nod, then his mouth descended. His lips were warm and

tasted like barbecue sauce. I let him lead, feeling lightheaded as he pressed harder, hungrier, and pried my lips apart.

His tongue didn't move in gentle, calculated, swipes or pokes. No, it delved deep, forcing my eyes open as I gasped and pulled back.

"You okay?" he asked.

"Yeah." Heat crept up my neck, making a beeline for my cheeks. With the moment ruined, I dropped my head, defeated by the truth. "I haven't exactly kissed a lot of people."

"I know."

My head shot up, brows puckering and my eyes searching.

"It's not a bad thing." His finger swept across my cheek. "You're gorgeous, but when you blush, you're damn near irresistible."

I smiled, even as my cheeks reddened further. He was real. As real as the blood rushing faster through my veins.

This was happening.

After flashing a quick grin, he fused his mouth to mine for a brief, gentle touch.

His hand stayed in mine the whole ride home, but this time, the silence wasn't awkward. It was a comfortable silence, and as I gazed out the window to the blurring summer colors of the cove, I couldn't rid my smile if I tried.

We exchanged numbers before I got out, and I made it to the porch before my smile wilted.

Dash opened the front door right as Byron was pulling away, his truck grumbling down the quiet street.

TEN

Dash

"So what did he do, fine dine you with food you hate?" I leaned against the doorjamb, assessing the Barbie who'd taken over my best friend's body.

What the fuck was that dress? Yeah, it looked great on her, hugging curves I didn't even realize she'd had, but it wasn't her.

"Move," she said, tone crisp, and some juicy scented perfume permeating the air between us.

She wouldn't look at me. In fact, her entire body seemed tense, coiled tight and ready to spring, but I didn't give a fuck. "You didn't answer my question."

"And I'm not going to." Her eyes met mine then, ice crystallizing the gray orbs. "Move."

She was mad. At me. What the hell did Woods do that'd caused her to be upset with me?

"Did he touch you or something?"

Her long lashes, coated in a thick layer of mascara, butted against her brows. Then she shoulder checked me, pushing past to get inside.

She tried to shut the door, but I was in the way, and I wasn't moving. "The fuck, Freckles?"

The screen door smacked shut behind me, and Peony looked up from the couch as Peggy breezed down the hall to her room.

"Did you have a good time?"

The slamming of Peggy's bedroom door was her answer.

Peony looked at me, eyes narrowed, and I tipped my

shoulders. "Don't look at me. I just got here." That wasn't exactly true, and we both knew it. I'd been in her room for the better part of an hour, staring at the hairspray, clothes littering the bed, and the empty space on it where she should've been on a Friday night.

"She'd put a lot of stock into this date." With her head shaking, she gave her attention back to the TV. "Fix it, Dash."

Stock? I almost scoffed but gathered an ounce of self-control and went to Peggy's room.

The door was locked, and I knocked, incredulity spiking my blood pressure. "Peggy, did you seriously lock me out?"

No answer.

I knocked harder. "Let me in or I'll pick the lock."

Three seconds passed before I sighed and fished out my keys, then the door opened. "Go home, Dashiell."

"Dashiell?" I couldn't remember the last time she'd called me by my full name. A name she knew I loathed. I stepped forward, uncaring that she wouldn't move, and tried to read her flushed, tense expression. "What happened?" I tried to soften my voice. Tried. I should've gotten a damn merit award for effort considering the storm rising within me. It didn't work.

"You happened." She stepped back, and I walked into her room as she went to shut the door. "You warned the guys at school off me?"

"Warned them off you?" I reared back, trying to play dumb, but she saw right through it.

Tears glossed her eyes, turning her voice raspier. "Why would you do that?"

Fucking hell. She really was mad. Hot sauce in her shampoo kind of mad.

I concentrated on breathing for a beat, hating the way the sight of her tears made my chest ache. "You're easy to take advantage of, Freckles. And believe me, they'd fucking take advantage."

"They can't take what I'm willing to give," she seethed, her chest rising and falling in a way that had her tits straining, cleavage bared.

I swallowed and looked away, my words struggling to clear my gritted teeth. "I'm going to pretend you didn't actually say that."

"Well, I did. All this time, I thought you were just a little overprotective. All this time, I thought something might've been wrong with me." I frowned, about to tell her she was stupid, when she almost knocked me on my ass. "Turns out that something isn't me. It's you."

The ache in my chest started burning as though the organ in there might catch fire and disintegrate. I steeled my jaw and tried to push down the anger and injustice. "Did you kiss him?"

She threw her hands into the air. "Why the fuck do you care?"

"Peggy?" her mom called. "What's going on?"

"It's fine." Peggy rubbed at her cheeks. "Sorry, Mom."

And that was the crux of it, really. Why the fuck did I even care? I kept my voice low. "Because he's a fucking douchebag who'll hang around long enough to fuck you, then ditch you."

A bitter laugh fled past her glossed lips, and she stabbed a finger at me. "Pot meet kettle, you hypocritical asshole."

She had me there, but this wasn't about me. It was about her and her stupid decisions and crazy-ass tantrums. "What the hell has gotten into you?" It was like an alien had stolen my best friend. A sexy, angry, emotional alien, but an alien all the same.

She blew out a breath, then walked in small circles in front of her sticker-covered closet doors. "You don't get it."

I took a hesitant step forward. "Try me."

"You've never had to worry about it, Dash. What it's like to wonder if you're not good enough."

"Because I couldn't give a flying monkey's dick what people think of me."

"Yeah," she said, following up with a nod. "Well, not everyone is like you. I do care." She stopped, tapping a finger at her heaving chest. "I care. I wanted to date. I wanted to experience what most other girls my age already have. But you had to be your typical controlling, selfish asshole self, leaving me to think that I'm not good enough …" She shook her head, swiping at a tear that'd raced down her cheek. "Just go home."

A thousand cutting insults sat on the tip of my tongue, but I swallowed them, felt them slice deep, and stalked back through the house.

For untold minutes, I sat in my car and stared at a patch of their yard illuminated by their back porch light.

Once home, I parked behind Dad's BMW and stayed there a moment, staring at it as I tried to shake off the bullshit that'd transpired. She'd be fine and hopefully back to her usual self by tomorrow.

A tapping on my window startled me, and I jerked out of my daze to find Dad's face there. He gestured for me to put down the window. "You getting out of that thing? Because if you are, move it over first. I have a late dinner meeting."

I turned the car on, shifted into reverse, and moved it behind Mom's car.

"What's eating you, boy?" Dad asked, leaning against his car and swinging his keys around his finger.

The familiar act made me cringe. Did I really take after him that much? As one of the best attorneys in the state, he was a dick, but every now and then, he'd make time to check on me if he was home.

"Nothing. Maybe that's the problem."

He chuckled, then smoothed a hand over the blond and gray hair atop his head. He'd recently turned fifty, though he looked at least ten years younger. "Your mother's in a state, so I'd steer clear."

"What'd you do this time?"

"Whatever the hell I want, as usual." He opened the car door, winking at me as he slid inside the sleek interior. "Don't buy yourself a wife, kid. Most are non-refundable."

It was something he'd said to me countless times, and my response was always the same. "Noted."

I walked inside to the sound of crashing and followed it down the hall to the kitchen.

In a sparkling golden gown, Mom sat on the floor, cutlery and broken plates decorating the tiles around her. Mascara blackened her cheeks, and even though I stood there for a solid minute, not once did she take notice of my presence.

Her problems were always too big.

And as I had enough of my own, I had no room to care about hers. Not that I ever did.

ELEVEN

Peggy

I spread my sheets out before me on the dining table, but none of them were calling to me.

"Try the purple birds," Willa said, opening her small traveling kit. "Paired with some white and the picture from the party, and the effect will be stunning."

She was right. I pulled the purple sheet close to me and plucked up one of the pictures Willa had printed.

I hadn't told them about my fight with Dash. I wasn't sure why, but every time I tried, it felt like a betrayal. He was my best friend but so were Willa and Daphne. And though I'd easily talked about Dash with them before, this felt different. Big and far too scarily personal.

"Back to the important matter here," Daphne said, squirting a dollop of glitter glue onto her page and grabbing a small brush. "He kissed you, and you clearly survived. So what was it like?"

"You're so funny." I rolled my eyes. "And it was, I don't know, pretty nice?"

Willa snorted. "Butterflies? Toe curling? We need more than just nice."

"There were flutters, yes." I spread some glue onto the page, then fixed the photo onto it. "He's a good kisser." I wasn't lying. I'd replayed the kiss over and over. It was a decent first kiss, if not a little too much. I couldn't exactly be the judge of that, though.

"How did you know what to do?" Willa asked, not unkindly.

"It's not exactly rocket science. You let them take the lead until you're comfortable."

I looked at Daphne, wishing I'd had some of her confidence. Maybe then I wouldn't have felt inclined to kiss my best friend for practice. "You've done it, right?"

"It?" Willa asked.

I tried not to blush. "You know …"

Daphne narrowed her eyes. "Thanks for assuming." My cheeks reddened, then she sighed. "Yeah, I have."

"Willa?"

Her eyes widened comically. "Uh, no, I would've told you."

"You've done other stuff, though." Daphne took a sip of her lemonade.

I was glad Mom was out grocery shopping. She'd tried to talk about sex with me once, but when I'd kept laughing, she'd given up. I kind of regretted that now.

"I have." Willa's face was so red, I couldn't help but think if I touched it, my skin would burn.

"You don't want to elaborate?" I asked at the same time Daphne said, "With who?"

"I can't say, so please …" Willa's cheeks puffed. "Drop it."

Daphne tapped the tip of her brush against the table as she stared at Willa. "This is going to bug me now. Why can't you say?"

Willa shifted in her chair, and one of her hands trembled.

I decided to let her off the hook. "What should I expect next?"

Daphne turned to me, and Willa gave me a grateful smile. "Has he asked you out again?"

"Well, not exactly. But he implied that he wanted to."

Daphne nodded. "He'll probably save getting dirty until he gets you someplace private. So, if you're not ready, don't let that happen."

"Dirty?" I asked.

"You know, take you through all the bases."

I nodded, trying to absorb all that would mean. I was ready, though. At least, I thought I was. I didn't have to love him to experiment and have fun with him.

"You want to do more with Byron?" Willa asked.

"Yeah, I mean," I blew a curl from my face, "I want to know what it's like, and Byron's really sweet."

Daphne beamed at me. "Our little Pegs is growing up."

I flicked some pink confetti at her. "Shut up."

A little while later, after Mom got home, we began cleaning up. "Pegs, you do know Dash has been in your room since I got home, right?"

Dash hanging out here wasn't exactly news to Daphne and Willa. They knew he came and went as he pleased. But the fact he hadn't made his presence known raised brows.

I forced a smile. "He can wait a few minutes."

"I need to get home." Willa shut her kit, drained the last of her lemonade, then set the glass down. "Bye, Peony."

Daphne joined her, waving over her shoulder.

"Okay." Mom wiped her hands on a kitchen towel, watching them walk off with her head tilted. "Bye girls."

Mom grabbed my shoulder before I could leave the room. "I'm cleaning it up."

"Not that. Dash." She hung the towel up. "What happened Friday night? It sounded like you guys had a fight."

Her voice was quiet, but with or without Dash being here, I still didn't want to talk about it.

"He's just being his usual self. Interfering and too bossy." I tried to play it off, but I knew she could tell it was more than that this time.

Even so, she let it go with a nod. "I picked up the last of your uniforms today."

"Thank you." I couldn't believe my last summer as a high school student had passed, and we'd be back in school the next day. It seemed I'd been waiting years to become a senior and experience this magical turning point that would help shape the course of my life. And now that it was finally here, my confidence and excitement had vanished.

"They're still in the car, but I'll iron them later and bring them to your room."

Dad gave us a credit card years ago. There was no way Mom could afford to send me to Magnolia Cove Prep without his help. As it stood, he paid for the ghastly yearly tuition, supplies, and had even said he'd buy me a car. Mom drew the line at that, seeing as Dash took me to school on most days.

But my eighteenth birthday was right around the corner, and I hoped that he'd ignored her. I didn't want to rely on Dash anymore.

It was surprising to some that Mom and Dad were amicable, considering he still loved her. When I'd asked, he'd stated he was too old to try to keep someone who didn't want to be kept. He'd respected Mom's decision to have her own life, as well as her honesty, no matter how much it'd pained him when she decided to leave him.

He'd never remarried. Though I knew at fifty-six that wasn't likely in the cards, I still wanted him to be happy.

When the table was spotless, and I figured I'd ignored the devil in my room long enough, I squared my shoulders and decided to get it over with. It was my freaking room, after all. He didn't get to make me avoid my own personal space.

He was playing the Xbox, his boots kicked to the floor, and his eyes bloodshot.

"Are you stoned?"

"Who cares if I am?"

I shook my head and shut the door. "What are you doing here?"

He cursed as his player died and then tossed the controller aside. "School is starting tomorrow. This tantrum needs to stop; it's been forty-eight hours."

"I haven't been counting." I moved to my desk, pushing some magazines aside to set my box back in the corner.

"But you admit to having a tantrum, right?"

I counted backward from ten, then turned around. "I'm not being a brat about this. You deliberately interfered with my life, my feelings, and my self-esteem."

He looked like he was about to roll his eyes, then caught himself. "If it walks like a brat, talks like a brat, and is still carrying on like a brat …" His gaze fell on me, blank and callous. "Then it's probably a brat."

Fuck this. "Okay, bye Dash. Window is that way." I grabbed my phone, then the door, and shut it behind me, annoyed beyond reason that I had to leave my own room.

Byron had been texting me since our date, but I had no new messages today. I'd contemplated texting him, but I didn't want to come across as too eager.

Dash remained in my room, or left, I didn't know. I plonked down onto the couch and unlocked my phone. When I went to open a new message to Byron, I frowned as I discovered some marked as read from him that I hadn't read yet.

Byron: What kind of flowers do you like?

Byron: Ok, so that was probably random. But I'm excited to see you tomorrow.

Rage engulfed me when I realized what Dash had done.

He'd opened my messages and read through them all. There was nothing too embarrassing said between us, but that didn't matter. He'd taken this stupid game a step further and snooped.

Thankfully, he hadn't responded.

Me: Sorry, Daphne and Willa were over. I love sunflowers, and I'm excited too. :D

Byron: Sunflowers, huh? What were you guys up to?

After texting back and forth for a while, I finally returned to my room. It was empty, and the window was closed.

TWELVE

Peggy

The giant ivy-covered gates of Magnolia Cove Preparatory were opened.

The two acres on which the castle-like structure sat upon a cliff face was a glowing green, the summer heat no match for the top-of-the-line irrigation system and the landscapers kept on payroll by the school.

The gray wood and stone building, which was larger than most mansions in the area, was draped in moss and serpentine whorls of greenery, disguising the age and dressing it in classic beauty.

The hedges were trimmed, the lampposts polished, and the parking lot almost full as Mom's car crept closer to the drop-off zone.

At least when I rode with Dash, no one snickered at Mom's small, ordinary SUV.

"Let them be shallow dicks," Mom said, giving the stink eye to a few onlookers as we pulled up. "I've driven cars even their fat trust funds couldn't afford to buy. It's only money on wheels."

"Love you, Mom." I blew her a kiss, which she caught and pocketed, then I dragged my backpack from the back seat and shut the door.

Daphne was waiting by the fountain, tapping away on her phone as Reese Dillon tried to talk to her. Daphne's light green blouse was tight over her chest, and her plaid skirt barely hit mid-thigh. She wore her black socks to her knees like most girls and finished off the ensemble with black heels. Me? Well, I just threw my blouse, skirt, and shin-high socks on, then did my best to lace my boots while I was still fast asleep most mornings.

This morning, I had every intention of getting up early to do my hair and makeup, but I'd hit snooze on my alarm and passed back out. I'd managed a quick brush through my hair and an application of mascara in the car on the way here, though.

"Thank God," Daphne said beneath her breath, grabbing my hand and pocketing her phone. "Bye, Reese."

I waved at Reese, who stared after us with his hands in his pockets. "Reese is nice."

"I don't want nice. Nice is boring."

"Nice is underrated, trust me," I said, tugging my skirt down when I felt the breeze kiss my thighs.

"Dash is apparently one hell of a hookup, so don't judge before you try."

I feigned ignorance even as my stomach dipped. "Ew." My nose wrinkled as we neared the steps. "I haven't been awake long enough for that."

Willa joined us as we walked inside, wearing her uniform much the same as Daphne did but with black ballet flats instead of heels.

"Well, I hope you're awake enough for that," she said, gesturing to the small crowd of guys from the lacrosse team who just happened to be standing halfway down the hall and looking right at us.

My eyes grew wide at the sight of them. "Um."

"Um is right," Willa said between her almost closed lips.

"Are those sunflowers?" Daphne asked a little too loudly.

My eyes grew bigger with each step we took toward our lockers.

Three weeks ago, we'd picked up our new schedules and

IDs. After comparing them over the summer, we found out we only had a few classes together each day, but thankfully, our lockers weren't too far apart.

And Byron was standing directly in front of mine.

His friends drifted away, jeering and sending suggestive looks as they moved on down the hall.

"I'll see you in third period," Daphne said, dragging Willa with her to their lockers.

That left me alone with the giant sunflowers and the giant holding them. "So, wow."

So, wow? Jesus.

Byron's chin dipped as he smiled, endearing and confident at the same time. "So maybe not totally random." He stepped forward, handing them to me. "For you."

I took them, finding a small card attached that read, *just give me a heads-up before you sneeze.*

A laugh sputtered from me, disbelief staining the sound and my cheeks. "Thank you. They're beautiful."

"You didn't need the flowers to look like an ass nugget. Those tap shoes you call loafers already do the job just fine." I turned, mouth agape, to find Dash leaning against my locker. "A word, Freckles?"

Fear and mortification joined forces, and I struggled to say anything.

"Dashiell, forgive me. I'll be sure to remember your flowers next time."

I blinked at that, and Dash's jaw worked, eyes hard on Byron. "Flowers aren't the way to my heart, Woods. And they sure as shit aren't the way to hers." His lips curled, and his teeth flashed. "But then again, you've known her five minutes. So what would you really know at all?"

"Dash," I hissed.

"How about that word now?"

I shook my head, words evading me.

"I think she's made it pretty clear she doesn't want to talk to you. So why don't you go and burden someone else with your gloomy presence?"

Seeing Dash was about to lunge, I turned to Byron and laid a hand on his chest to keep Dash, who was breathing heavily at my back, from getting suspended on the first day. "Let me put some things away, and I'll catch up with you at lunch?"

Byron was staring over my head, but with a tap on his granite chest, he lowered his gaze. After a nod, then a quick, calculated peck to my forehead, he was swaggering down the hall.

I opened my locker and my bag, trying to stuff notebooks inside and the flowers on top. All the while, Dash just watched me.

"Kayla doesn't exactly look thrilled today, does she?"

I hadn't looked, and I didn't think I wanted to now. "Dash, seriously."

"What?" He pushed me aside then squashed the flowers in enough to shut the door.

"You squished them."

"Who gives a rat's ass? They're weeds anyway."

"I like them."

"You like a lot of things you probably shouldn't." He eyed me a moment. "Only now, you're picking those things over me."

He started strolling down the hall to where Lars, Jackson, and Raven were hanging outside the boy's bathrooms.

Guilt sliced deep, and I called after him. "Dash, wait."

He stopped, his shirt half-untucked and his pants sitting too low on his hips, as he fiddled with his collar, raising it higher.

"This is ridiculous," I said once I'd stopped in front of him. "Why can't you just say you're sorry?"

"Because I did nothing wrong."

I met his hard stare with one of my own. "Interfering with my life isn't wrong?"

He stepped forward, growling low into my face. "Not when it's only ever been to protect you."

My lashes dipped as he skirted around me to join his friends.

His words sat there, hovering like a ghost as I squeezed my books close to my chest and headed for class.

Kayla's gaze felt like a flatiron had seared into the back of my head during biology that morning.

"She seems pissed," I said, not needing to look across the cafeteria to know she was still glaring at me, gossiping and hashing false truths about me.

Daphne dragged a fry through her puddle of ketchup. "He totally claimed you in front of the whole school by bringing you those flowers." The fact Daphne was sitting with us and not with Kayla and her pep squad probably didn't help.

"I didn't think she'd be this mad."

"She cheated on him," Willa said. "Like she has any right to be mad that he's moving on."

I didn't think that mattered much to Kayla.

I almost squealed when Byron fell into the seat next to me, tearing a chunk out of his wrap. "Hey."

"Hi," I said, trying not to laugh when he attempted to smile around his chewing.

"Your girl is mad," Daphne said.

Byron frowned, glancing over to the cheerleaders' table. He lifted a shoulder. "She'll get over it."

Daphne's pursed lips said she thought otherwise.

That, combined with the way he didn't dispute the words *your girl,* had the sandwich I'd just eaten threatening to make a reverse trip.

Byron finished chewing before saying, "Wade's hosting another party this Friday night. A return to school, fuck senior year thing."

Willa raised a brow. "What's his problem with senior year?"

Byron looked at her as if she was crazy, then shook his head. "Hey, think you can ask Jack to bring some green?"

Willa's hazel eyes darkened at the mention of her stepbrother. "Why don't you ask him?"

"Because Dash isn't exactly my biggest fan right now, which means neither is the rest of his stoner crew."

The way he'd said *stoner crew* itched at my skin. Granted, they got high a lot, but I still didn't agree with the name.

Daphne arched a brow but otherwise kept eating her fries.

Willa sighed. "Sure."

With a slap on the table, Byron stood. "Sweet, thanks." I thought he was just going to leave, and I was kind of hoping he did, seeing as I knew eyes were watching us, but then he grabbed my chin and bent over. "Think about coming to the party. I'll call you tonight?"

I nodded, braced for a kiss and fearing it, but it never came.

I exhaled my relief, then took a long sip from my water bottle.

"He was totally about to kiss you," Willa said with excited eyes.

Daphne smirked. "Yeah, if you hadn't looked like a deer caught in headlights."

Scowling, I stole a fry from her plate.

"So are we going to Wade's again?" Willa tapped her nails on the table.

Daphne nodded, wrapping her red lips around her straw.

I glanced around the cafeteria but couldn't see any sign of Dash or his friends. They were probably outside or sneaking a cigarette in one of the deserted classrooms.

I had English with him before lunch, and though he'd taken his usual seat next to me, like he did whenever we shared the same class, he hadn't said a word.

Still, going to the party was another way to hang out with Byron. Convincing my mom to let me go was going to be tough, though. "Mom probably won't let me go again. Not so soon."

Willa and Daphne both groaned. "Tell her you're staying at my place, duh."

I glared at Daphne, at how easily she expected me to lie, but as the day dragged on, and I'd thought about it some more, all the reasons why I shouldn't fell away.

Until I couldn't see how the lie wouldn't work.

THIRTEEN

Dash

Fucking cocky Prince Charming wannabe.

If it wouldn't put me in an even worse position with Peggy, I would have introduced his balls to his stomach, and my fist would have made pancake batter out of his nose by now.

Church meowed, and I ran my fingers over his head when he plopped down next to me on the couch. I'd wanted to dunk myself straight in the pool when I'd arrived home, but after walking out there and hearing my mother's moans, I'd stalked right back inside and slammed the door.

I'd been so distracted, held hostage by rage, I hadn't even seen Emanuel's old Chevy parked off to the side of our long drive.

A message came through on my phone, and I exited out of the game I was playing to read it.

Freckles: Come over?

The petty part of me—which let's face it, was a lot of me— wanted to tell her to fuck off. But my desperation to have things return to normal won out, and I leaned forward to snatch my keys off the table.

Church protested as I got up and pocketed my phone right as Mother Dearest's heels clacked over the floor. "How was your first day?"

"Not as good as yours."

Her cheeks turned crimson, her mouth hanging open.

I made haste for the door before she could say anything else.

Peggy's window was already open, a sign that maybe she was up for negotiations. My spirits lifted as my body did, and I rolled inside onto her bed. "Ready to grovel?"

Peggy set her homework down, already out of her school clothes and wearing one of her preferred super-long men's T-shirts. Most of the shit she wore was from the thrift store, but I didn't like the idea of her wearing some strange dude's old clothes, so every Christmas, I bought her some new men's XL T-shirts.

I tried to keep my eyes off her thighs as she took a seat on the bed. Tried. I got points for that, because fuck if I could. Why did it feel like it was the first time I'd seen them? Had they always had that tiny dip between them?

She quickly stuffed a pillow over her lap and attempted to fix the craptastic job she'd done of putting her hair into a messy bun. There wasn't enough of it anymore, so ringlets sprang free, caressing the elegant slant of her neck and dusting the slim curves of her face.

"I owe you nothing. But I'm willing to put this aside on one condition."

"One?" Shucking off my boots, I peered up into her face, getting comfy on my side of the bed.

"You don't interfere with my life anymore."

"You're my best friend. Are you saying I'm not supposed to care?"

She blew a wayward curl from her lips. "I'm saying you need to quit being a controlling dick."

I slapped a hand over my chest. "Well, I'll be. This isn't exactly the apology I was hoping for."

"You'll be hoping for a while if that's what you're expecting."

We scowled at each other, but I could feel my face grow lax as I watched her lashes open and close and studied the tiny bow to her upper lip.

"Fine."

"Fine."

"Can we play now?" I asked.

In answer, she grabbed a controller and handed it to me.

The next morning, I picked Peggy up for school, satisfied that things were back to normal in that regard, yet something was still irking me.

It was like having an itch I couldn't find. As I watched her scroll through the music on my phone, then stroll down the hall to meet up with the douchebag extraordinaire, I found myself in a constant state of tension.

"Her tits sure bounced like they were real," Raven was saying when I joined them at my locker. "Nice handfuls too."

"Who cares if they're real or not? They're fucking insane." Lars stuffed a handful of Cheetos into his mouth, then dusted his hand off on his trousers.

Jackson messed around with his tie. "She's still got one hell of a lady boner for Woods, though."

"Damn right. She's probably thinking about him when she fucks you," I tacked on.

Raven flipped me off. "Good morning to you too, shithead."

"We hitting Wade's again this Friday?" Jackson asked. "Get this. Willa said the team wants me to score them some green."

I barked a laugh. "As if."

"That's what I said. Fuckers can do their own dirty work."

The bell rang, and I plucked my notebook out, slamming the locker closed to find Byron all up in Peggy's face.

Rave snuck in a low taunt. "Those fists of yours clench any harder, you'll burst out of your clothes. Hulk style, baby."

I went to punch him, and he chuckled, dodging as he slipped into the dispersing crowd.

"No flowers today, Prince Charming?" I asked as I sidled up nice and close to Peggy.

Peggy spun, shoving me back a step. "Quit, Dash."

I righted my messed up shirt, making sure it was messed up just how I liked it. "Just saying. No need to get all bent out of shape over it."

Byron's grin needed to be wiped off his smug face. Yeah, he thought he had me pegged, but he didn't know shit. He had no idea.

Peggy muttered a goodbye to Byron, then joined me as we headed to class. "Would it kill you to be nice?"

"I'm not sure, but I kind of like being alive, so it's best we don't tempt fate, right?"

Peggy tried to smother her laugh, but it snuck out, and I bumped her shoulder. She bumped me back, hard, and I chuckled as I side-stepped to catch myself.

"We still need to finish the last season of *Game of Thrones*," she reminded me as we took a seat in the back of the room.

I grinned, some of the tension easing away. "After school."

FOURTEEN

Peggy

I walked back to my locker between classes and froze.

A tiny pink letter was peeking out of one of the cracks. I looked around, finding a few students lingering, then tucked my lip between my teeth as I unlocked it.

It fluttered to the floor. After shoving my books inside, I picked it up, taking it with me to my next class. My nail flicked it open as I took a seat at the desk beside Daphne, and my heart bottomed out.

Break up with him, or I'll take something of yours.

Daphne snatched the note before Mr. Roth came inside, her brows gathering as she read it, then looked at me. "Is she talking about Dash?"

I hadn't even thought of who she might've been referring to, but the thought of Kayla and Dash caused everything inside my head and stomach to spin. "I don't know."

She ripped it up, then swept the pieces to the floor. "Ignore her. Are you and Byron even going steady?"

The class started to fill, so I just shook my head. We hadn't labeled what we were doing. In fact, after almost a week of texting daily, I didn't even hear from Byron last night.

I supposed I could've reached out first, but I was still worried I'd come across as needy. Thanks to Dash interrupting us this morning, we'd had less than a minute to say hello.

Steady. If we weren't going out or dating for real, then what were we doing? Getting to know one another? I guess that's what it was, which was fine with me, but I had to wonder if I really wanted to take this thing further with Byron.

Just then, he walked inside the classroom, right by two of his teammates, and took the seat directly in front of me. "Hey, Pegs."

I smiled, and Mr. Roth dumped his briefcase on his desk. "All right, sit down, sit down."

My eyes stayed glued to the back of Byron's head as the note, whatever it was we were doing, and Dash clouded my head like a bad fog.

Maybe I'd done something. Maybe he was sick of trying to vie for my attention. Or maybe, I'd been making myself too available to him. I resolved to talk to Daphne about it at lunch.

Daphne had told me if we weren't going steady, then I needed to pull back. Let him work for it. Whatever that meant.

So even though I was dying to message Byron and check if everything was okay and ask him what was happening between us, I didn't. I liked him, sure, but I wasn't next-level obsessed. I could wait him out.

I snatched the popcorn bowl to put back on my side of the bed. My eyes were on the TV as White Walkers descended on the Wall, but my mind roamed anywhere and everywhere else.

Maybe it'd be like last time, and I'd just show up at the party, and we'd eventually run into each other?

I hoped not. We might not be able to call each other boyfriend and girlfriend, but I thought we were at the stage of getting to know each other where he'd at least make plans with me.

Dash's face interrupted as he loomed above me. "For fuck's sake, are you high?"

I blinked up at him. "What? No." I laughed then. "Wait, were you just singing Manfred Mann?"

"You wouldn't even need to ask that if you'd quit daydreaming for one damn minute."

His eyes were hard, jaw set, and I poked him in the cheek. "Don't be mad."

His dimple appeared, his eyes dropping to my mouth. "Wanna practice again?"

I pushed him off me. "I'm good, thanks."

Dash laid on his side, his head in his hand, and his shirt riding over his waist. "You don't think you need to?"

"I've kissed him already."

His jaw clenched. "When?"

"After our date, in the parking lot." I shoved another handful of popcorn into my mouth.

Dash watched me, silent for some minutes, then said, "Just once?"

"Yeah." I leaned up on my elbows to grab my water bottle, popping the top and taking a long sip.

His voice was scratchy as he asked, "Have you kissed him again since?"

I shook my head. "No, but I think he might try again this Friday."

More silence.

When I couldn't take it anymore, I slammed my drink down on the nightstand. "Ugh, just speak."

Dash smirked. "Just saying, how do you know you're ready for what comes next if you've only kissed him once?"

"Are you being serious right now?" I couldn't tell because his expression wasn't giving anything away.

"Deadly. You need my training as much as you need your next breath, and you know it."

I stared at his mouth, remembering the velvety touch of it on mine. Kissing him didn't suck, and it didn't make things awkward, but the thought of doing so now felt wrong in different ways.

"Wouldn't that be cheating in a sense?"

He scoffed. "He's an eighteen-year-old guy who hasn't asked you to be his girlfriend. As far as I know. Who's to say he's not hooking up with other people?" Dash softened his next words. "He did just get out of a long-term relationship, Pegs."

The whole *"he's a guy"* thing didn't fly with me. Dash was right, though. Byron hadn't promised me anything, and he hadn't said he wasn't seeing other people. He hadn't even hinted at it. I swallowed the sting that tried to swell my throat.

"It feels wrong," I said, planting a hand on his chest when he drifted closer.

His hand wrapped around mine. "That makes it even better." His face hovered over mine, giving me a chance to stop this, but I didn't.

His gaze narrowed, sharpening the bright blue of his eyes. My heart kicked faster, sprinting as his nose brushed mine and strands of his hair rained down to lick at my forehead.

My eyes closed at the first glide of our skin, and my stomach ceased knotting when his bottom lip fitted itself between my lips. Gentle, caressing, hypnotizing strokes had my body pliant and growing warm as his hand left my cheek and started drifting down my body to my hip.

When my mouth opened farther, and my tongue stroked hesitantly at the underside of his top lip, he groaned. "Good, that's so good."

I did it again, swiping a little deeper, and his teeth caught my tongue, gently scraping over it. I fizzed and faded beneath him, a desperate sound leaving me.

"Pegs." Mom knocked, and Dash flew to the other side of the bed. "Is Dash staying for dinner?"

She opened the door as I stuffed a heap of popcorn into my mouth.

Setting a basket of clean clothes on the floor, she looked over at us, her lips puckering. "Don't tell me you've filled up on junk the one night I actually decide to cook."

"I've always got room for your cooking, Peeny."

Dash had called her that since he started talking, and ever the sucker for it, Mom smiled. "You'd better." She shut the door, and the popcorn sprayed out of my mouth as we both rolled over and started laughing.

FIFTEEN

Peggy

I rounded the corner, dropping my hall pass as I saw a couple making out against the wall.

"Such a dirty fucking girl," Lars said against Daphne's neck.

My eyes almost popped out of my head, a small squeak escaping when I saw where his hand was. Under her skirt.

Lazily, as if he didn't even care who was watching, his head rose, and Daphne opened her eyes, her breasts straining against her blouse, and the top buttons undone.

I scrambled to grab my pass, gesturing with it down the hall. "Um, pee break."

Daphne grinned. "Run along then."

I nodded, continuing past them.

After I did my business, I decided against splashing water on my flushed cheeks. Instead, I stared at my reflection, waiting for them to cool.

The humidity had ruined my attempt to straighten my hair, but it sat a little longer, waves skimming past my shoulders, thanks to the effort.

I patted the remaining drops of water from my hands, then flipped my head forward and gathered it all into a small ponytail, using the rainbow scrunchy I had around my wrist.

I suppose Lars and Daphne weren't exactly a secret, but that was the first time I'd actually seen them together.

Lars was here on a scholarship, and most people thought

it was due to his mom dating the principal. Some would say Daphne was slumming it, including herself, and even though Willa and I had pushed, she still wouldn't divulge much about their relationship.

If you could call what they did a relationship. Who was I to know? One and a half dates and I was still clueless about everything.

Yet as I remembered the sight of his hand on her thigh, I knew I didn't want to be. My cheeks threatened to flush again as I thought of someone touching me that way while whispering wicked things into my ear. I marched out of the bathroom, taking the other hallway back to class even though it was the long way around.

Dash eyed me behind the thick frames of his glasses, slouched low in his seat with a pen hanging between his teeth as I skimmed past the tables to my seat next to his.

"What's up with you?" he asked when I kept doodling circles on the page instead of reading the five pages instructed by the teacher.

"Hmm?"

"You went to the toilet, right?"

I withheld a laugh. "Yes."

"Well, what the hell happened in there that's making you draw like a four-year-old again?"

"Mr. Thane," Mrs. Cruthers said from behind her desk. "Eyes on your own table."

With one last withering look at me, Dash did as he was told, but I knew he was still waiting for an explanation.

When someone started coughing down the front, I lowered my voice to a whisper. "I saw Daphne and Lars."

His brows pulled in as he tipped his head toward me. "And?" When I felt my cheeks begin to color, he grinned, his eyes glinting. "Oh, you saw them fucking around."

"Mr. Thane. Care to share what you're talking about with the class?"

Dash pursed his lips in thought. "That's probably not a good idea, so I'm gonna have to say no."

Mrs. Cruthers stabbed a finger at the door. "Outside. You can finish your reading in the hall."

Dash was still grinning as he stood and grabbed his things. "Later, Freckles."

He didn't see me later, though. I peeked around the cafeteria but couldn't see him.

I gave up my search and plowed into my leftover macaroni.

"What's up with you?" Willa asked.

"Peggy Sue caught me and Lars in the hallway." Daphne took a bite out of her burger.

"In the hallway?" Willa asked a smidge too loud.

"Shh. Shit." Daphne picked some lettuce from her lip, tossing it to the table with a splat. "Sometimes we meet up really quick. It's not a big deal."

I just remembered. "There are cameras."

"Not in every corner." Daphne winked.

I looked over at the table of cheerleaders, noticing Kayla was actually eating and not staring death daggers at me for the first time this week. Which could be because Byron hadn't shown today. "Do you miss your old friends?"

Daphne scoffed. "No, but the few who are real still talk to me. When queen Mcbitch face isn't around, of course."

"That makes them real?"

She twisted her lips. "Good point. Now they're on my shit list too."

My eyes bulged. "Ah …"

Waving a hand, she snatched a napkin, patting her mouth.

"Don't give me that."

"What?"

"That face you make when you think you've done something wrong."

Willa laughed as Daphne tried to imitate my supposed face, her eyebrows dropping low and her eyes widening.

I flipped them off. "Shut up."

They cackled harder.

Lunch ended, and we headed to our respective classes. The afternoon dragged, and I found my mind swirling in dizzying circles. Where was Byron? I could text him and ask. Why did what I saw in the hall still leave a lingering curiosity? It felt kind of weird, being that they were my friends.

Dash was waiting for me, smoking beside his car as the teacher on duty debated whether to walk over and ask him to put it out.

I got there before he could and jumped inside, thankful Dash had already started the engine. Cool air blew over my arms. Through the window, Dash watched me redo my hair, a cloud of smoke blurring the glass for a moment.

Once inside, he was quiet, fingers tapping the wheel as some hardcore band blared from his speakers. When he neared the bridge, I decided I didn't want to go straight home.

I turned the volume down. "Show me your new TV?" Apparently, he'd gotten one for his birthday at the start of summer. I didn't typically go to his house, but it wasn't by choice. He was just always showing up at mine before I could ever consider it.

He peeked over at me, then shrugged, turning around and heading toward the bay.

Dash's house was a weird mix of old meets new architecture. Sloping and flat rooftops met provincial-styled columns in various shades of cream and dull blue. In the meticulously kept gardens, hedges intermingled with May's favorite flowers, roses, and a gurgling fountain sat in the middle of the pink stoned circular drive. When we were kids, we'd TP it for Halloween or draw moustaches on the statue of the naked man, who spewed water from his mouth.

"It's still the most ridiculous fountain I've ever seen."

"I think its dick fell off." Dash hit the brakes, turned off the ignition, and jumped out.

"You're joking." I shut the door, leaving my bag in the car as I traipsed over to the fountain.

"Looks like Emanuel glued it back on."

Sure enough, it looked as if a line of clear glue sat over its shaft. I snorted, then bent low to drag my fingers through the cool water.

Dash tugged at a piece of my hair. "It's hotter than Satan's scraped up asshole out here. Let's go."

"You say the nicest things."

Dash huffed, holding the door open for me, which shocked me a little.

"Dash, oh—hi Peggy." May was standing at the end of the hall, holding a martini in one hand and her sunglasses in the other.

"Hey, how are you?"

"Good, good." An awkward pause settled as she stared at me, and I kicked off my boots, not to be nice, but more for something to do. "How's your mother?"

"Great, thanks for asking."

Dash cleared his throat. "Why don't you go drink that martini, Mother?"

May blinked, then forced a smile. "Yes, why don't I?" She took a sip, then disappeared.

"Nosy fucking woman," Dash said as we traversed one of the long halls to his room, and then another hall, and then stopped at the last door on the left.

"You're like a cynical old man," I said as he slammed the door behind us. "With the slippers and cat to match."

"What? I am fucking not."

I raised a brow at Church, who was asleep on said slippers.

"Don't talk shit about Church."

His room was bedecked in dark browns and grays, and having the drapes pulled shut gave it a modern dungeon-esque feel.

Framed records hung on the dark brown walls. The Rolling Stones, Arctic Monkeys, and varying other bands' records were signed and protected by a sheet of glass. He'd gotten tickets to see the Arctic Monkeys live for his seventeenth and had taken me with him. His dad had scored the signed record from the Stones.

Half a dozen boots of the same design in different shades of black and gray littered the floor, hiding beneath jeans, T-shirts, ties, his leather jacket, empty chip wrappers, and textbooks.

And then there was the giant TV hanging from the wall opposite his giant king-size bed, the latter sitting low to the ground.

"How do you even watch that?" I asked.

"With great ease." He stripped out of his blazer, tossing it on the brown leather sofa in the corner.

"It's so fucking big."

"That's what she said."

I coughed out a laugh, then lowered to his bed, my school skirt fanning up around my thighs.

"You're curious, aren't you?"

"About?" I pretended to take an interest in my nails.

The bed dipped, and then his voice was directly behind me. "Lie back."

"We don't need to—"

"Cut the bullshit excuses, Freckles. We know why you wanted to come over, and it wasn't to see my TV. Lie back."

I did, though I was tense, and a nervous breath sat stuck in my throat.

"Good," he whispered when my back settled against his chest. His hands brushed down my arms, rubbing until he could feel my breathing steady. "What exactly did you see?"

We both knew what he was talking about, so I didn't bother pretending otherwise. My eyes had shut. The gentle touch of his hands lulling my body to relax and meld into his. "Well, he was kissing her."

A swift caress had my ponytail shifting, warm breath heating my neck. "Where?"

"Her mouth and …" I swallowed when his lips grazed my neck. "Yes, there."

"What else?" I could've imagined it, but I swore his voice turned huskier.

"His hand was up her …" I licked my lips as his rubbed over the curve between my shoulder and neck. "Her …" I stopped, a gasp leaving me when I felt his other hand bunch up my skirt. "Skirt." My exhale tumbled out of me when the pads of his fingers hit my thigh.

"What do you think he was touching?" The words were nothing but heated air, barely audible, and my stomach flooded with drunk bees, buzzing and flipping.

"Her … her …" Oh God, I couldn't even say it, but he didn't force me. He tilted my head back with his fingers at my chin, his mouth crashed down on mine, and his other hand climbed between my parted legs.

"Wider," he rasped, and I shifted them apart even more. "Good. And I believe the word you were looking for is cunt, pussy, vag—"

I shoved my tongue inside his mouth, and he groaned, meeting me sweep for breathless sweep. "Do it," I said on a pleading exhale, pulling at his lip with my teeth. "Please."

His eyes opened, hooded and dilated. Then, keeping them on me as we breathed each other's next breaths, his finger skimmed over the wet patch of my panties.

Something moved over his face, and his grip on my chin became firmer, as did the hardness I could feel digging into my lower back.

I shivered as his fingers crawled over the fabric, tickling, rubbing, until he'd reached the edge, and then he pulled.

The elastic snapped, and a bite of pain met my lower hip. I ignored it, my opened legs trembling as his fingers snuck beneath the weakened cotton and found me.

"Shit." The word was a wheeze, his eyes shutting. His swallow was loud next to my ear, but no match for the thudding tempo of my heart. "Fuck me. Shit."

It was all I could do to sit still as he slid his fingers through me and began rocking into my back. I never thought having someone touch me there would feel like this. That it could feel a thousand times better than doing it myself.

"Dash," I croaked.

His gaze snapped to mine, his chest heaving, each inhalation lifting my body with it. "Do you think he was doing this?"

I nodded, then grabbed the side of his face, wanting his lips on mine. Our teeth and tongues started a slow dance in gentle torture, while his finger pressed against where I was most swollen. Sweat beaded at his temples and slicked down my spine, but we didn't stop. I wouldn't have let him if he'd tried.

"It's …" I tore my mouth away, my eyes struggling to stay open. I was all but lying over him by that point, draped over him like an electric blanket about to catch fire.

"Coming?" he asked, then probed my entrance. He inserted the tip of his finger while the other ran tiny circles over me. "God, look at you."

I took one ragged breath after another, panting as my thighs started to quake. A pitiful sound left me, and I became impossibly lax against Dash, feeling him hot and heavy against my slick back while a thousand mini earthquakes rocked through me and tossed my brain into glittering confetti.

Dash cursed, and when my eyes reopened, the world crashing in like a tidal wave, I turned as he scooted back. My saliva thickened as he undid his pants, pulling himself free.

Reality took a step back when I gazed at the bobbing, angry, thick looking steel his hand wrapped around. "You weren't joking about the she said thing."

He chuckled, but then the sound broke off. "Ah, fuck, I'm gonna come any second. Wanna put your mouth on it?"

I licked my swollen lips, then crawled over his legs, feeling the cool air on my bare thighs. "What do I do?"

"Lick it, suck it, deep throat it, kiss it, squeeze it, fondle it. I'm not picky."

I laughed, and with his pained grin, I felt like there was no pressure to perform to a certain standard. Practice is practice after all.

I grabbed him, rubbing my thumb over the engorged head. "Wow."

"You're good for my ego."

"Well, considering the last time I saw it, it was the size of a twink—"

"Don't finish that sentence. Let's start with licking."

Laughing again, I lowered my head, swiping my tongue up the underside of his shaft. I stopped when I heard purring, and it wasn't coming from Dash. Peeking over to the other side of his bed, I saw Church kneading the bedding, his bright yellow eyes on us. "Church is watching."

"He's fine. Ignore him and love my dick."

I swiped my tongue under the head, tasting salt, and he twitched, then cursed as I pulled away. "He's judging us, Dash."

"Church, fuck off." He nudged the cat. Church hissed, then plopped to the floor and stalked off toward the bathroom.

I pinched my lips, then wrapped my hand tighter around him and decided to try to put him out of his misery. My mouth took as much of him as it could fit, and then he jerked, cursing and groaning as hot liquid squirted down my throat.

I coughed, swallowing quickly to keep from vomiting, then swiped below my lip. "God. Yuck."

Dash peeked one eye open, a satisfied curl to his upper lip. "Fucking awesome." He dragged his hand through his hair, exhaling a rough sigh. "What's next? I should be good in a few minutes."

"I need to go. Mom's probably going to be home soon." I smacked my lips together, cringing as I crawled off the bed to fix my skirt and straighten out my shirt.

Dash sighed again. "Fine, just give me a minute."

I smiled as I headed into his bathroom to rinse my mouth.

SIXTEEN

Peggy

I raced outside as soon as Dash's Rover pulled up with my lunch bag scrunched in my hand.

After climbing in, I stuffed it into my bag, then flipped the visor down to finish applying some mascara as he took off.

"Watch it," I said, almost poking my eyeball out when he drove over a roundabout instead of around it.

"You don't need that shit anyway."

I ignored him and quickly dipped the wand in to slick some on my other lashes. "What's that smell?" It was citrusy and woodsy at the same time.

Dash tossed his cigarette out the window. "New aftershave."

Shoving my mascara inside the front pocket of my backpack, I peeked over at him. His collar was pulled high, as per usual, but his hair didn't look like his typical I-just-rolled-out-of-bed-like-this mess. Today, it was a strategic mess; golden blond strands swept over to the right as though he'd fingered them just right for five minutes in front of the mirror.

He was clean shaven, which wasn't always the case. He wasn't one to shave every day, but rather, he would let the overnight growth shadow his defined jawline. His cheekbones were starker, more prominent, and the strong line of his nose begged a finger to trace it. I wasn't sure if it'd always been that way, or if, after what we'd done together, I'd started paying more attention.

"Not that I'm complaining or anything, but why the hell are you staring at me so damn hard?"

"Your face looks extra smooth," I lied, kind of. Extra smooth? God, I was so awesome.

"I'm just going to file this random ass conversation away as too fucking random. Moving on," he said, driving over the bridge and turning right to the school. "What are you going to tell your almost boyfriend? That you have a 'best friend with benefits' situation going down, and you no longer require his attention?"

I snorted, grabbing my bag and unclipping my seat belt as he drove through the school gates. "That would be a huge hell no." Once he'd parked, I opened the door, jumping down and swinging my bag over my shoulder.

"Why?" He slammed the door and grabbed his bag from the back.

"What do you mean why?" We crossed the lot and stepped onto the grass, my boots sinking into the plush green.

Dash took his time to answer as I stared ahead, looking for Daphne, Willa, or Byron. "I just don't get it. You and me—"

"Yo, Thane!" Lars jogged over, his shirt undone and flapping in the breeze. He was wearing a wifebeater underneath. Slowing once he'd reached us, he jerked his head at me. "Sup, Pegs."

I waved, then saw Daphne standing with Willa on the steps. "I'll see you later."

I skipped away, ignoring the heat from Dash's glare on my back.

"I heard she was making out with Coach Lenton after school," Daphne said, licking ranch from her fingers.

Dash and his friends were sitting in the back corner, tossing food wrappers and crushing soda cans. Annika from the cheerleading squad sidled over, standing next to where Dash was sitting on top of the table with his legs apart. A biting sensation pricked at my stomach when she placed her hand on his leg, her pretty oval face scrunching with her forced laughter.

Willa dropped her fork, snapping my attention away from Dash. "No way."

"Who are you talking about?" I resumed picking at my sandwich.

"Kayla. Apparently, she's making the rounds."

I looked back over at Dash, who was scowling at Annika—not that she seemed to care.

A thud hit the table next to me, and my nose pricked as I caught a whiff of Byron's cologne. I'd seen him in chemistry this morning but had only returned his wave.

He straddled the bench seat, his eyes alight. "You're a sight for sore eyes."

I offered a smile. "How are you?"

He blew out a breath. "Been dealing with some shit at home. I was going to text you last night, but it got too late. I had to hit the gym to make up for missing practice."

"Everything okay?"

"Yeah." Though he didn't sound so sure. "Just had to make sure my mom went to some appointments is all."

They must have been important if he was skipping school and practice. "She okay?"

"Getting there. So," he said as he stole a fry from Willa's plate, "what have I missed?"

Willa and Daphne shrugged, the former saying, "Oh, not much."

I sucked my lips and peeked over at Dash, who was now scowling at me or, rather, Byron.

"You free to chat tonight?"

The bell rang and students started throwing their trash out before heading to the doors.

"I suppose I can be." Yep, I was great at making myself a little less unavailable.

Outside the cafeteria, he pulled me down the hall, and I squeaked as he crowded me against my locker. His hand softened around mine, fingers curling and causing a herd of tingles to spread up my arm. "Not gonna lie, I was kind of disappointed that you didn't even text me yesterday."

I struggled to meet his gaze. "Well, I wasn't sure if you'd have wanted me—"

"You still wanna do this?" His eyes dropped to my lips, then lifted to mine, questions filling them. "Because I really like you."

Did I still want to do this? I did. At least, I was pretty sure I did. "Yeah, of course."

He lifted my hand to his lips, and Dash made a gagging sound as he passed us.

I sent his back a scathing look. Byron's fingers gripped my chin, directing my focus back to him. "Ignore him. He's just jealous."

I reared back, almost smacking my head into the locker. "Jealous?" I laughed, loud and shocked. "I don't think so. He's just an ass."

Byron's gaze narrowed on mine, then he shook his head. "That too. Come with me to the party tomorrow night?"

Damn. I'd almost forgotten about that. I still needed to tell Mom I was sleeping over at Daphne's. "As opposed to meeting you there? I'm getting ready at Daphne's."

"Whatever you want," he said, his arm finding purchase on the locker behind my head, his head, his entire body moving closer to mine. He ran a finger down my cheek. "I'm thinking I just might make this thing between us a bit more official."

My stomach did a backflip, and I hoped my eyes weren't bulging. "You are?"

He nodded, his finger reaching my lips and tracing them. "Wanna kiss you so bad."

"Yeah, well you can't," Dash said. Then Byron was shoved away. "She needs to get to class before your Romeo ass lands her with a late slip."

Byron's hands and jaw clenched.

I wanted to slap Dash, then tug at his stupid, perfect, messy hair. "What the hell, Dash? Don't shove him."

Dash moved me aside, then opened my locker to grab my history book. "I was clearly doing you a favor. Thank me when you're not late." Since when did he care about being on time for class? Slamming the locker, he didn't even let me look at Byron, so I waved over my shoulder as Dash snatched my hand and hauled me with him to class.

"What was that about?"

Dash didn't answer me. He flipped his book open and tugged his glasses from his shirt pocket, sliding them on as Mr. Andrews addressed the class.

I kept sneaking glances at him, but as the clock ticked on at the front of the room, and Mr. Andrews started getting amped about ancient Egyptians, I found myself going back to the same thing.

More official. Did that mean what I think it meant? I was pretty sure it did. And cue the storm of butterflies flapping and bouncing in a drunken jig inside my stomach.

It was happening. He was my boyfriend.

Oh, my God.

After school had finished, I found Daphne and quickly went over the plan. I'd meet Byron at her place or near her place and catch a ride with him. However he was getting there.

Daphne was grinning like the Cheshire cat. "Your first official boyfriend."

I frowned at that. "Let's not word it that way again, okay?"

She laughed, and then I raced off to the parking lot, climbing inside Dash's car which was already parked in the drop-off zone.

"What's got you smiling all weird like that?"

"Can't a girl smile?" I put my seat belt on, shoving my bag between my knees.

"Depends on what's made her smile, if you're asking me. Which you did. So who? Or what?"

I didn't see the point in not being honest. My excitement was too real. A blazing inferno of exhilaration. "Byron wants us to be official."

The car jerked as Dash hit the brakes too hard, almost running up the ass of Annika's Skoda in front of us. "Sounds riveting."

"So are you going to Wade's tomorrow night?"

"I hadn't planned on it, but I'm guessing you have?" He turned out of the school. "What's your mom going to say about party number two in a matter of weeks?"

"I'm not telling her."

Dash was quiet for a beat, and the silence, usually comfortable between us, became stifling. I rolled the window down and tried to think of something to say that'd smooth the pensive, hardened edges to his features. "What are you doing this afternoon?"

"Heading to the skate park for a bit, then I was going to come over and have you fondle my dick."

I coughed out a laugh. "*What?*"

"You heard me."

I blinked five times before I turned to him, still laughing.

"Dash, we can't do that now."

"Because fuckboy Romeo says he's claiming you?" He chuckled, the sound dry. "We were having fun. Fuck him."

I studied his expression, the hard set to his jaw, but I couldn't see his eyes behind his Ray-Bans. "That would definitely be cheating, and well," I hemmed, "I like him. I don't want to ruin things."

"Like Kayla did," he said. "You're right. He doesn't seem like the type to stand for betrayal all that well."

A sour taste eroded over my tongue as those words sluiced through me. He didn't. And even though I was new to this, and we weren't official, I knew Dash was right. Byron probably wouldn't take what Dash and I had been doing too well at all.

"I'm curious, though. What's there to like about the guy?" Dash asked. "His horrible taste in shoes? Not to mention, Kayla's not done with him. Drama, drama, drama."

"It sure sounds like she is." I opened the door when he reached my place, yanking my bag out. Leaning inside the car, I sighed. "Dash, please just let me do this."

His elbow was resting on the door, his head tilted as he surveyed me from behind dark frames. "I'm just failing to see why you even want to."

"I've already said why."

He waved his fingers. "Yeah, you like him. Supposedly. But you know …" His head dipped, gaze moving over my body. "Too much practice never hurt anyone."

I smirked, then shut the door. "Bye, Dash."

SEVENTEEN

Peggy

Coughing, I doused my hair in another layer of hairspray, then shoved the can down on my dresser.

I'd donned my aqua green tutu and paired it with an off-the-shoulder, ripped white T-shirt.

A text came through on my phone, and I picked it up, smiling.

Byron: one hour. :D

Me: 59 minutes :D :D

Gone was my fear of seeming too eager beaver, and in its place, excitement brewed steadily, keeping an almost permanent smile on my face. I wondered whether we'd sneak out, like Byron had said when he'd called me last night. "Find our own place to party," he'd said in a tired yet oh, so sexy voice.

While I wasn't ready to hand over my V-card to him just yet, I felt more than ready to try all the things Dash and I had tried. I was confident it'd feel just as good, just as exhilarating, breath stealing, and daydream worthy, and maybe even better.

Dumping my phone, I selected some silver hoop earrings and put them on as I tried to keep my feet from dancing on the spot. The window beside my bed was cracked open to help with the fumes, the breeze drifting off the creek stirring the lace curtains.

Dash had been quiet on the way to school this morning, and I'd gotten a lift home from Daphne after he'd texted me to say he was bailing early due to a headache. I'd asked if he was okay but hadn't gotten a response.

I was about to text him again to check when the wooden floorboards creaked with Mom's footsteps. My heartbeat stalled, then exploded, booming erratically. She was supposed to be at Phil's for dinner.

"Peggy," she said, more of a sigh than a greeting, leaning into my bedroom. "Take the earrings off. You're grounded."

My hands fell, my heart still rioting. "What?"

"Don't you raise your voice at me. I said you're not going. Now get changed."

Dazed, I just stood there. I'd asked if I could stay at Daphne's last night, and she'd said yes instantly. I'd slept over at Willa's plenty of times, Daphne's a few times too, and never once had she questioned it. Hell, she'd never once said no, so it wasn't even a matter of asking anymore, and more about letting her know what my plans were.

"I don't understand," I said the thought aloud.

"Wade's party?" Her brow rose sharply. "I wasn't born yesterday, sweetheart."

I groaned, yanking off my earrings. "Mom, I wouldn't have—"

"You should've just asked me like last time."

"I didn't think you'd say yes to another party, not this soon," I pleaded, feeling my eyes water.

Her own softened marginally. "I guess now you'll never know. Now strip and wash the makeup off. You're grounded for a week."

A week was pretty good, I thought, considering. But I'd only ever been grounded once before, and that was when Dash decided I should try some pot during last Thanksgiving break outside near the creek.

I should've known that wouldn't have been easy to hide, seeing as I'd laughed my ass off over nothing for an hour straight, ate everything in sight, then vomited it all up.

I hadn't done it again since.

I sighed, the sound a pitiful gush of air, throwing my arms around my body like a six-year-old who didn't get her own way. "This is so not freaking fair."

"Heard that."

I scrunched my nose, then yelled, "How'd you find out anyway?"

It took her a minute to respond, and I yanked off my skirt, throwing it into the corner of the room. "It's Magnolia Cove, Pegs. You think you kids are the only ones who gossip?"

Touché.

"We'll figure something out. Your birthday is soon right?" Yelling ensued in the background. "Mark, you fucking psycho, how you doing?" Laughter reached my ears, and I started swinging my legs up in the air on my bed. "Right? It's bomb as fuck. All right, later. You there, Peg?"

"Yup." I couldn't exactly go anywhere else. For a whole week.

"Sorry, haven't seen that idiot in ages. He goes to the public school."

Great, so not only was there a party I couldn't attend with my new boyfriend, but it was potentially one of the biggest parties to happen this year. I faked a yawn. "You should go, have fun."

"I am," he said, swallowing something, likely alcohol. "Wish you were here. I can't believe you got found out."

"I know."

We made plans to talk tomorrow, and I hung up before chucking my phone to the end of the bed. I'd texted Daphne earlier, telling her our plan had been thwarted. She wanted to know how, and I told her gossip. It didn't sound like she believed that, but at this point, I didn't really care.

I switched on the Xbox, but no one was online. Playing with a bunch of strangers was fine, though not as fun. I switched it off ten minutes later and went in search of a snack.

I was in bed before ten, wanting nothing more than to sleep this night off so I didn't have to think about Daphne, Willa, Byron, and probably Dash having fun without me.

Around midnight, I was almost asleep when the sound of cussing followed by a hard body came through the window. "Dash?"

"The one and only," he slurred, crawling up the bed commando style.

"You reek of booze."

"Probs because I drank a shit ton of it, probs." He slumped down next to me. "How's about a kiss?"

"How's about you should probs go home?"

He blinked slowly, then laughed. "Good one, but nah, I made it here, and here is good."

Grumbling, I tugged the duvet back over myself, well aware of the fact I was only in panties and a tank. "How was the party?"

"Pretty fucking crazy. How was the no party?"

I huffed, then paused. "Wait, how'd you know I wasn't going?"

His brows gathered, eyes shutting. "Ah, because you weren't there maybe?"

That had me laughing, and so did he, though it was more like bursts of drunken sound. "Quiet," I hissed. "Mom's already pissed at me."

"What happened?" he asked, rolling over to face me. His fingers reached for my cheek and his entire hand fell on it, heavily petting.

I shoved it away. "She found out I was going to Wade's, so now I'm grounded for a week."

"Bummer."

"Uh-huh."

"Wanna make out?" His hand went under the duvet, finding my hip and pulling me closer. My nose almost touched his, and all I could smell was bourbon and cigarettes intermingling with his new aftershave.

"No," I said, not sure if I meant it when his hand gripped around the curve of my hip, fitting so perfectly.

"You sure?" he asked on a whisper. "Because I'm so hard for you right now."

I laughed, then turned my face, trying to smother it in my pillow. "God, how did we get here?"

"Well, I walked. I'm assuming you've been here since school got out." I gave him a look that said that wasn't what I'd meant. He exhaled, his warm breath fogging my lips. "Who cares? It's a pretty great place to be."

"It is, is it?"

His lip curled, teeth and dimple appearing. "Best not to overthink it."

With his mouth unbearably close to mine and drifting closer, I pushed my hands against his chest. "It's always best to overthink it when you have a boyfriend."

His mouth snapped shut, and I could hear his teeth grind together. "He didn't seem to miss you too much tonight."

I sat up. "What's that supposed to mean?"

Dash rolled to his back, tucking his arm behind his head. The moon danced through the window, highlighting the tormented look etched upon his face and the muscles clenching in his upper arm. "Never mind."

"But I do mind. Did he do something?"

"Other than act like a fucking idiot? No, nothing you need to worry about."

I lowered to my back, and we both stared up at the patchy paint on the ceiling a long while.

Dash passed out before me, the sound of his snoring lulling me into a restless sleep. When I woke up, he was gone.

EIGHTEEN

Peggy

After watching my phone like a hawk all day Saturday, wondering if Byron would call, I almost missed it that night when I decided to throw my phone in my sock drawer.

He was tired and hungover, so therefore, he sounded disinterested in anything I talked about. Which was understandable.

He called again on Sunday to apologize, saying he'd never drank that much in his life and that half the night was a blur.

"Oh, goodie," Dash said, who'd also been quiet on the drive to school. "More weeds."

I shushed him, then pasted on a smile when I walked over to Byron, who was holding more sunflowers in front of my locker. "Thank you." I took them from him, toying with one of the luminous petals.

He slid his hands into his pockets, his tie still undone. "Open the note?"

I flicked it open and read the small inscription.

Do homecoming with me?

Homecoming was just under two weeks away, and I hadn't even thought about it until now. Which was strange, given I'd already bought my dress.

I looked up at him and nodded. "I'd be delighted to do homecoming with you."

He grinned, wrapping an arm behind my back. We squished the flowers between us when he grabbed my face and quickly pressed his lips to mine, pulling away before we got caught. "I've wanted to do that for days. And that felt more like a tease."

I bit my lip, then unlocked my locker to grab my books and put the flowers inside. "I'll see you at lunch?"

He tipped his chin up, winking as he walked backward to his own locker. "Count on it."

"Damn," Daphne said from behind me. "Someone has it bad."

"Or someone is trying a little too fucking hard," Dash chimed in, unlocking my locker and inspecting the card. "Homecoming?" He threw an accusing glare at me. "You said at the start of break that we were going together."

I didn't remember that, but maybe I had. Thankfully, I was saved from answering when Lars approached with a sucker hanging between his lips.

Daphne bristled, and I frowned as he gave her a once-over, then jerked his head for Dash to head to class with him.

"This conversation isn't over, Peggy."

"Oh, I'm sure." I waved.

He stopped, his tone hard and his eyes slightly crazed. "I'm dead serious. I'm taking you. So fix whatever the hell you just agreed to with Prince Shit Shoes over there." He flicked his eyes to where Byron was laughing with Danny, one of his teammates, down the hall.

Then he was striding away, Lars glancing at me over his shoulder as they walked to class.

"Told you," Daphne singsonged.

"Told me what?"

She and Willa rolled their eyes, then started talking about what a mess some of the cheerleaders were at Wade's party.

"So what do you want for your birthday?" Byron asked, unwrapping his chicken wrap and taking a huge bite.

I watched him chew, then dragged my eyes to the rose gardens lining the sitting area outside. Now that fall had begun to turn the heat down somewhat, it wasn't a death sentence to sit outside and eat lunch. Thank God, because being cooped up, having people's glares directed at you when you were simply trying to eat, wasn't my idea of a nice break from class.

"You don't have to get me anything, really," I said around a bite of cheese.

"Are you kidding? Of course, I do."

I paused mid chew, swallowing too hard. "What makes you think that?"

His brows knitted, face bunching. "Uh, because when a girl usually says they're fine, they're not."

I didn't say I was fine, but I let that be. "Honestly, I'm happy with cake. Lots and lots of cake."

"What kind?"

I flicked some crumbs from my lap. "Caramel. Double chocolate. I'm not picky." Those last words electrified my chest, and I quickly smothered the memory.

Byron pondered that as he finished his wrap.

"So," I said, remembering Dash's statement about homecoming, "about homecoming."

"Oh yeah. I've already spoken to my dad, and he's rented us a limo."

"What?" Shit.

He nodded, swallowing the last bite and scrunching the paper. "Yeah, sweet huh? We can have it all to ourselves, or you can invite Daphne and Willa to come with."

That was sweet. "Wow, well, thanks."

He grinned, then popped the top of my soda for me.

I wasn't sure what I was going to do about Dash, but it was clear I couldn't exactly ditch my boyfriend for my best friend. Especially when that best friend was Dash.

Daphne and Willa joined us for the remainder of lunch, and I couldn't help but notice the way Willa kept staring at her phone on the table. "Something wrong?"

Willa looked up. "Huh?"

"You keep staring at that thing, you'll go cross-eyed," Daphne said, turning the page in her book.

"Waiting on a call?" Byron asked, peering around the gardens, his knee bouncing beneath the wooden table.

"No," Willa snapped, then shoved her phone away. "It's nothing. Just needed an appointment, and the doctor won't call me back."

I didn't believe her, but I could tell she wasn't about to spill the truth. Not here. Possibly because of Byron's presence, or possibly because she just didn't want to share whatever was eating at her.

I chose to leave it alone but made a mental note to keep watch.

We headed in when the bell sounded, and Byron tugged me to him with an arm around my neck. "Did I ever tell you that those boots you wear, the way you wear them, does some really awesome things to me?"

I flushed, shaking my head. "No." I laughed. "But, thank you?" A question. A thank you as a question. Who the hell was I?

He merely laughed, then pressed a kiss to the side of my head. "Well, they do. Really awesome things," he whispered to my skin. "I'll text you later."

I watched him swagger to the doors of the cafeteria, then joined Daphne and Willa outside at our lockers.

"What are you doing for your birthday?" Daphne asked. "Being that you're grounded and all."

"That blows," Willa said, grabbing her fluffy pencil case and nabbing a pen from inside it. "We need to do something, though."

"Peony is cool," Daphne said. "She'll let us come over and at least watch some movies, maybe spike some OJ."

Mom had been pretty cool about the whole almost sneaking out thing, but I was most definitely still grounded.

"I'm not sure …" I trailed off as a flash of pink caught my eye. My heart pounded as I looked around the hall, but there were too many people getting their things for class to see where she was. I opened the locker and plucked the note from inside, unfolding it with a tremor racing through my hands.

Last warning.

"What the fuck?" Daphne snatched it from me. "Last warning? Who does she think she is?"

"How can you tell who it's from?" Willa asked, sneaking a look over Daphne's shoulder to read it, her dark eyes growing.

"I was BFFs with Kayla for years. I know her handwriting."

I took it back, but then Daphne plucked it from my fingers. "Oh no, you don't. Where is she?"

"Can we let it go? I don't want any drama."

Daphne was glancing around. "Too late for that, Pegs."

"There were other warnings?" Willa asked.

"There was one." I exhaled roughly, then raked a hand through my hair. "It said she'd take something of mine if I didn't leave Byron alone."

Daphne cackled, then gave me my books and slammed my locker shut. "Come on."

"Uh," Willa started. "Do you really think that's a good idea?"

"Yeah," I said, speed walking to keep up as the crowd parted for Daphne, and we followed. "Leave it alone. She can't do anything to me anyway."

The second bell rang, and I tensed even more.

"She can, but we're going to make sure she won't."

Kayla was checking her makeup in the mirror stuck on the inside of her locker. She wound down her lipstick and capped it when she saw us approach. "Hey, ex-friend. How's life down in the trenches?" With a whack of her hand, she shut her locker.

"A lot less miserable, thanks for asking." Daphne held the note between two pinched fingers, her golden nails sparkling. "What's this shit about?"

Kayla swiped a tendril of black hair from her forehead. "Oh, that? Just making sure a certain someone knows the score."

"And what score would that be?" Willa surprised us all by asking.

I wanted to slink away into the fading crowd, preferably run home and forget this was happening.

"That when people try to take something that doesn't belong to them, there's bound to be"—she paused, directed her freezing gaze to me—"consequences."

"You cheated on him, and then you broke up. Get the hell over it."

Kayla scowled at Daphne. "I didn't cheat. He said we were on a break."

"Whatever. Just stay the hell away from Peggy. It's not her fault Byron's into her."

Annika tittered. "Oh, you didn't just go there."

"I did," Daphne said. "And by the way, it doesn't exactly look like you care that much about him when you've been sleeping with half of Magnolia Cove's male population."

Annika and Annabeth gasped, manicured hands trying to hide their huge smiles.

Kayla growled, stepping into Daphne's face. "Jealous? Come on, we both know you love sloppy seconds. I'll try to make sure I leave some other scrappy, broke guy for you to ruin next."

Daphne lunged.

Willa and I grabbed her just as a teacher passed. "Isn't there a classroom waiting for you girls?"

"Yes, Mrs. Truncheon," we all said at once, then disappeared to those respective classes.

NINETEEN

Peggy

Kayla's and Dash's warnings plagued me, yet try as I might, I couldn't figure out a way to fix everything.

It all came back to Byron. I didn't want to dump him. He was sweet, nice to look at, and sent me good night messages.

I'd always wanted good night messages.

Dash had been acting weird all week. Gone were the suggestive looks, words, and the angry glares. The car rides to and from school consisted of talking about *Blitz*, his bikes, my birthday, and discussing some of the books he'd been reading.

Back to how we used to be.

I didn't know why that bothered me.

"So I'll pick you up at seven?" Dash called out the window after dropping me home on Friday. We were going out for Mexican before heading to see the new *Avengers* movie. Byron had made dinner reservations in town for tomorrow, so when Dash said he was taking me to the movies, I told him it'd have to be tonight.

To my surprise, and a bit of annoyance, he didn't protest at all.

"Yep, later." I waved and hauled my bag inside, then almost screamed as Mom and Phil popped up from behind the couch.

Phil was holding a large chocolate cake, and Mom was holding two metallic pink balloons with the numbers one and eight. "Happy birthday to you, happy birthday to you ..."

I stood there, trying to take the well-meaning assault as best I could, and smiled in relief once it was over. "Thanks."

They both gave me a hug, and Phil set the cake on the coffee table. "Made it myself."

"Thank God," I joked. "Because it looks so good, and I really want to eat it."

Mom slapped my shoulder. "My cakes are not that bad."

Phil and I made a face, and she squawked, throwing her hands in the air as she left the room to grab some plates.

After we finished, I helped them clean up and put the cake in the fridge. "So Dash is taking you out?"

I halted in the doorway, realizing I hadn't cleared that with her. "I'm not still grounded, am I?"

She walked over, brushing some curls from my face. I was at least half a foot taller than her now, courtesy of Dad's genes. "No, honey." She jabbed an acrylic nail between my eyes. "But don't you lie to me again."

With a wince, I gently pushed her finger away. "I won't."

"Come, let's go open your presents," Mom said, grabbing my hand and tugging me to the living room.

"What'd you get?" Dash asked when I climbed inside his car.

"Some special shampoo, a new flat iron, my own push-up bra, and a gift card to spend online."

"Nice." He turned out onto the street. "Are you by any chance wearing that bra right now?"

And so the flirting was back. "I'm not. It needed to be washed first."

He forced a pout. "What color?"

"Not telling."

He groaned. "Seriously? What's the harm in telling me the color?"

I suppose there wasn't. "Candy pink."

"Candy pink," he repeated, almost missing a red light.

"Dash, red." I grabbed the oh-shit handle.

"Did you by any chance get matching panties?"

"This conversation is over. I'd like to live to see my nineteenth birthday, thank you."

"So sure of yourself."

I burst out laughing, then frowned when I saw he'd taken a wrong turn at the light. "Where are you going?"

"Just feel like taking the scenic route. So what'd you do with the balloons Romeo got you?"

"His name isn't Romeo, and shit." I cringed. "I left them in the teachers' staff room."

Dash barked out a laugh. "Oh, that's too good."

"Shut up." I moaned. "This is so bad. What do I tell him when I get them on Monday?"

"That you didn't want them, so you abandoned them."

"You're no help. I love balloons."

He blew a raspberry, waving me off.

My eyes narrowed when he turned down a long, tree-lined street that sat opposite the bay.

I almost punched him in the chest as my arm flung out when he pulled into the long gravel drive that led to my dad's place. "Okay, what the hell are you doing?"

"Thought we'd swing by and see your old man." Dash didn't say anything else as he jumped out of the car.

Clad in his usual tight white T-shirt, leather jacket, black denim jeans, and combat boots, he stood on the drive, dragging a hand over his thick hair as he waited for me to get out of the car.

Confusion held me in its befuddling grip as I followed him up the drive to my dad's three-story yellow and white vintage restored home.

I used to swear to my parents it was haunted. I would hear creaking noises and mumbled shouts on the third floor long after my parents had gone to bed. But whoever it was that stalked the attic, office, and guest rooms never ventured down to the other floors.

"My dad's away."

"Ah, but he returned early."

The front door opened, and there he was, a smile as glowing as the sun on his aging face. Wearing his jeans and a plaid shirt, he checked his Rolex. "Just in time, birthday girl."

"For what?" I shook my head, then raced over, throwing my arms around his neck and inhaling the scent that could only ever belong to him. Cigars and some kind of cherry-scented soap used to wash his clothes.

His hold was strong, and when I stepped back, I smiled up into his green eyes.

I had him to thank for my blonde hair, but his was now mixed evenly with gray.

"You look good, Dad."

"You look like you've shot up in a matter of months, not years." His hands landed on my shoulders. "Eighteen." His smile was nostalgic. "I got you something." He turned and headed toward the four-car garage, clicking a button on the keys he'd plucked from his pocket.

My lungs almost collapsed, I sucked in a breath so hard and fast.

In the garage sat a bright red Volkswagen Beetle. I steeled myself, and the burning in my eyes, turning to him with a smile that hurt my face. "I wasn't aware you were a fan of red." The other two cars in the garage, a Lamborghini and a Porsche, were black.

He bellowed out a laugh, then walked over and wrapped an arm around my shoulders. "Very funny. It's yours."

"Dad …" I didn't know what to say.

"Your mom was a bit pissed, but she's held me off since you turned sixteen."

"It's freaking beautiful."

That earned me another chuckle, and he pulled me closer, unlocking it and forcing me to take a seat inside.

My hands spread over the leather steering wheel, fingers floating over every dial and screen inside. "I can't believe this."

"Soon enough, you won't need me for much at all."

I'd almost forgotten Dash was there, and I got out of the car, grinning at him. "I'm sure you'll think of something."

His answering smile made my heart thrash, and heat spread up my neck. Looking back at Dad, I wrapped my arms around him again. "Thank you. I love it."

"Dashiell helped me pick it out." My dad was one of the only people Dash allowed to call him by his full name, but his nose still twitched whenever it happened. "Picked the color, model, all of it."

"Didn't get paid for out of my bank account, though," Dash said, chuckling. "Thank fuck."

I took a step back, gazing up at Dad. "You didn't need to do this, especially one this expensive."

Dad's bushy brows met. "Don't tell me what I did and didn't need to do. No one was taking this opportunity from me." He jerked his head at Dash. "Despite his smart mouth, if he didn't like driving your tushy around town all the time, he'd probably have done it too."

Dash shrugged. "Nah, I got her a yearly pass to Hooters.

Much cheaper, and let's face it, nicer things to look at."

Dad's lips twisted. "Your dad hasn't thrown you out yet?"

"Will you take me in when he does?" Dash's eyes lit.

Dad chuckled, then thumped Dash on the back. "Come on, Peggy Sue. The fun isn't over yet."

I struggled to drag my gaze away from my car. My. Own. Freaking. Car. But I did, catching up with them as they headed up the stairs and inside.

"Surprise!"

I screamed, my hands slapping my face as Mom, Phil, Daphne, Willa, Suella, Lars, Raven, Jackson, Dad's closest friends, and more people from school jumped into the foyer.

Streamers flew into the air, cameras flashed, and music turned on as they all crowded me. Everyone was dressed in skirts, dresses, heels, half-suits, and nice shirts.

Still feeling petty about the fact I hadn't shown it off, I was wearing the same outfit I'd planned to wear to Wade's party the previous weekend. But after looking at some of the guests mingling and drifting through my dad's house, I felt woefully underdressed and every inch my age.

Half an hour later, after yet even more people from school arrived, I cornered Mom in the kitchen before she left. "How'd you do all this?"

"Wasn't me." She shouldered her handbag, then fluffed my hair. "If you drink, just don't get too crazy."

I nodded, hugging her tightly, then Phil as well, and asked, "So Dad organized it?"

Mom smiled. "He allowed it, but no." She looked through the kitchen, and I followed her gaze to where Dash was stacking presents on the table in the dining room.

She and Phil walked off. A knot rose up my throat, lodging there as I felt my eyes grow wet. Scratching his head, Dash stepped back, studying his handiwork. He'd made a color-coordinated tower out of all my gifts.

When he was satisfied, he grabbed his drink, then spun on his heel, freezing when he saw me watching. "Freckles, apparently people like you."

I didn't trust myself to talk, so I didn't.

He strolled over, swinging a thumb over his shoulder to the pile. "Figured you'd want a photo for the cut and pasting shit you do. Speaking of, I got you something. Come with me."

I followed him into the dining room and stopped when he pulled out an unwrapped box. He'd stuck a purple bow to the top and shrugged, handing it over. "If I'd wrapped it, it would have looked worse."

I took it, setting it on the dining chair.

"Hey, birthday girl," Daphne called. "Someone missed the memo and got here late."

I turned to find Byron heading toward me with a flat look on his face. "Hey, you." I went to him as he held his arms out.

He kissed my forehead. "Sorry, I was told to be here at eight."

I groaned, pulling away to glare at Dash, but he was gone. My frown wilted as I tried to search for him.

"I know you said you didn't want anything but cake, so …" Two gentlemen carrying an extra-large cake came in behind him, my dad directing them to the kitchen.

"Holy shit." I raced in there as they set the cake down, my eyes roaming up and over the four giant tiers.

Hanging from the top was an envelope. Byron grabbed it, handing it to me as my dad saw the two men out.

I tugged out a card that read Happy Birthday with bright yellow sunflowers. Inside, two pieces of paper almost fell to the floor. "I know you probably need to clear it with your mom, but

I thought, if she's cool with it, that you'd wanna come see some snow with me over winter break."

"I love snowboarding," I said, smiling.

"I know." He grinned, poking me in the cheek. "Willa and Daphne told me."

"That doesn't mean I'm any good, though." I gave him a pointed look.

He chuckled, and I rose onto my toes to kiss his cheek. His head turned, and I was thankful my dad was no longer in the room, for his mouth opened mine and his arms caged my body to his.

His lips devoured, and his tongue glided. I bit his bottom lip before smiling against his mouth. "Thank you."

"Did you open my present?"

I stumbled back from Byron at Dash's question and couldn't meet his eyes as he stood against the kitchen doorway. As if he'd been standing there for way longer than I would have wanted him to.

"I will soon," I finally said, putting the airline tickets back inside the card.

"You were told to buy a cake, not to whip your dick out and show everyone how big you wish it was."

Byron stilled. "The fuck is your problem? Because I'm pretty sure you solved any you had with Annika last Friday, right?"

Annika? My head snapped up, flying to Dash. He'd come over right after the party and tried to hook up with me. A curdling sensation roiled inside, souring those minutes I'd shelved as something sweet.

Dash scratched at his cheek, laughing beneath his breath. "Low blow, but I'm feeling generous, so I'll let you have it. Later, Pegs."

"Where are you going?"

"To get my dick wet. Want it to be you this time?"

Willa's eyes popped as she halted outside the kitchen, hearing Dash's words.

She looked at his retreating back, then at me, questions abuzz in her startled eyes. "Later," I mouthed.

Byron scrubbed at his chin. "He's really—"

"Oh, my God. It's amazing!" Willa purposely cut Byron off, and I gave her a small smile in thanks. "When can we eat it?" She clapped her hands, bouncing in her heels.

"How about now?" Dad said, coming into the kitchen with a pack of candles and a lighter in hand.

After being mortified in front of God knows how many people as everyone sang "Happy Birthday" and each took a slice of cake, Dad and his friends retired to the pool house to give us some space.

But when the bass started thumping through the walls, I started feeling unsure. It was one thing to attend parties, but a whole different beast to host your own. Especially while your parent was present, even if he wasn't in the main house.

I spent the next few hours cleaning as everyone danced, laughed, and drank—though I didn't know where they'd gotten the alcohol from.

Byron found me when it was nearing eleven with a beer in his hand and some fruity looking drink in the other. "You're like the little cleaning fairy, disappearing whenever I think I've finally caught sight of you."

I took the offered drink, tired, a little sweaty, and somewhat irked. "I just don't want anything to get messed up."

Byron nodded, then swayed a little on his feet. I frowned. "You okay?"

"Think I've had a little too much." He pinched his fingers together.

Offering a weak smile, I popped the top on my melon concoction, tossing the cap into the trash bag I'd been carrying from room to room. "How'd you guys get the alcohol anyway?"

He used his beer to point at some of the guys out by the pool. "Danny's older brother."

"His brother is here?" More and more people had shown up, and if I was being honest, it was starting to make me anxious.

"Nah, just bought it for him. Come dance." He tried to grab me, but I ducked left.

"I'm okay. I'm going to clean up a little more."

Byron pouted, then backed up when someone called out to him, and left me there.

I didn't wait for him to come back and quickly grabbed some empty chip bags from the coffee table, then some rogue soda cans rolling over the Indonesian rug.

I tossed them in the trash bag, then took a long sip of my drink, pausing with it in the air when I caught sight of Dash out by the pool.

Some of the anxiety fled my shoulders when I saw he wasn't doing what I'd feared he was. Though why I'd feared it, why I still felt sick over what Byron had said Dash did at Wade's party, well I didn't know why or how to figure it out.

He was walking around, collecting bottles and cans in his arms and taking them to the bin he'd wheeled over to the pool fence.

He was also shirtless.

While he didn't have the washboard abs the guys on sporting teams at school liked to flaunt, he had some, and he was still fit. His skin sun-kissed and smooth. He'd developed lean muscles from the small amount of weight training and cardio he did—when he could be bothered—to ride his dirt and BMX bikes.

His golden back faced me, his shoulders expansive, tapering gradually to his hips. His chest was mostly hair free, but as he turned and my eyes dipped lower, my mouth dried. His ripped stomach contracted as he bent over to grab a bottle, then straightened. The tiny trail of hair leading inside his pants had me pondering whether I'd touched his stomach at all in any of our practice sessions.

In fact, I couldn't help but think I'd maybe overlooked too much of him in general.

I took the trash bag outside, a cautious smile at the ready when he caught me heading toward him even though what Byron had mentioned earlier still poisoned my stomach.

He held the lid open for me, closing it when the bag was inside. "This isn't birthday girl behavior."

"I can't relax," I said.

He ran a hand through his damp hair, then dragged the trash over to the sitting area by the porch. With a jerk of his head, he gestured for me to follow him inside.

I did, taking long sips of my drink as I tried to ignore the make-out sessions, body grinding, and copious amount of drinking happening in my dad's meticulously kept backyard.

"Did you get your you-know-what wet?" I asked, the beverage in my hand warming my limbs as he headed upstairs.

Dash huffed. "Dick? And yeah."

I almost tripped up the steps, and he caught my arm. "How many of those have you had?"

"This is my first one." I pushed some hair from my eyes, unable to meet his, then kept walking upstairs.

"I took a swim. Been a while since I've been in that pool."

I laughed. "That's what you meant by getting your dick wet?"

He reached me as we hit the landing, and we moved down

the rug-covered hall to my room. Arched windows lined the walkway, and I remembered sitting at the biggest one at the top of the stairs as a kid, pretending I was a princess in a castle, getting annoyed with Dash when he refused to play my prince.

"You always wanted to be the villain," I said.

Dash followed my gaze over his shoulder to the big arched window, knowing what I was thinking about. "And you always tried to make me something I wasn't."

I bumped his shoulder with mine, smiling. "Or maybe, the person you were always supposed to be."

"Careful, now. If you think too highly of me, you'll only be letting yourself down in the end." I snickered as we found my old room. He switched on the light and shut the door halfway.

It was pink. Everything. The duvet, the walls, the old wooden dollhouse in the corner, and even the drapes. Nothing had changed. My white twin bed sat exactly where it had the day Mom and I left.

I exhaled a wistful sigh, then spotted the box Dash had given me on the end of the bed and walked over to it. "You brought it up here?"

"I didn't want to risk anyone ruining it. You'll see why when you actually open it."

His last words held some bite, causing guilt to gnaw quick and sharp.

I picked up the box, taking a seat with it on my lap as Dash started messing with my old *Goosebumps* collection.

"I'm sorry," I said. "I got distracted. I didn't mean—"

"Just open it."

I tugged off the silky purple ribbon, then opened the cardboard flaps to reveal what was inside. Photographs, possibly hundreds, dating back to when we were newborns.

Tears collected, and I couldn't contain them as I started

sifting through the memories. "Dash," I croaked, closing my eyes to try to steady myself.

"You do all that scrapbooking shit with your friends, but I've yet to see you make an album for us. So it's a selfish present, but I don't even care."

It was the furthest thing from selfish he'd maybe ever done. It would've taken him weeks, maybe months, to find, collect, and print all of these. We both knew that, but I let him keep his brick and mortar shield in place and reopened my eyes to finish looking through them.

Soon enough, he'd fetched more drinks from downstairs, then took a seat beside me as we replayed and retold as many memories as we could remember.

"I did not wear a diaper until I was four."

"Pictures don't lie, Freckles."

I shoved him. "It was Halloween." I drained the rest of my third drink. "I was dressed as Pebbles, and you were Bamm-Bamm."

His lips puckered as he studied the photo. "I didn't wear a diaper, and I was George of the Jungle."

"You were Bamm-Bamm."

"Bamm-Bamm and Pebbles don't wear diapers."

"They do, puffy Stone Age diapers."

He flicked the photograph, and I took it from him, trailing my finger over his chubby four-year-old face.

"Why the hell did they dress us up as that anyway?"

"Hell if I know," I said. "Probably because we made cute Flintstone babies."

"Didn't they end up together?"

I snapped my gaze to his, grinning. "Shut up. You've watched it?"

"A time or two," he said with a shrug, then finished his

whiskey, likely stolen from my dad's office. "Don't get too excited."

"So they get married?" I tucked the flaps of the box shut, sliding it to the other side of the bed.

"I think so. Just like you and I will."

I fell backward, laughter howling out of me.

"You find the idea that ridiculous, do you?" He leaned over me, blue eyes smiling.

"Imagine that." I squinted up at him, my head dizzy.

"Actually"—he swallowed, his Adam's apple shifting—"I do." His words made my heart pause. "Imagine it."

My breath caught. "Dash." *He was drunk*, I tried to reason with the burning in my chest.

With his eyebrows dipped low, he licked his lips. "You shouldn't be with him."

My heart began racing, and my lungs failed to keep up. "Why?"

"Because ..." His head lowered, his hair falling forward and grazing my face as his nose touched mine. "You should be with me."

We crashed together in a tangle of heated lips, rough hands, and desperate sounds.

"I want you so bad. I swear it's all I think about," he said, his voice dry and punctuated between heavy breaths. His tongue licked up my neck as his hand sank behind my head, and his body lowered over mine, grinding between my spread legs.

They wound around his back, and I panted, hands greedy in his thick hair. "I don't know what we're doing, but ..."

"But?" he asked, eyes meeting mine as he rocked into my core.

I moaned. "But it scares me."

"Good," he bit out, his teeth nipping at my lip. "Because

you fucking petrify me."

His words paralyzed. "Yeah?"

"Yeah," he said, his eyes twin storms of charged electricity. Then his tongue dived into my mouth, and mine was ready to meet it.

My leg hiked higher up his back, and one of his hands skimmed lower, crawling between us and dipping inside my panties. He froze, his lips leaving mine bereft and cold. "You're bare."

My eyes narrowed, and I blinked the cloud-like haze from them. "Um, yes?"

His forehead creased, his gaze dark and filled with something unnamable. "For him?"

And just like that, what we were doing, what I was feeling, seized the moment within its brutal grasp and crushed it all. It fell away like broken petals on the wind, scattering in a million directions, too far out of reach.

I threw myself off the bed, stumbling to my feet.

"Wait, where are you going?"

"I have a boyfriend," I said, my hands scrubbing at my cheeks. "I can't, ugh." I gave up trying to talk, too wrapped up in my latest mistake and what it could mean for Byron and me.

"Hate to break it to you." Dash smirked, his kiss swollen lips rubbing together as he watched me pace the fluffy pink rug in the center of my room. "But he's not your boyfriend."

I halted. "What?"

"He's no more your boyfriend than I am. If anything, we're more together than you and Woods are."

Exasperated, I laughed, sounding crazed as I shook my head and held back a scathing retort. It wasn't Dash's fault I'd messed up; it was my own. And although he wasn't making this confusing place we'd gotten to any easier to traverse, I wasn't about to put the blame on him.

Needing to catch my breath and gather my thoughts, I was halfway to the door when a crash down the hall met my ears.

I turned my wide eyes to Dash. "I thought people knew they weren't allowed up here?"

Dash stood from the bed, taking his time to meet me at the door. "They do know. Wait here."

I didn't. I followed him down the hall to the parlor located between my room and my dad's.

The frosted doors had been shut, but that didn't mean much. We could still see the naked back of a woman pressed up against them, and we could definitely hear her moans. "Jack," a soft voice said.

The door banged, a male groan reaching us as the female let out a squeak. I gripped Dash's arm. "She okay?"

The doors started rattling, and Dash grinned, patting my hand. "Oh yeah, I'd say Willa's doing better than okay."

"What? Wait," I said when he started pulling me back down the hall. "Willa? Jack." My mouth fell open. "She's having sex with her brother?"

"Stepbrother," Dash amended. "Now let's go kick these assholes out. I don't wanna be cleaning until three in the morning."

My feet unglued. "But they've been siblings since they were babies. It's, it's …" Willa's silence about boys and the daydreaming glow to her eyes; it all clicked into one shocking piece.

Dash stopped at the top of the stairs with a brow raised. "Like what we just did?"

I groaned. "That's not really the same."

"Keep telling yourself that, and maybe then you'll get over whatever hang-ups you're holding on to."

"What the hell, Dash?" I followed him to the kitchen where he grabbed some more trash bags.

"Chill, it's your birthday. Let's just …" He sighed, resignation sinking his shoulders. "Finish it in style."

"By cleaning?"

He glanced out the window at all the guests, most of whom I didn't even recognize. "First one to get a full bag gets dibs on where we order pizza from."

I snatched the bag and raced out of the kitchen, laughing as Dash cursed, then gave chase.

TWENTY

Dash

*I*t scares me.

I'd waited her out the rest of the weekend, confused out of my mind over what I should do. Or if I should even do anything.

When Monday morning rolled around, and I realized she'd be driving herself to school, annoyance, anxiety, and anger festered into one giant ball, leaving me liable to snap at just about anything or anyone.

I arrived at school late on purpose, not wanting to risk seeing Woods clamor for something he didn't and never would get to have. By the time I slunk into second period, I was primed and ready to fight, my feet shifting in agitation beneath the desk.

"Dash," Annika cooed when the teacher slipped out to use the bathroom.

I didn't bother turning my head around.

After a tap on my shoulder, a pink gel pen was roaming up my neck.

I flicked it away, and Annika giggled. "Heard Peggy had some party last weekend."

"And?" I asked, scooping a handful of sour gummies from my pocket and slipping them in my mouth.

"And you didn't invite me," she said. "We had fun at Wade's, right?"

She'd sucked my dick like an addict, but not even her skilled mouth compared to the hesitant exploration that'd gone down in my bedroom with Peggy.

My best friend was turning my mind into a sludge pile of confused desperation. "I don't want a repeat, if that's what you're rambling about."

She made a tutting noise. "You came so hard. I don't believe you."

"Because I wasn't thinking about you." I didn't feel bad for saying that, not one fucking bit. She had it coming with her incessant pestering. "Take a fucking hint and find someone else's balls to bust."

"You're a piece of asshole shit, Dashiell."

My teeth gritted, but I ignored the jab as Mr. Denkins reentered the room.

I wasn't sure how much longer I could take this. This feeling that ate and ate and ate at my chest, leaving nothing but bleeding need behind.

She wanted me, that much I was certain of whenever I'd gotten my hands on her, but as soon as they were off, I was back in the friend-zone. A place I thought we'd stay, that I'd been content to stay, for the rest of our lives.

But now, that'd changed.

I couldn't watch her morph into a woman with someone else. No goddamn way. I didn't know how I'd never seen it before, or when exactly it changed, but maybe that was why I'd shied away from anything that resembled commitment.

Because it was supposed to be her all along.

Peggy and Dash—more than just best friends.

As everyone filed out after class, I headed to study hall to stew on my feelings until lunch. There, I resolved to ditch my scumbag friends and steal the seat beside Peggy before Byron got there.

We entered the cafeteria at the same time, and as both our

eyes saw Peggy take a seat with Willa and Daphne, we charged.

He pushed; I shoved. He cursed, shoving me back. Laughter sounded as I almost stumbled to the floor, and then I chased, my shoe colliding with the back of his knee, sending him to the ground right before he'd reached the girls' table.

I slipped into the seat, stealing a piece of Peggy's carrot. "What?"

Peggy blinked, her curled lashes holding me hostage over her gray eyes. "What the hell was that?"

"A little friendly competition never hurt anyone."

"Competition? Dash." She scowled, her gaze moving to Byron. "You okay?"

Byron winced, lowering to the seat next to Willa, who scrounged around in her bag for something. "Yeah. Not sure about my pride, though."

"Guess Coach Gorerro doesn't work you hard enough, Romeo." I chomped down on the carrot, displaying as many teeth as I could.

Byron bristled, the look in his eyes a promise of retribution. Let him try. While he was doing that, I moved my mouth to Peggy's ear. "I want you to suck me again."

Her eyes went wide with shock, worry, and a hint of excitement. "Dash! Oh, my God. Shut up."

"What, was I too loud?" Her hand grabbed my thigh under the table, squeezing. And holy hellfire did she have sharp nails. "Ow, shit. Fine. Sheath your talons."

She slowly released me, and I made a face at Daphne, who was eyeing us with a knowing look. Yeah, she knew, maybe even Willa too. Though how much remained to be seen. I didn't give a fuck. I'd stand on this table and shout how great her pussy and mouth were to the whole cafeteria if I wasn't worried that Peggy wouldn't speak to me again.

"Have a good time on Friday, Willa?" I stole another piece of carrot, having not grabbed anything due to wanting my spot next to Peggy.

Peggy grumbled, slapping at my hand, but she was too late.

Willa's doe eyes bounced up from her apple slices. "Uh, yeah?"

I nodded, my smile wider than the sun. "Yeah, indeed."

Her mouth popped open as she realized I knew. I'd known for a while something was up with her and Jackson, but I didn't have any proof until Friday. Dirty, sneaky tyrants. No wonder the guy was either perpetually stoned or looked like he didn't know his ass from his face. Fucking your sister, technically step-sister, who'd lived under the same roof as you for almost your entire existence would probably do that to you.

Made me feel a lot better about the filthy things I wanted to inflict on Peggy. Not that I'd ever felt all that bad anyway.

"Don't you have a blunt to smoke?" Byron asked, his eyes still heavy on me, jaw twitching with barely veiled rage.

"Saving it for later. I like my weed best after food or …" My eyes slid to Peggy. "After sex."

Byron legitimately growled.

"Problem?" I poked the bear.

His face was growing mottled. "I don't know, you tell me."

"I'm fine, thanks for asking." I gave my attention back to Peggy, who was turning bright pink.

"Fine, huh? Is that why you ratted on Peggy to her mom about Wade's party?"

My head swung to him, my fists and heart clenching. He didn't know that. No one knew that other than Peony when I'd expressed my concern to her on the phone the day before the party.

Did I feel bad for being the reason she got grounded for a

week? Maybe. Okay, no. Not really.

Peggy gasped. "What?"

"I don't know what you're talking about," I said to Byron, albeit, a little too late. He had me, and he damn well knew it.

He folded his beefy arms. "I wasn't sure, but hey, now I am. It was totally you."

I stood, leaning over the table and baring my teeth. "And I'm totally going to rip your dick off and shove it down your herpes infested throat."

"Enough. What's going on here?" Mr. Andrews said, nearing the table.

With every ounce of strength I had, I dragged myself away from Byron's smug face. "Nothing."

"You can finish your lunch outside, Mr. Thane."

I didn't point out that I didn't have any lunch, but I stood, glancing down at Peggy. "Pegs."

She wouldn't look at me. "Just go."

Fuck.

Lars bunny-hopped, then did a bar-spin over the ledge, bringing his bike to a stop beside mine at the top of the bowl. "You going to ride that thing or just sit on it all afternoon?"

I'd come here to clear my head, gain some damn clarity, and figure out how to get Peggy to talk to me.

For the first time in forever, she'd locked her window.

It'd been three days since she'd decided she wanted nothing to do with me, and though I'd hoped she would, like a naïve idiot, she'd yet to ditch the loafer-wearing fuckstick. If anything, what I'd done had only opened her arms farther for him.

"Fuck off," I said around the cigarette dangling between

my lips.

Jackson down whipped, then rolled over, wiping beads of sweat from his forehead before dumping his cap back on his head. "He's butthurt over Peggy."

"I said fuck off."

A bunch of younger kids rode in, took one look at us and the middle fingers I gave them, and rode back out to the basketball courts. We didn't do well with sharing, especially not me. They could wait their damn turn.

Lars rolled his bike back and forth, arms hanging over the front bars. "I've gotta say, Thane. I never thought this would be you."

Jackson huffed. "Pussy."

I didn't want to take the bait, but fuck if I could help it at this point. "Elaborate or take a hike."

"And leave you to mope all on your own?" Jackson checked his phone, frowning, then leaned forward to pocket it. "Because that's what you're doing, you know. Moping."

"Mopey as fuck." Lars nodded.

"I don't mope. I fucking brood."

Jackson laughed. "This sure as hell isn't brooding. You look like someone's diagnosed you with an incurable disease."

Love was a disease.

The thought sparked, sending shockwaves through every nerve ending of my body and electrifying my heart.

I couldn't be. I didn't think it was possible, but then again, if it was going to be anyone, these past few weeks had made it crystal clear it was going to be her.

"Well, go on, wise asses." I stomped on my cigarette. "What would you do?"

"Quit letting her ignore you for a start."

Lars agreed. "The longer you let that happen, the more

room you're giving them to get even more serious."

"You really wanna let Woods get between Peggy's legs?"

I growled at Jackson. "Watch your putrid mouth."

"Pot black kettle."

My brows met. "What?"

Jackson waved a hand. "Whatever. Just get your girl or get over it."

"Is that what you're doing?"

About to launch into the bowl, he froze, Vans skidding over the concrete.

I laughed. "The taste is always better when you're eating something forbidden."

Lars looked back and forth between us. "What are you even saying?"

I kept my eyes glued to Jackson, and he swallowed, a plead within them. I wasn't one to keep other people's secrets, but in this case, knowing the fallout would be too fucking devastating and potentially life-ruining, I smirked. "Just Jackson's penchant for hooking up with the unavailable."

Lars's frown said he wasn't completely buying it, but he was too selfish, we all were, to care for too long.

"So what are you going to do?" Lars asked as we wheeled our bikes out of the skate park an hour later.

"I don't know, but I'm sure I'll think of something."

I was still dazed by my earlier revelation. Still trying to wrap my brain around the truth that had laid dormant for who knew how long.

A hidden truth unearthed. It was official. I'd fallen for my best friend, and she was breaking my black fucking heart.

TWENTY-ONE

Peggy

I parked my car on the street outside the house, not wanting to block the driveway.

It seemed a little weird that my ride cost more than Mom's and Phil's, but at school, it fit right in. Though the flatness that overran me when I'd parked it in the lot first thing Monday morning made me realize I really didn't care.

I'd been too caught up in the events that'd blown my mind and confused my heart over the weekend. Did Dash like me? Over and over, I'd replayed everything that'd happened that night and in the weeks before. The culmination of it all had my chest constricting as I'd had dinner with Byron, chatted with Dad on the phone, and even now, days later.

He liked me more than a best friend should. Though what scared me the most was knowing I had to ask myself if I liked him too.

Mostly because there was no need to ask or answer. I didn't know how it'd happened, but somehow, I'd handed even more of my heart to him. More than what a best friend should give. But it would be a mistake to take it any further than we already had.

As it was, we stood to lose way more than we could ever gain.

Dash Thane wasn't capable of loving anyone but himself, and I'd do well to remember that.

"You never told me Dash was the one who told you about the party," I said, dragging my fork through my spaghetti the Wednesday after my birthday.

"That's why you won't let him in?" Mom asked, sipping her wine. Dash had tried to use the front door after I'd locked the window in my bedroom first thing Monday afternoon.

"He betrayed me."

Phil took an interest in his phone, minding his own business. He never tried to step in on parenting related matters, which I think Mom preferred. I knew I did, and I think Phil did too. He didn't have kids of his own, and after teaching teenagers over at the public school all day, he was probably happy not to have to deal with any more teen drama.

Mom's brow arched. "He was concerned. It's not like you to lie to get what you want."

I sighed. "I know, but he did it so I wouldn't see Byron. It's so freaking stupid, I can't even comprehend it."

Phil snorted, and both Mom and I looked over at him.

Feeling our eyes on him, he looked up, startled. "Sorry, just ah, funny picture on Facebook."

"Don't tag me in it," Mom said. "What you think is funny usually isn't."

I smirked at that, shoveling more food into my mouth.

Phil frowned. "Excuse me?"

Mom waved her fork at him. "Never mind. Back to Dash. Don't leave him out in the cold too long. It's not good for that boy." I knew she was referring to the way his parents often forgot about his existence until it suited them.

Phil made another sound, and Mom groaned. "Go on, out with it."

He hesitated, glancing at me. I tipped a shoulder, waiting.

"Don't tell me you don't see it?" he asked, his gaze darting back and forth between Mom's and mine.

"See what?" I asked.

Phil blinked, and Mom gave him a warning look. His face was

reddening, so I twirled my finger for him to spit it out.

"He likes you."

I rolled my eyes. "He's my best friend. He only likes me because some other guy is peeing all over something he thinks he owns."

Mom coughed on her next sip of wine.

"You okay?" Phil moved to pat her back, and she pushed his hand away.

"Fine," she said, fanning her face as she set her glass down. "Peggy, I really do think that maybe you should talk to him about it. I get what you're saying, I do, but—"

I pushed my chair back. "There are no buts about it. That's exactly what this is." It couldn't be anything else because everything would change. Dash wasn't boyfriend material. We'd crash and burn and lose the friendship we'd spent a lifetime creating. "I'm going to finish my homework."

"That hideous thing you call a dress has been dry-cleaned," Mom called as I took my plate to the sink and rinsed it. "It's in your closet."

"It's not hideous, but thank you." I stacked my plate and utensils in the dishwasher, then grabbed a water bottle from the fridge to take to my room.

"Is Byron taking you?"

"He sure is."

"Are you going to the football game?"

"Hell no."

My sneakers squeaked over the polished floor as I left the sound of slamming basketballs and closed the door to the gym behind me.

I was on the tail end of my period, and though I was thankful I wasn't going to have it tomorrow night for homecoming, I still hated doing any physical activity when I had it.

My pad fell from my hand, and I bent over to pick it up, slipping it inside the pocket of my gym shorts after making sure no one saw.

I rounded the corner, traipsing down the hallway that led to the girls' bathrooms.

A hand latched around my wrist, pulling me down the opposite hallway. "You need to break up with him."

His touch was kerosene, but I didn't want to catch fire.

"I'm not talking to you." I pulled my hand free and crossed my arms.

Dash's smirk was infuriating. "You just did."

"Ugh. We're not ten anymore."

"Don't I fucking know it," he said. "End it, Peggy. He's a superficial twat."

I dropped my arms, scowling at him. "He's sweet. He buys me flowers."

"Flowers? Flowers die, Freckles. I'll give you my dick. He only needs ten minutes after each round before he's ready to come back to life."

"He?" A laugh slipped free. "You did not just say that."

He raised his hands into the air.

"Dash, stop it."

"No." He crowded me back into the locker. "If you think I'm going to leave you alone and just let that asshole have you, you're crazy."

"The only asshole I see is you. You betrayed me."

He laughed. "It was a party. Big fucking deal you didn't get to go. It was for your own good."

"Bullshit." We both knew why he'd done it.

"Yeah? So you're telling me he wouldn't have tried to take advantage of you?"

"I'm his girlfriend, you moron. I wanted to see him."

He made a hissing noise, face contorting. "You don't know what you want."

"I know I don't want you."

His chest rose high, then collapsed. "You're lying, and you know it, Freckles."

He didn't get it. He wasn't thinking through every worst-case scenario. He was acting on what he felt now, what he wanted now. Mere moments in the present weren't worth sabotaging a future. "I won't subject myself—*us*—to that. We'd never work. The only person you ever worry about is yourself."

"Not true. Who helped you clean up at the party? Not that cocksucker. It was me." He swallowed, a thick sound, and then lowered his voice to a growl. "Who got you a present that'll actually last instead of only trying to impress you? Me. And who kept fucking kissing you, knowing you were only doing it to better kiss someone else?" He punctuated his words by stabbing his finger on his chest repeatedly. "Fucking. Me."

My eyes ached, but it was nothing compared to the burn in my chest. "Stop it."

"Never. I've always been there, and I always will be. Who cares if I'm a little conceited? A little too honest? I show up for you because you're one of the only people I care about. Isn't that enough?"

"We're friends, Dash. Don't ruin that." My voice was scratched, breaking. "Please. You don't want me; you just want me because you feel threatened."

His hand slammed into the locker beside my head, making me jump. "That's it. Continue lying to yourself, and then

maybe you won't want me just as much as I want you, right?"
He shook his head, searching, waiting for my response, but I
kept my mouth shut. "Right."

He stalked off, leaving me limp against the cool metal with
my heart pounding a bruising beat and sucking back tears.

TWENTY-TWO

Peggy

The limo pulled up to the curb, and Mom quickly ushered us into position in front of the small hydrangea bush in our front yard.

Byron's parents weren't here. He said his dad was away on business, and well, his mom was still working some stuff out.

I didn't pry. Partly because I knew Byron would talk to me about his mom when he felt comfortable, and partly because Dash, even though he wasn't here, kept invading my every breath.

"Okay, a little closer," Mom said. "That's it. Cheese!"

We grinned, and I barely felt Byron's arm around me as Mom took shot after shot, and when he shifted to lay a kiss on my forehead, Mom cooing behind her phone, I fought back a wave of exhaustion.

Daphne and Willa arrived a few minutes later, and I grabbed the layers of bubblegum tulle, my boots scuffing over the grass as I joined them and took in their dresses.

They'd decided upon matching cocktail attire, seeing as they'd decided to forgo dates and attend together. In shimmering bronze and plum, their skirts puffed out around their thighs as if they were wearing hoops beneath them.

I lifted the hem of Willa's, discovering an abundance of tulle, and almost regretted not going shopping with them last Sunday. "These are amazing."

"Check out the back," Daphne said, spinning to display a

large bow with tails draped over the sides of the skirt, ending right at the hem. "Cute, huh?"

"You girls look like sexy Easter princesses," Mom said, snapping photo after photo.

"Easter?" Daphne questioned, her red lips thinning.

"Ignore her. You look incredible." I reached out to touch one of Willa's long curls.

They were both wearing fake lashes, and though I wished I'd done the same, I'd curled and applied a dozen layers of mascara to mine instead.

"Group photo." Mom gestured for us to huddle.

Just as we smiled, another car pulled up. I heard doors shut and watched Mom's face drain of color. "May?"

"Good evening, Peony."

We spun around and saw Dash and his mother walking over the driveway toward us.

May sniffed, her chin rising as she surveyed our small house. "Good grief. It's worse than I thought."

"Great to see you too. You can go now," Mom said, her hands moving to her hips.

"Sorry, Peeny." Dash tugged at his sleeves. "She insisted on being here to take some pictures of her own."

"Well, it's my son's last year of school. I'd think it perfectly understandable." She opened her handbag, pulling out a camera the size of my head. "Now, how do I work this thing?"

Dash sighed, pulling at the lapels of his slate gray tux, then snatched the camera from her and clicked a few buttons.

Slowly, I shut my mouth, swallowing to rid the dryness that'd infested it.

Byron cleared his throat. "Um, Pegs? What's he doing here?"

"Taking Peggy to homecoming," Dash said.

My hands twitched when I saw he was wearing a bow tie. A bow tie the same color as my dress. Byron had decided against it when I'd offered the idea, saying he wasn't a fan of pink. Dash definitely wasn't a fan of pink, yet … I shook my head, blinking rapidly. "Dash, we spoke about this."

"You spoke; I chose not to listen. Selfish, remember?" He winked, but he was anything but happy as his eyes settled on me, then moved to Byron.

May slapped at her arm. "Damn mosquitos. Let's hurry this up before I catch malaria or something."

"Catch malaria?" Mom asked, incredulous.

Knowing this couldn't end any other way unless we all dived into the limo idling by the curb and left, I trudged over to Dash. "Make it snappy."

May frowned, holding the camera up. "I don't remember you being so snotty, Peggy Sue."

"Probably because you paid no attention to anyone but yourself." Mom was beside her, phone already poised. The sight of them together for the first time in years was startling. So different yet almost as if nothing had changed.

"Haven't you got enough photos?" May grumbled, taking her twentieth or thirtieth as Byron stood with Willa and Daphne, scrolling through his phone. "Don't be such a damn hog."

"I can't believe you actually just said that."

May lowered the camera, turning to Mom. "Believe it, hog."

"What are you, four years old?"

"You wouldn't know because you've missed too many of my birthdays, y-y-you selfish slum living witch."

Mom's cheeks flushed, and I gripped Dash's arm a little tighter, taking comfort in the scent of his aftershave. "What were you thinking, bringing her here?"

Dash grunted. "I wasn't. Besides, she was a stowaway. I didn't know she was hiding in the back seat until I was halfway here."

"Oh, I'm the selfish one, am I?" Mom said.

"Uh, yes. Yes, you are." May waved her camera around. "You didn't even tell me that my son was going to homecoming with Peggy."

"Because you told me I was a classless whore for not staying with a man I didn't love and waving goodbye to my McMansion."

"Did she really?" I asked Dash out the corner of my mouth.

"Probably."

"I didn't say you were a whore. I said you were an idiot. There's a big difference."

"Because that's so much better."

"Should we …?" I pointed at the limo.

Dash nodded. "Yep."

I waved at Daphne and Willa, who looked as though they wanted to stay and keep watching years of hurt and frustration blow up in front of my cozy little house.

We all piled into the car, the door shutting on the yelling match, and then Dash started laughing.

"What?" I asked, taking a seat next to Byron.

Dash settled in on my other side, pointing out the window. They were still screaming, but all we could make out were red, enraged faces and flying hands.

"Who wants some champagne?" Daphne asked, cracking open the top of a bottle that'd been cooling in an ice bucket.

She poured us all a glass, and Willa sighed. "Do you think they'll make up?"

Dash and I spoke at the same time.

"No way."

"Not a chance in hell."

"Pity." She clucked, taking a swig from her glass.

Byron sat silently beside me, and I could feel the tension start to creep inside the air-conditioned space. "So this limo is nice."

Byron huffed, and no one else said a word.

Daphne raised a brow at me, drinking her champagne to hide what I knew was a shit-eating grin.

The silence stretched on. My palms grew clammy.

Dash leaned into me. "So your place or mine afterward?"

I could've punched him square in the nose. "Shut up."

"What did you just say?" Byron asked, leaning away from and around me at the same time.

Dash moved an arm behind my head, and I knew without even looking at him that he wore a taunting grin. "Just seeing what our girl's plans are for later this evening. Nothing to worry your pompous head about."

"And why would you think those plans would involve you?"

I turned to Dash, pleading with tight lips and huge eyes. He wasn't looking at me, though. He was staring straight over my head as he said, "You didn't know? Peggy and I had this sweet 'friends with benefits' arrangement."

Daphne or Willa coughed.

I died.

"Peggy?" Byron asked the back of my head. "What's he talking about?"

"Nothing," I said through gritted teeth. "It's nothing. Not anymore."

Dash set his eyes on me then, his brows furrowed. "Nothing, yeah?" His lips curled as his gaze stayed steady on mine. "I wouldn't say making sure our Peggy Sue was ready for you is nothing. But you can thank me later."

The girls gasped, and I heard a thud on the floor of the limo.

"Dash, Jesus." I was about to cry or slap him. I couldn't decide on which.

"Ready?" Byron's tone was filled with warning.

Dash ignored it. "You know, making sure she gained just the right amount of knowledge." He lowered his voice, leaning over me. "When you kiss her, you need to make sure you hit that soft and sweet, work your way up to ravishing her mouth the way we're dying to. Know what I'm saying?"

I slapped him hard in the chest, speechless and unable to catch my breath as the limo turned a sharp corner.

Dash steadied me, and I ripped my arm away before turning to Byron.

He swallowed, his fists two balls of concrete in his lap. "You've kissed him, Pegs?"

Laughter sprang from Dash. "She did more—"

Willa practically shouted, "Oh, look. We're here."

I'd never been so thankful to see the gates of school before, and I all but leaped over Dash to get out into the fresh air.

I inhaled one crisp breath after another, resisting the urge to fan my heated cheeks.

After sending me questioning looks, Daphne and Willa linked arms, heading toward the gymnasium's entrance.

An arch teeming with roses and a petal-lined path led inside. Streamers littered the grounds. Music pounded through the doors. Laughter, catcalls, and some shouting pierced the darkening gardens. I stopped walking well away from the entrance, not exactly sure what I was supposed to do with my two unlikely dates, especially now that Dash had opened his traitorous mouth.

Dash hadn't been invited to go with me. After just showing up and what he'd done, the right thing to do would be to ditch him and head inside with Byron.

Byron took that opportunity away from me when he walked ahead, not even looking back to see if I was following.

A hand grabbed mine, and Dash tugged me with him toward the path riddled with soft pink petals. It almost killed me to crush them beneath the weight of my boots. Though it helped to picture Dash's balls as I tried to remove my hand from his death grip.

We stopped to have our photos taken, and I found myself smiling for real when Dash whispered into my ear. "You look like heaven."

The camera flashed, and then we walked on, my palm growing slick in his as people turned to watch us enter the crowd. Before we got lost within it, he walked us over to an empty corner, and before I could step away, he framed my face with his hands.

"You just love causing trouble for me, don't you?" I whispered, wondering if Byron would even speak to me after this.

His lips hitched, his eyes dark blue beneath the dancing disco lights above our heads. "That will never change."

I licked my lips. "Never? Dash—"

"I love you." His expression volleyed the admission, yet it still stunned me. "More than a friend should. The kind of love you fall into and desperately try to crawl out of, but it's fucking futile."

"What?" I shook my head, trying to peel away from his hold. "No, you're lying."

"Think about it, Peggy. Climb back down to reality and think about it." His grip tightened, and he stepped forward, his voice holding a determined edge that scraped at any resolve I had left. "You know I'm not. I won't cause any more trouble for you tonight, but if you think you might love me too, ditch him.

For the love of God, please just ditch him." He pressed a firm, desperate kiss to my forehead. "Then come find me."

Then he was gone, a large shadow lost in a sea of color.

Wet trickled down my cheek. I swiped it away, trying to wrangle the emotions that wanted to send me hurrying after him.

I couldn't. I couldn't make sense of anything, and the longer I stood there, my thoughts swirling and my heart thrashing, the more confused, scared, and isolated I felt.

Looking around the room, I saw Byron over by the tables of finger foods. I gathered my skirts in my hand, and some courage, and walked over there quickly so as not to lose him again.

"Hey," I said, tapping his arm. "Way to just leave me outside." I laughed, trying to make it sound like it wasn't a big deal when it kind of was.

He took a moment to answer, and when he did, his eyes fell angry and hard on my face. "You didn't seem to need me."

"What?"

He sighed, adjusting the light blue jacket of his suit. "When did you kiss him?"

My mouth opened and shut. I didn't want to lie, but I couldn't spit out the truth. "Not since we started dating." The urge to admit that wasn't exactly true tugged at my vocal cords, though I knew admitting so would just cause more trouble. Fear, so much fear, swelled within. Unshakable in its control. I liked Byron. I liked Dash. I hated this indecisive game we'd wound up being players in.

A sharp brow rose as he studied my face. "I want to believe you."

"So believe me." I straightened my shoulders. "I can't make you, but I didn't invite him here. I had no idea he'd show up the way he did."

"Yeah? Well, I guess it doesn't matter what you do or don't do."

"What's that supposed to mean?"

He flicked a hand, forcing a smile to someone behind me, then gave his attention back to me, his voice rough and low. "That means you don't care enough to stop him, and I'm starting to wonder who or what you want. Me? Or him."

With his loaded plate, he stalked off to talk to some of his teammates.

I wanted to scream at him that trying to stop Dash from doing anything was a one-way trip to insanity, but that wasn't entirely correct, and there was little point.

I spent most of the night sitting on the outer edge of the room, wondering what to do. Wondering about all the ways I should've done so many things differently.

Willa and Daphne pressed me for information about Dash, but I just shook my head. They tried to coax me into dancing with them, but I wasn't interested. My eyes kept skating over the dance floor, but whether I was looking for Dash or looking for Byron, I wasn't sure. Dash was nowhere to be seen, and Byron was busy stealing shots out of a flask he'd tucked inside his jacket pocket while stomping on balloons with his friends and talking to some of the cheerleaders.

It was far from over when everyone was kicked out and told to head home. I rode with Daphne, Willa, Byron, and some of his teammates to a party two streets away from school at an old warehouse someone's parents had rented.

Only, we didn't make it inside.

After everyone else got out, Byron shut the door, then told the driver to circle the block until he said otherwise.

"What's going on?"

He poured me a glass of champagne, and I took it, taking

a greedy sip as he scooted over to sit next to me. "I was being a dick earlier. I think we should talk."

My brows furrowed, and I lowered my glass to my lap.

Byron's eyes swam with remorse, but his next words had me deflating. "Kayla really screwed me; you know that." He puffed out a laugh. "Everyone knows that. And then there's the shit with my mom and dad." He took a long sip of champagne, his throat rippling as he swallowed, then swiped his hand over his hair. "I guess I'm just afraid of being fucked over again."

Unsure of what to say, I drank a little more, then set my glass down. My fingers curled, and I met his eyes, confusion enfolding me like a tsunami when I tried to think of what to say or do. "I get that."

I picked the glass back up, draining it. Slumping back against the seat, I exhaled slowly, my limbs and heart heavy. Where was Dash? I pictured him waiting for me at the party, if he was even going. Maybe he and his friends went to the skate park to drink and get high.

"Byron," I said when I looked up and found his eyes on me. My breath hitched as he took my empty glass and set it with his on the small table before sliding close.

"Maybe we can talk later." His hand rose, caressing my cheek with his fingers. "Maybe I just need to feel that you want this too." Then he was kissing me, his body leaning into mine and forcing it backward over the seat. I could hardly feel the leather beneath my skin as he tugged my dress up to my hips with one hand and used the other to tug the straps down. It wouldn't budge, and being old, the strap snapped as his tongue plundered my mouth.

"It's about fucking time, Peggy Newland. Open those pretty thighs for me," he rasped into my mouth.

His fingers found my panties, and I shut my eyes as cracks

formed like fissures in my chest. I waited for the heat, for the electricity I'd felt with Dash, or even the flutters I'd encountered with Byron.

They never came. Perhaps that was for the best. You can't get burned if you don't ignite. Byron was good. Byron was safe. Byron wouldn't destroy years of friendship.

It was nothing like it should've been. Nothing like I'd dreamed it'd be. Fear and despair warred to keep me chained beneath him as his fingers met my skin. Memories of Dash's being there infiltrated, and all my fake reassurances folded like wet cards. I gasped, trying to pull away from his mouth. He rose over me, and I blinked, tingles clouding my bloodstream from the few drinks I'd had. Before I could talk, my panties were gone, and his fingers were between my legs.

For long moments, I became lost, a sheet of thawing ice as pleasure ignited. My eyes slammed closed, and my body turned to mush as he kissed and gently explored.

"God, you feel so good. Are you going to come?"

I could hardly swallow let alone answer as he tried to insert a finger and the pain, accompanied by the sound of his voice, sent me careening back into reality. His tongue plunged deep into my mouth as he removed his finger and rubbed me with it. "I can't wait to be inside you."

I thought I knew what feeling sick meant until that moment. Until I realized what was happening and what was going to happen.

I tried to tear my mouth from his. I tried to shut my legs and move my hand between us to pull his away. When that failed to get his attention, I sank my teeth into his lip, hard.

"Fuck," Byron barked, and the coppery taste of blood filled my taste buds. I spat it out, narrowly avoiding his face.

He rolled off me to the floor. "Shit, Peggy. What the fuck?"

"Sorry, but I can't," I said, guilt stabbing at my eyes.

He hissed between clenched teeth, dabbing a finger at his lip. "You're a savage." I banged on the window, wanting out of the car. "You said you liked me."

I laughed even as tears started falling down my cheeks. "I do, but I can't do this right now. I'm too ..." I sniffed, words evading me. "Confused."

His eyes widened, and he scrambled over the floor to the seat. "Confused? Don't just try to bail, talk to me."

I sucked my lip, glancing down at his lap to where his pants were tented, but then forced my eyes away. "I don't know how to explain it. Or if I should." I tried to smile at him. "We've both been drinking, so maybe it should wait."

"You were enjoying it, though," he said, a tad too vehemently for my liking. "Where did I go wrong?"

Regret, I'd learned, was something that didn't arrive slowly. It barreled in with the force of a thousand sharp knives to the gut and shredded everything inside.

Byron was my boyfriend, and I liked him. So why did I suddenly feel as though I could hurl at any moment? I didn't know much when it came to being in a relationship, but I knew enough to know I shouldn't feel like this. Like maybe I'd been wrong. Maybe I was in the wrong place with the wrong person.

Withholding a cringe, I shook my head and ignored the hand that tried to reach for me. "Just get the driver to pull over, please."

Something banged on the windshield, and the limo came to a screeching stop. The door opened, and Willa gestured for me to climb out. Without looking at Byron, I hurried out to find Daphne putting her shoe back on.

"Did you throw that at my car?" I heard the driver ask.

I righted my dress, then tried to fix my hair as I wobbled a little on my feet. I wasn't even wearing panties.

"You wouldn't stop when I waved at you, so yeah, I did. And your fucking windshield wiper scratched it. They cost more than your weekly wage, asshole."

The driver backed up, sensing from Daphne's glare that she was going to play nasty if he tried to argue with her. He climbed back inside.

"Peggy, please. Just wait a damn minute," Byron said, climbing out of the limo.

"What did he do?" Willa said, helping me stay steady as the blunt edge of the night's events threatened to send me sitting on the hard ground.

"Nothing. I'm going to call a cab and head home."

"Peggy!" Byron tossed his arms out, moving toward me when a group of guys started heading our way.

"Yo, Woods! Sweet ride." I recognized one of them from math. "Think you can give us a lift? We've got some shit to pick up."

Byron looked over at me, and I smiled, hoping it wasn't a grimace, then turned my back to fish my phone from my bra.

"Your dress." Willa gasped. "Did he try to …?"

"No. It's fine. I just want to go home," I said, giving in to temptation and slumping down onto the concrete as the limo pulled away.

They sat with me, and I cried as I explained what happened while we waited for a cab.

TWENTY-THREE

Dash

I'd waited outside the gym, drinking with the guys in the far end of the football field, as the rest of the school acted like a bunch of dingbats, all trussed up like peacocks as they fawned over who looked best and whose shit didn't stink.

Then we hightailed it to where the real fun would begin at the after party.

But they never showed.

Not Peggy, and not Byron, hell, even Daphne and Willa were only there for a few minutes. All weekend, I'd tried not to let what that could mean send me careening over the edge I'd been balancing on for weeks. But fuck if it wasn't becoming harder and harder to keep pinwheeling my arms around with the constant state of whiplash that kept slamming into me.

"No friends to be a teenage dirtbag with this weekend?" Dad asked as he flicked through the Sunday paper.

I removed my glasses and set my book down, pinching the bridge of my nose as Mom flitted around the dining room, pretending to reorganize things and look busy.

"Go pour a martini, Mom. You're making me jittery just looking at you."

"So don't look at me and mind your tongue."

"Dashiell," Dad said in a tone that conveyed he didn't want to reprimand me, but he was about to anyway. "Don't speak to her like that."

I pushed away my half-finished plate of scrambled eggs.

"She tell you about the fight she had with Peony?"

Dad looked over at Mom, lowering his glasses on his nose to peer up at her. "Fight?"

She dropped the frame she'd been holding, and it hit the cabinet with a clatter. "It was a minor squabble."

"Is that what you call telling someone she's a classless whore?"

Dad removed his glasses, tilting his head. "Come again?"

"I did *not* call her that. I called her a classless idiot."

I smothered my laughter behind my hand. Dad blinked at her.

She swiped a wayward strand of hair from her face. "Oh, come on. Don't look at me like that."

"What else did you say?"

It was one of those rare times in my life when I saw my mom's cheeks color with something other than makeup. Feeling. "It wasn't a big deal."

"She said she was a hog and selfish." I drained my orange juice. "Among other things."

Dad's mouth gaped open. "Really?"

Mom growled, stalking over to me. "For once in your life, could you at least pretend to love me?"

"Pretending takes effort."

Now it was Dad who growled, and I pushed my chair back. "Okay, I'm out."

Book and glasses in hand, I made my way to my room, but what I heard trailing me had me almost missing a step and then stopping.

"Come here."

"Mikael, I don't need your reprimanding and reminders right now."

Dad said it again in a tone that brooked no room for

argument. "Come here." I could almost picture her dramatic sigh before she did as he'd asked. "What happened?" he asked, voice soft.

Then came the tears. "Oh, it was just horrible."

I shook my head, then escaped to my room.

Kicking my door shut, I dropped my book on the nightstand and shoved my glasses back on as I flicked on the TV and waited for the game to load. As much as I didn't want to call her to find out why she never came to find me—and whether that meant what I feared it did—it was killing me not to know for sure.

But I think I'd rather die slowly than be put out of my misery via the sound of her voice.

She wasn't online, and after playing a few games with Jackson, I tossed my glasses and controller on the bed and decided to distract myself with happier thoughts. If only to keep from texting her until my fingers bled.

Thoughts of when she'd been in here, in this very room, rushed in. Her legs spread between my own, opening like a blooming flower for my fingers to explore her soft depths.

My hand tunneled beneath my plaid pajama pants, wrapping around myself. My eyes shut, my head falling back as I remembered how she'd looked, all innocent, curious eyes and lust-stained cheeks, as she'd swiped her tongue beneath my shaft.

Combined with the sound of her panting breaths, the mewls of surprised pleasure I'd pulled from her, and the way she'd soaked my hand, I came, frantically reaching for the tissue box by the bed to catch everything she'd caused to erupt.

After tossing them into the trash and rolling over to stare at a picture of us tacked to the wall by my bed, I wished every other feeling she evoked could've been expended in the same way.

Torture.

The wondering, the hoping, the freefalling on my own—it was nothing but torture.

The crowd parted in whispers and laughter. All the usual bullshit for the Monday morning soundtrack.

My eyes looked for Peggy, but she wasn't at her locker and neither was Byron. I'd gotten here just in time for the bell, so I continued to my own, unlocking it and changing out my books before dragging my feet to class.

I whipped out my phone as the teacher chatted with another teacher in the doorway, and for the first time since Friday, I logged into Facebook.

I wasn't a big fan of it, but just like most people who weren't, I still used it when I could be fucked and had nothing better to do. Thumb scrolling, I felt the wind get knocked out of me when I saw someone had tagged Peggy in a passive-aggressive post about good girls going bad.

She hadn't responded to it. Why didn't she untag herself? I stared at it until a hand thumped on the desk, and Annika tipped back on her chair, smiling like she'd eaten rainbows and unicorns for breakfast.

"What?" I snapped when she didn't say anything.

"Just trying to figure out if you know what our very own Peggy Sue got up to with a certain someone in a limo Friday night?"

My heart disintegrated, falling like ash into my stomach.

Annika pouted. "Guess not." She lowered her voice to a whisper when the teacher backed into the room. "Let me be the bearer of such joyful news then. She fooled around with Byron. I hear he's got expert fingers, and Peggy has terrible taste in panties."

She turned around when I did nothing but stare at her, dumbfounded and drifting away.

The teacher called my name twice before I finally jerked my hand up. As soon as the bell sounded, I stormed out of there.

Being out in the hall surrounded by the gossiping student body wasn't much better. The walls started to melt, lockers and doors looming closer with each step I took to the front entrance.

My heart was sinking with every lurching step, my hands trembling as I wiped drops of sweat from my hairline, shoving past a group of jocks.

"Hey, watch it, Thane."

"Fuck you," I spat.

Hennessy's laughter bit at my skin. "You mad your little girlfriend got it good last Friday? Don't be. She's primed and ready for you now."

The word primed did it.

I threw myself at him, pinning my arm against his bulky, roided neck. "You want to die?"

He sputtered, face growing a dull shade of red as he struggled to breathe. "Chill out. I was just m-messing with you."

Hands tugged at my shirt, and I felt it tear as Lars and Raven pulled me back.

Hennessy shook out his shoulders, grinning even as he coughed. As if he hadn't almost had his ass handed to him.

"Outside, man. Come on." Lars jerked me toward the doors as students started heading to class.

I pulled away, my hands sinking into my hair as soon as we stepped into the crisp air. Walking over to the steps, I bent over. "Fuck." The word dragged out of me on a hoarse groan.

It felt like my heart was stuck in a vise, squeezing and squeezing even though nothing was left. I'd been wrung dry, drained empty, and I couldn't fucking breathe without feeling it with every rattling inhale.

"Want a joint? I've got some tucked away in my car," Rave offered.

"Dude, he doesn't need weed," Jackson's voice reached through the fog.

"Looks like he needs something."

I groaned again and straightened. Fuck this.

Fuck this and fuck them.

Maybe it wasn't even true. If it weren't for all the practice we'd done, I'd most definitely not believe that shit. But that was what she'd wanted from me. It was the only thing she'd wanted from me.

Experience to use with him.

"You spoken to Peggy since Friday?" Lars asked.

"No," I said, clearing my throat when the word came out as a husk. "I thought I'd give her some space. I told her ..." I stopped. "I asked her to ..." I stopped again, my eyes clouding with a haze of disbelief.

"You asked her to what?" Lars said.

I pushed my hand through my hair. "Doesn't matter now."

"I haven't even seen her yet," Raven said. "But if she's here, go find her, dude. Just talk to her or something."

"Don't know if there's anything to talk about anymore." And I didn't want to fucking talk about it with them or anyone for that matter.

I stalked back to the doors, then halted when I saw Peggy's car pull into the lot.

The guys fell silent behind me as she took her time getting out, boots on, hair curled and bouncing around her shoulders.

She locked the car, her mustard leather bag hanging over her arm as she crossed the lawn.

Rage and betrayal brewed inside, creating a wildfire of heat that needed a way out. Silently, I begged for her to just look at me, lift her head and show me that what I'd heard wasn't true.

When she reached the stairs, she glanced up, tilting as she almost tripped on the first step. I saw her chest heave as she inhaled, and then it happened. Tear soaked eyes searched mine, and I knew.

They weren't gossiping for no reason. There was always a reason among the lies, and today's reason was my best friend.

The girl I'd stupidly gotten hung up over.

I headed for the other set of stairs, taking the long way around the gardens to the parking lot.

"Dash?" Her voice was like ice over a burn, but I wouldn't let it soothe me, not when she was the one who'd inflicted the pain in the first place.

"Dash!"

I heard Lars tell her to leave me be, and then I heard nothing but the quiet, pitiful thud of my own heartbeat as I shut myself in my car and got the hell out of there.

I didn't get far.

No, that was impossible.

I parked, and I waited. And when the clock struck two, I drove back and parked right next to his ghastly fucking truck.

The trees ceased their swaying, and the air felt stickier than it should as I balled my fists at my side, clenching and unclenching while he took his sweet-ass time to get to his car.

Come on, asshole. Look up and see the wrath that awaits you.

As if hearing the silent command, he skidded to a stop, the smile he'd worn while typing on his phone slipping as quickly as he pocketed it. "Wondered where you might be."

Was that resignation I detected? Good. He should be re-signed to this. But that wasn't enough. I cracked my knuckles, and his steps slowed as he heard the sound. I didn't want him resigned. I wanted him dead or as close to it as possible.

He threw his hands out, his gym bag hitting the asphalt. "What can I say, man?" His lips wiggled into a smile. "I'm so far from sorry I forget what the word even means."

I launched at him, taking both of us to the ground. The concrete bit into my elbow, jarring my arm, but I didn't care. The thud and pained sound that came from Woods as he hit the ground was music to my ears. My fist smashed into his face, and he landed an uppercut to my jaw. My head spun, but my rage couldn't be stopped, and blindly, I kept landing blow after blow. His chest, his cheek, his mouth, and then I heard a pop, and blood gushed over my fists.

Yelling and shouting had ensued, but I was too far gone, trapped beneath waves of agony that needed release, to hear much of anything.

Hands wrenched at my shoulders, and a fist met the side of my mouth, the tang of blood smearing over my tongue as I shouted, struggled, and cursed for them to release me.

"Fuck, stop." Raven's voice penetrated.

"You're going to kill him or give yourself a damn heart at-tack. Fucking chill." Lars slapped at my face as Rave and Jackson held me back, and a teacher helped Byron sit up on the ground.

"Mr. Thane." Principal Denham stomped over in his croco-dile knock-offs. "My office. Now."

I ignored him and the hellfire look twitching his pudge-infused face, tearing my arms out of my friends' grip. "No need. I'll see myself out." I wiped at my lip, my heart thrashing like a wounded beast as I watched Byron stand, one of his eyes already swollen shut.

It wasn't enough. The fact he'd wake up and maybe be able to see a slit of sunlight wasn't anywhere near enough.

"Mr. Thane, I won't tell you again."

"What about that dickhead?" Lars pointed at Byron while I spat blood on the ground, then finally, I took a good look at the crowd that'd gathered.

"Language, Lars," Denham said.

Half the school had left, but the other half that hadn't were all there, whispering or quickly stashing away their phones after recording the fight.

"He didn't start it."

I barked out a dry laugh, but really, I didn't give a shit. They could do whatever they wanted, and I would do the same. I opened my car door and jumped inside. Lars and Jackson pounded on the windows, but I'd locked the doors. I didn't need them to come with or follow me like I was on some kind of suicide watch. As the principal pulled out his phone, likely to speak with my mom or dad, I peeled out of the lot, forcing students to jump out of the way as screeches and screams left their mouths.

Blood dripped onto my cheek, and I figured I'd probably been hit more times than I recalled. The guy hit the gym every day and was all about training in the off season, so it made sense he knew how to use his bulk.

Too bad he'd muscled his way into the wrong girl's life, consequently ruining mine.

I drove around town for however long. Long enough to be able to think a little more rationally.

All that went to hell when I saw the red Volkswagen parked outside the wrought iron gates shielding my driveway. The sight of her—her arms crossed over her chest, her lip between her teeth, and her face blotchy from crying—was almost enough to send me back to school to finish what I'd started.

Almost.

I drove in once the gates opened, and she jogged in behind me before she was locked out. Dirt sprayed, a few rocks pelting the car as I sped down to the garage, then slammed on the brakes.

She was there within seconds of me shifting into park, panting and breathing heavily.

The sound had tormenting thoughts clenching my fists.

"Why'd you leave?" Her question sounded like an accusation, and I shook my head, a sinister laugh departing my thinned, bloodied lips.

"Fuck you. You got what you wanted, right?" I stepped closer to her, noticing how puffy her eyes were. "Did I prep you just right?"

She shook her head, her lips wobbling. "I'm sorry. I know—"

"I hate you," I said with every ounce of ruin I felt.

"Dash …" Her voice broke. Her face, shoulders—all of her—seemed to crumple as she took an unsteady step back.

The sight of her misery was about to send me to my knees, but my revulsion kept me standing. I hit the remote for the door, my chest heaving. "I fucking hate you, Peggy."

The door closed on her shattered expression.

TWENTY-FOUR

Peggy

I fucking hate you, Peggy.

As if it wasn't bad enough that rumors had spread about me throughout the entire school, the one person I needed most had believed them without even hearing me out. The look on his face, the anger wrenching his voice—it hurt worse than anything that'd transpired since homecoming.

I'd stalked through the halls silent, my head down and my heart weary as whispers and disgusting overtures found me at every turn. I wanted to scream at them, but I knew it'd only give them further ammunition to use against me. Instead, I'd spent too much time crying in the girls' bathroom, drowning in my own reckless decisions.

Class was hardly a reprieve because even the teachers looked at me as if I'd disappointed them.

I'd wanted a boyfriend, to feel wanted, to experience what it was like to have another human being touch you and look at you in a way that painted the world in fresh color.

I never expected this to happen.

I'd made a mistake, which was evident in the way Byron so easily shared what'd happened between us. Not once did I think he'd share something personal and maybe, under different circumstances, special between us. Regardless, I couldn't live with that kind of guilt for long. I'd sat at home all weekend, trying to devise a way to tell Dash myself. To tell him I had feelings for him too.

That was pointless now, and I wondered if Byron had somehow hoped or planned for that, or if he even cared that he'd made my life hell in the days after. Maybe I'd never know because every time I'd tried to talk to him, he'd make himself scarce and ignore my calls.

Words held too much power. It was clear he'd wielded that power for his own personal gain, uncaring of how it would affect anyone besides himself.

It wasn't fair, and it was all I could do to drag myself out of bed Tuesday morning and throw myself to the wolves once more. I'd allowed it to happen. I'd even enjoyed it before everything I'd been smothering was brought to the surface. Complaining and playing the victim wouldn't get me anywhere, but nevertheless, it was impossible to keep it from gnawing at every beat my heart took.

Dash was nowhere to be seen, and by lunchtime, word had spread that he'd been suspended and that Byron had received a week of detention.

Rumor was he apparently needed to see a plastic surgeon about his nose, and that was why he hadn't shown up at school on Tuesday. I found that hard to believe, albeit not entirely impossible. I'd only caught the tail end of the fight before heading to Dash's house to wait for him, but I'd seen enough to know Dash had given him one hell of a banged-up face.

Dash had a busted lip and some swelling beneath his right eye, but it was clear that no matter how much muscle Byron had, it was no match for the rage coursing through Dash yesterday afternoon.

Rage that I'd caused.

Rage that shouldn't even exist because while I'd allowed things between Byron and me to go too far, I hadn't allowed him to take our make-out session and transform it into entertainment for the masses. He'd betrayed me, and now I couldn't even get close enough to break up with him, let alone howl my hurt at him.

It was Dash, but maybe, just maybe, he wouldn't have been suspended, maybe he wouldn't hate me, not entirely, if he'd found out what I'd done via me instead of the student body.

"It'll blow over," Daphne said as we walked to our last class for the day. "As soon as someone else does something fucked up, which, let's face it, will be soon."

"It wasn't fucked up," Willa tried to defend. "He was her boyfriend."

I smiled at her, weak but grateful.

Daphne laughed. "No one cares about the finer details, especially not when Dash and Byron are both involved."

That didn't exactly make me feel better. "That's stupid."

"It's hot gossip."

"Still nothing from Dash?" Willa asked, stopping outside the door.

I squeezed my textbook to my chest. "His phone's been off."

They knew the score now. Well, as much as I was willing to admit, which was mostly everything except for chasing Dash's Range Rover down his driveway like some lunatic.

But it hadn't really hit me until I saw he was going to close those gates on me—until he'd shut the garage door and spewed those venomous words in my face—exactly what I'd done. That by trying to keep things from escalating between us, by trying to salvage our lifelong friendship, and by trying to find something I wanted from him in someone else, I'd ruined it all.

No, I hadn't just ruined it, I'd emptied a bucket of fuel over an already burning fire and caused our entire world to explode.

"He'll calm down. You'll see." Daphne tucked some glossy hair behind her ear. "I know it sounds cliché, but you do just need to give him some time. He's a hothead, but he's obsessed with you, so he won't stay mad forever."

I wanted to believe her, and some tiny part of me did, but as the days crept by and the weekend approached, I was beginning to lose hope, and I'd run out of tears and patience.

Sick of Mom's coddling and constant nagging for me to tell her what was wrong with me, I drove to my dad's house on Saturday and stayed for brunch.

"Are you going to tell me why you look like you've eaten too many sour gummies?" Dad asked, sipping his coffee.

"No," I said, then pushed my almost full plate of fruit and bacon aside. "Just teenager crap."

His moustache twitched as he tried to contain a smile. "Teenager crap?" He shook his head, setting his coffee mug down. "As long as you're not downplaying your feelings, Peggy Sue." A bushy brow raised. "No use in doing that, it'll only eat you alive from the inside out."

I sighed, then got up from the table. "It's not a big deal." It was the biggest kind of deal. "I'm going to grab some of the presents from my room."

After eyeing me for a long moment, Dad nodded.

My feet felt like lead as I hauled myself up the stairs and down the hall of the second floor toward my forever pink room. A shuddering breath left me as I shut the door and saw the little brown box still sitting on my bed.

The gloss printed memories between my fingertips co-alesced into vivid images that played out like a movie reel in my mind. Flicking through them, I paused on one from when I was nine, dressed in my school uniform, and felt something crack wide open in my chest.

The silver slide glistened in the midday sun as kid after kid shrieked, throwing themselves down the hot metal, then smacked the backs of their thighs, whining while laughing.

"Hey, clothes peg," Louis Charles called with his hands around his mouth. "Come have a turn."

I set my lunch bag aside, unsure but feeling excited I'd been asked. Slowly, I stepped over the crunchy sun warmed grass, then inside the play area where bark littered the ground. "Isn't it hot?" I asked, moving closer to where he stood with his arms crossed over his pudgy chest.

He lifted his shoulders. "Eh, maybe a little."

I gazed at his small brown eyes, the glimmer in them unsettling my stomach. "I don't know ..."

"Oh, come on," he groaned. "Just one time won't hurt." He gestured to the other kids who were no longer near the slide but playing jump rope in the shade. "They did it."

They did, and if they did it, I could too. Dash was one of my only friends, but Dash was bossy and mean. Maybe this would make me some more. And so with my lip between my teeth, I climbed up the rope ladder, my sneakers thudding onto the wooden landing.

I didn't often play on the play equipment, due to it usually being overrun with other kids. Excitement coursed inside, sending a zinging sensation through my limbs until my lips hitched into a smile when I reached the slide. It was hot, sure, but I could be quick, just like the others were.

My hands hit the metal as I took a seat, and I could feel the heat sear through my school skirt. Excitement faded into trepidation. I looked down at Louis, who was nodding with an eager smile playing on his lips. "Go on, just go quick."

Right. I could do that. My hands landed on the edge of the slide, and the burn ignited my skin, but it was too late. I'd already propelled myself down, and my school skirt rose, my bare thighs grazing the metal the entire time I descended. My panties crept into my butt, making my skin stick in every place.

I howled, tearing myself off it once I'd reached the dip at the end. I hadn't even reached it; I had to crawl toward it due to the way my skin stuck instead of slid.

"Peggy Newland," Mrs. Primrose said. "You know the slide is off-limits when the weather is this hot."

"Sorry," I said, my throat clogged. "I forgot."

She nodded, flicking her eyes over me in a brief glance. "Don't do it again."

Laughter and snickers filled the air, and Mrs. Primrose took a bite out of her apple before moving to the other side of the playground.

"Nice pink underwear, Peggy Sue." Louis sneered.

Bryce Humling slapped his leg. "Yeah. My grandma wears the same kind."

A basketball came out of nowhere, slamming Louis in the side of the head and sending him to the grass. "Ow!"

Bryce turned to see where it came from and got smacked square in the forehead with a tennis ball. His hand went to his head, and he winced, bouncing back a step.

I looked over to find Dash and Jackson approaching, the latter eating a sandwich. "How do you know what type of panties your grandma wears, Bryce? You sick freak."

Jackson laughed as did the kids who were just laughing at me a minute ago.

Dash stopped beside me as I adjusted my skirt. "You seriously fell for that idiot's goading?"

My cheeks were crimson. "I wanted to slide."

Dash's granite expression softened, then he punched me in the side of the arm. "Dad's built one into the side of the pool. We'll try it out this weekend."

He then pulled a handful of sour gummies from his pocket and held them out to me. I took them, smiling as I dumped them inside my mouth.

*"You almost knocked me out, you psycho!" Louis rubbed his head
as we headed to an empty bench beneath an old maple tree.*

"Yeah? Fight me, pig nose."

I bit my lips to keep from laughing.

Dash turned to me as we took a seat. "How's your butt?"

*"Stings a little," I said around the mouthful of candy setting fire
to my taste buds.*

*Dash and Jackson laughed, but it didn't make me feel like a loser.
It made me laugh too.*

I set the photos back inside the box, then dragged my fingers over my damp cheeks.

He'd always been there, no matter which rumor had spread,
or who had tried to mess with me. Always.

Except for now.

Everything had changed now, and it was all my fault.

Anger flared in my heart for the way he'd so easily shut me
out and for the way I'd accidentally thrown us away. I knocked
the box off the bed, watching as the photos spilled out, scattering over the rug and wooden floor.

TWENTY-FIVE

Peggy

To say school felt foreign without Dash's brooding presence would be an understatement.

The halls felt smaller, the floor lacking its usual sheen, and I could hardly stand to look at Lars, Jackson, and Raven.

I wanted so badly to ask them how he was, if he still hated me, and if I could maybe use their phones to call him. Perhaps his wasn't always off. Perhaps he wasn't not online. Perhaps he was simply avoiding me.

The words that'd scraped over his tongue and flew through the air to slam me in the very core of who I was couldn't be erased. Neither could what I'd done. He hadn't even given me a chance to explain, but he wasn't Willa or Daphne. He wouldn't rationalize it the way they had.

He might have been my best friend but not in the same way. He wouldn't understand.

Not when he'd told me he'd fallen for me just hours before I'd broken his heart.

Kayla twiddled her fingers at me, then mouthed the word, "Whore."

"Jesus," I breathed, dragging my eyes away from the pleased look on her pretty face.

"Ignore it, Peggy," Willa said.

I tore a bite out of my sandwich, tasting nothing as I chomped, then forced it down with some water. "It's not fair," I said, my head aching as the chatter and laughter pummeled me. "He gets to continue as if he hasn't been a complete asshole, and I have to just take it?"

Daphne threw a look over her shoulder to where some of the guys on the lacrosse team were sitting in the back corner of the cafeteria. "I know, but at least he looks like a squashed grape."

Byron didn't look too good. His eyes were still swollen, as was half his face, but he tried to smile it away as if it was nothing.

When his eyes met mine, he stared for a half minute, then looked back at his friends.

"That's it," I said, standing. "Fuck this."

"Whoa," Daphne said, following me as I forced my shaking legs to their table.

It was mere meters away, yet it felt like I was walking a mile as every eye watched my approach.

I squared my shoulders. "A word, Byron?"

A few guys laughed, trying to hide it by ducking their heads. Byron took his time giving me his attention, and I almost flinched at all the multi-colored bruising up close. "You finally breaking up with me?"

I withheld a shocked laugh. "Just follow me."

I didn't know if he would, but as I neared an empty table in the opposite corner and Daphne returned to her seat at ours, I felt his gaze on my back.

I only bothered sitting because everyone was already paying us enough attention. Standing would only make us more of a spectacle, potentially attracting Mr. Andrews' attention.

Byron sighed as he sat with his legs facing away from the table as though he was ready to bail. "So what's up?"

"What's up?" I repeated.

He tipped a shoulder. "Figured this was coming, so let's just get it over with."

"You figured?" I didn't think I'd ever felt so angry, so quickly in my entire life. Not even the time Dash hosted a sleepover at his place in seventh grade compared. When he'd told everyone I had head lice so I couldn't play spin the bottle. Nothing compared to the boiling tensing of every limb as I stared at Byron's nonchalant expression. Well, as nonchalant as one could appear with half their face bruised to hell. "If you thought you needed a formal breakup after all this, you're not just a spineless dick, you're a clueless one too."

He rubbed his lips together, staring down at the table. "That it?"

"No," I said, leaning forward and hissing through my teeth. "That's not fucking it. What gave you the right to think you could betray me like this and figure I'd just be okay with it?"

My chest was heaving, and he had the audacity to glimpse at it before meeting my eyes. "So I told a few friends?" He spread his hands. "It's not a big deal, Peggy."

"It's not a big deal that the entire school has been talking about us? About me?"

His jaw tightened. "Calm down." He looked around, hands raised. "People saw us. My friends knew. We never showed at the party, and we'd left homecoming together. It was tell some teammates the truth or have them think we went all the way by not saying anything."

I sat back, still seething but stumped. "They thought we went all the way?"

"What else would you think they'd assume after knowing where we'd been?"

I could feel my face drain as I floated away, adrift and blinking. "I don't know."

He leaned forward. "Look, I never planned for this to

happen, Pegs. But I didn't think they'd get this crazy, and I didn't want lies spread about you. You're my girlfriend," he paused, "or you were. I hate to say this, but the only reason it's such a big deal is because you're walking around acting like you've been slapped."

"Are you kidding?"

"No. That was harsh, but it's true." He sucked his lip, then winced and ran a finger over one of the healing cuts on it. "I waited all weekend for you to call and assumed you regretted what we did when you never did." He looked at me then. "Which, it's clear now that you do."

"Byron—"

"Did you ever want me, Peggy?"

Guilt clogged my insides. "I did."

He frowned, his hand grabbing mine. "This doesn't need to be over, you know." Our eyes met, the remnants of Dash's hurt lingering over his face. My stomach roiled. "I know you said you were confused, but we can talk about it. If we walk out of here together, they'll shut up sooner."

I pulled my hand back and laughed, crazed and loud as I stood, my body engulfed in a cloud of suspended disbelief.

"Peggy, wait," he called.

I didn't. I waded back to my seat as jeers and laughter started up. I'd probably embarrassed him. Good. It was only a tiny morsel of what he deserved after leaving me to feel embarrassed for days.

"Are you okay?" Willa asked when I returned to our table.

"So not okay," I muttered as the ache in my head spread to my eyes. "I hate this."

Daphne patted my back, and then a commotion over by the doors had our heads spinning.

Lars had just stalked through them, and the teacher was

calling after him. Annika was standing a few feet back from Mr. Andrews with a pinched face.

Daphne's hand stilled. "What the hell?"

I wasn't sure what had happened between them, but as I spied the crease marring Daphne's forehead, I knew she was dying to find out.

The bell blared, and everyone started heading to the doors, but we waited.

"Aren't you and Lars seeing each other?" Willa asked, tugging at the hem of her blouse.

"Seeing each other's a nice little label for it," Daphne admitted, then sighed. "But yes, we're still seeing each other."

It was on the tip of my tongue to ask more, but Willa beat me to it. "Exclusively?"

Daphne swallowed, then started collecting her trash. "Yeah."

So it was understandable that she was wondering, probably a lot more than we were, about why Lars and Annika appeared to have had some kind of fight.

The rest of the day dragged, the clock in each classroom threatening to make my head explode as I twitched with agitation. My chat with Byron had changed nothing. He wouldn't try to change anything. It would kill his pride and deflate that ego at this point.

Asshole.

"Hey, Newland," Wade said during history, a pencil tapping at the edge of his desk. "You and Woods done?"

I didn't want to pay him any mind, but I couldn't help but say, "So done."

He turned his attention back to the board, and I gave mine to a dent in the table, chewing on my nails.

When class finished, students hustling for the door all at once, Wade lingered as I got up and collected my things. "Think

I can have your number?"

I blinked at his grinning face. "Um, no. Sorry." I didn't know why I bothered apologizing. Maybe it was the shock, but I hauled out of there in an instant.

At my locker, I grabbed my bag, stuffing the books I'd need for homework inside, when yet more whispers and gasps reached me. "You've got to be freaking kidding me," I said, slamming my locker and about to scream my way out of school.

I stopped as Daphne neared me, grabbing her books.

"Hey, Daph, if you're done with Annika's baby daddy, call me," Danny said, gesturing with his hand to his ear. He and his friends laughed as they backed down the hall.

"Baby daddy?" I turned to Daphne.

Her mouth parted, and she seemed to fade into the rows of beige-colored lockers behind us. "He knocked her up." It wasn't a question, but a statement soaked in shock.

Which was confirmed when Willa raced over, worry etching her face and words. "You heard?"

Daphne jerked her head.

We stood frozen as half the school departed, and when Lars shouldered his bag, his head lowered as he walked down the hall, he didn't even look at Daphne.

I passed the choc chip to Daphne and took the peppermint, dunking my spoon in.

We'd declared an emergency scrapbook meeting at my place, which had turned into an ice-cream pity party before we'd even made it here.

"Have you tried calling him?" Willa asked.

Daphne shook her head, her eyes red. I didn't know if I'd

ever seen her cry before, and I didn't know that it was fair she looked even prettier when she did. "I don't want to."

Willa and I both nodded in understanding.

"When did it happen, though?" I asked aloud, finally. "I mean, you said you guys have been exclusive."

"Only for a few weeks." Daphne stabbed her spoon into the tub. "We'd kissed at the start of summer, but I thought it'd be a one-time thing until I saw him at Wade's before school started."

"I heard he and Annika hooked up before break. I also heard that it could be his baby or Coach Lenton's."

I snorted. "Seriously? He's like forty."

Willa shrugged. "He's not bad for forty."

Daphne stared at her ice cream. "I think that second one is just a rumor."

I nodded. "But how do we know there's any truth to any of this, then?"

"There's a kernel of truth to every lie," Daphne said.

I scowled, hating how much I'd lied to not only Dash but also myself.

Willa knocked my foot with hers.

I blew out a breath, ditching the ice cream on the window sill and flopping down onto my pillows. "And the look on Annika's face at lunch."

"Oh, yeah," Daphne said, scoffing. "She's definitely with child."

"She looked scared," Willa said.

Daphne grunted, and Willa apologized.

"No," Daphne said. "You're right. But wouldn't you be? She's not even eighteen until next month, if my memory is correct."

The minutes ticked by as Daphne assaulted her ice cream while Willa and I stared up at the ceiling.

"How did we get here?" I pondered, my heart hurting. "Sad,

confused, and left in impossible situations."

Willa hummed.

When Daphne started crying again, harder this time, I sat up and took the ice cream, setting it aside as Willa handed her some tissues. While Daphne tried, unsuccessfully, to control everything she was feeling, I realized something.

She and Willa might have been in impossible situations, but I wasn't. I didn't have to keep feeling like this if I didn't want to.

I had to find a way to make him talk to me.

TWENTY-SIX

Dash

Pregnant.

I wished I could say that he had it worse than me, and yes, I was the kind of asshole who compared, but I was pretty sure he still had a functioning heart. Even if it was in a state of shock.

"What are you going to do?" Rave asked, sitting on the frame of his bike.

He was an idiot. He could fuck it up, and that thing would cost two grand to replace. We didn't ride cheap.

Paper crackled, and then Lars blew out a smoke-filled exhale. "I don't even know."

More silence.

I wasn't sure what it was about these kind of moments in life, the ones that came crashing in and wrecked everything to hell, reducing everyone to wordless wonderings, but I didn't like them. It was akin to playing victim, lying down and taking it.

I was no pushover. I was getting so fucking sick and tired of taking it.

I pulled out my phone, staring at the stream of texts from Peggy that I'd ignored. Well, ignore would be the wrong choice of word, considering I'd stared at each one for hours.

Freckles: I'm sorry, Dash.

Freckles: I need to talk to you. Please talk to me.

Freckles: Why won't you answer? At least text me back. I didn't mean for this to happen. I'm sorry.

Freckles: I think I've made a huge mistake, and I'm sorry. I'm so sorry.

My nostrils flared as I read the last one she'd sent, and then I pocketed my phone.

"Is she going to keep it?" I finally asked the question we all wanted an answer to.

Lars nodded. "She's already a few months along."

I didn't think that meant she had to keep it, but there was no way I was taking part in a pro-life debate. I didn't care enough to get that involved.

"What about Daphne?" Jackson asked, his hands hanging over the front of his handle bars. He was the only one not sitting. Instead, he hunched over his bike.

Lars made a grunting noise, and I glanced at him in time to see his eyes shut briefly. "Can we not? I …" He tossed his blunt, sighing as his head hung. "I don't know."

Maybe his heart was as fucked as mine after all. But I was still the winner.

"How did it happen? You didn't wrap beforehand?"

I huffed, plucking out a cigarette and lighting it. "Please. As if he needs lessons on safe sex now."

Rave grimaced. "My bad."

"It broke." Lars chuckled, the sound lacking humor. "It was hers, and when I'd asked if she'd butchered it on purpose, she'd laughed and said she would never tie herself to a guy on a scholarship with no money. She isn't that stupid."

"I beg to fucking differ," I said through a laugh, then shut my trap when Rave glared at me. The way Annika had all but begged to suck my dick came knocking, interrupting my gloom. The look of dismay on her face when I'd left the laundry room at that party without fucking her now made horrifying sense. She was desperate enough to try to pin the pregnancy on someone else, anybody else so long as their bank accounts were fat enough.

For once, I chose to keep my thoughts to myself.

"I put it on knowing it was too small but not giving a shit. I'd done it before."

We all mumbled our agreement. "Happens."

"But I didn't think it'd fucking break."

Again, more silence.

I'd been at home all week with nothing but silence. I wanted noise. I needed mayhem. "When and where is the next party?"

They all looked at me like I was nuts, but Lars tipped his head back, thinking. "There's a couple tomorrow night. One down by the bay and another at Rosetta Carmichael's for her eighteenth."

"You wanna go?" I asked him. "We can get fucked up."

Lars nodded. "Hell yeah, I do."

The other two nodded too, and then Lars moved the topic to me.

"Talked to Peggy?"

I flicked ash from my cigarette, laughing through a cloud of smoke. "Fuck no."

Jackson scratched at his stubble. "She handed Byron his ass at school."

I didn't want to know. I didn't need to know. "How?"

Mother of shit.

As if he could read the ongoing torment between my brain and heart, Lars smirked.

Rave kicked at his pedal, bending over to check it. "Marched over to the team's table and made him follow her to one of their own."

She'd let him touch and kiss her, then invited him to lunch? My fists clenched, and nerve-endings zinged as the cigarette crumpled, burning me. I dropped it.

"Pretty sure they broke up," Lars said.

Jackson belched. "Yup. In front of the entire cafeteria." He chuckled. "I've never seen Miss Peggy Sue look so mad. Not even that time you put ants in her lunch box."

I scowled. "I didn't do that."

Jackson's face scrunched as he prepared to launch into the bowl. "Ah, yes you did. And a million other fucked-up things."

"I was her best friend," I defended.

"And her biggest tormentor." He took off, leaving me stupefied.

"Damn," Raven said. "Ants? I reckon you should consider yourself lucky that girl even put up with you."

I growled, getting up and swinging my leg over my bike. "Fuck all of you, you don't know shit." They didn't. They didn't know how close we'd come to venturing into something life changing. Instead, we'd ventured into something neither of us could recover from.

And it was all her fault.

Lars heaved out a sigh as he stood and picked up his piece of shit bike. It wasn't shit, it was actually awesome, but it was old as hell. "I need a fucking drink."

"I fucking hear that."

Rave clucked his tongue. "So which one are we going to tomorrow night?"

"Any. Both," I said. "Don't even care."

I might have been grounded, considering I'd been suspended from school, but I'd been grounded over a hundred times in my life and never once had I actually abided by it.

Dad was too busy screwing his secretary when he wasn't doing actual work, and Mom was too busy floundering over Emanuel and her dumbass problems that weren't even problems to realize I'd left the house.

When Dad had asked me why I'd beat the hell out of Byron Woods, all I'd done was shrug. Mom told him it was about Peggy, and then Dad had given me a look that said he understood. He wasn't happy, but he knew she'd been dating the asshole.

It didn't matter that she'd been dating him. That had never mattered when I'd woken up to the idea that she was only ever supposed to be mine.

Nothing much really mattered now. If life wanted to keep throwing shit at me, I was going to move, dodge the spray, and no longer take it lying down.

It was time to throw shit back.

TWENTY-SEVEN

Peggy

I flicked through Facebook, realizing with a jolt that Dash had blocked me.

He hardly used it, and neither did I, but he'd gone and blocked me anyway.

I jumped over to Instagram, and sure enough, I was unable to pull up his profile there too.

"Talk about extreme measures," I said, heading back over to Facebook.

People were posting about the parties tonight. Selfies had been locked and loaded, locations marked, and I had to wonder if any parents in the cove who cared where their kids were bothered to check their Facebook posts. Unless, of course, they'd blocked them from seeing certain things.

"Smart," I said, shoving more potato chips into my mouth, uncaring that I was doing a lot of talking to myself.

"Pegs." Mom stopped at my door with her hair done in a loose updo. Phil must have been taking her out. "I'll be home around eleven. You'll be okay?"

I eyed the potato chip bag next to me and the jar of dip beside it, then my pink fluffy socks. "Yeah, I'm all set."

She smiled, about to leave, then walked into the room to sit by my feet. "Listen, I know you've been having a hard time, and I know Dash hasn't been here in an unusually long time."

"It's been a week," I said, a tad defensively.

"Like I said, a long time." She had me there. "And it's

killing me to try to give you space, but I need to know. What happened?"

I toyed with the chip between my fingers. I could tell her. I could tell her, and maybe it'd make me feel a little better, or maybe she'd have some advice for me. Or I could not tell her and just hope it all straightened itself out and then I'd never have to.

I set my phone down. "I'll make you late."

"I don't care." She settled onto the bed some more. "Spill."

After sighing so hard it emptied my lungs, I did. As I let it out, I realized just how bad it sounded, just how epically I'd messed up, and just how much force the gravity of the situation held. I would've been embarrassed to admit what I'd done with Byron, but the way she reacted rid me of any I'd felt while explaining.

Her first point of worry was Byron, and I watched as she stalked around my room, ruining her hair as she cussed up a storm. "I'll string him up by his filthy balls for opening his—"

"Mom," I said, a little shocked.

She blew out a breath, then straightened her green sweater. "You need to break up with him. He broke your trust."

"I know," I said. "I have, kind of." At least, I thought I had.

"Don't you dare give him another inch of attention," she warned.

"I wasn't going to."

"Give those tickets back, too."

"I've already slipped them inside his locker." I'd done it yesterday, faking a trip to the bathroom during class.

"Okay. Good." She quit her pacing, then started fixing her hair. "We'll head to the salon first thing tomorrow and get our nails done."

I nodded, then picked up my phone when I thought she

was leaving.

Dash had blocked me, but that didn't stop me from seeing useful comments coming in on someone's post. One of the commenters was Raven, telling someone they'd better show at Rosetta's eighteenth birthday.

Mom slapped her hands to her sides, alerting me that she was still there. "And as for Dash. That boy has crushed on you for years. It wouldn't surprise me if he was in love with you and you were just too blinded by your friendship to see it."

My throat constricted. "I know." I corrected myself. "I mean, I know that now."

"He'll forgive you, I promise." She bent over, kissing my head then combing her fingers through my hair. "Don't beat yourself up over this. You'll make many more mistakes in this life." That bit of wisdom had me wanting to lock myself inside for the rest of my days. "We'll talk more tomorrow but keep trying with Dash. He's an oddball, but he's oddly good for you." Her brows met as she stepped back, and her lips pulled tight. "In a way that shouldn't work, but it just does."

"Actually," I said, swinging my legs over the bed. "Do you mind if I head to a party?" When she tilted her head and raised a brow, I hurried to add, "I'll drive. Just to see if he's there and if he'll talk to me. Please."

Maybe it was the desperation in my voice, eyes, or stance, but after staring at me for a drawn-out moment, she nodded. "Don't stay if he's not there. After homecoming, I think you need to lay low for a while."

I agreed and told her I'd be home before she was, then tossed the chips into the trash to get ready.

Throwing my closet door open, I plucked a black frilly skirt out and a pair of black stockings, pulling them both on. I was already wearing a plain white T-shirt, so I left it on and added a spritz of perfume before dragging a brush through my tangled curls.

My eyes still bore the remains of the day's mascara, but remembering Dash's comment, *you don't need that shit,* I shrugged and grabbed my phone and keys.

The moon hung low in the sky, surrounded by dazzling, dancing stars. Hope became untamable the closer I got to Rosetta's place on the other side of the creek. She lived a five minutes' drive away from Dash's, so it'd make sense for he and his friends to wind up there.

I just hoped he was there, but even if he wasn't, I was done soaking in self-pity and fear. I'd try the party down at the bay, and then I'd go to his house and demand that someone let me in. I had to tell him I was sorry, and most importantly, I had to tell him I'd realized I loved him too.

Because I did. I'd always loved him but not like this.

Love, I'd discovered, was something that multiplied. With every kiss and every touch, it continued to change shape as we continued to fall.

Dash was a bastard. A selfish, immature, and, at times, scheming prick.

But that wasn't all he was. He was thoughtful, smart, generous, and loyal to a fault. Which he'd proved in more ways than one with how he'd fought with every breath to remain the main focus in my life.

Now, it was my turn to fight. I'd been a fool to think, even if it wouldn't ruin our friendship, that he'd be the worst kind of boyfriend.

He wouldn't. He was everything I'd been searching and hoping to find in someone else, never daring to look too close to home. I never thought it possible, not once, and the few times I had, fear would strike me hard and true. We couldn't risk it, and it wouldn't work. But we did risk it, and we did work. I'd just ignored it out of naïve self-preservation. After all, you couldn't ruin something that never was.

Until I did.

My breathing turned chaotic when I parked at the end of the long car-lined street and followed the thud of the music to the drive of the golden bricked home. A few people from school were outside smoking and drinking. I waved when a girl from biology smiled at me.

The music pounded alongside my frantic heartbeat as my eyes adjusted to the dim lighting inside. I slunk into the monstrous living room where couples were making out, or probably worse, on the couches while others danced around them. I ducked and weaved my way through.

I exited the kitchen without any sign of him or his friends and stopped at the base of the large oak stairs, peering into the crowd. Water splashed behind me, faint beneath the sound of the music. Fish. They had a pond filled with carp beneath their staircase. I tore my eyes away from the gurgling water, then pushed my way through throngs of people to head up the stairs.

Finally, on the second floor, I caught sight of Lars, who hadn't been at school today, smoking on the couch. Raven was next to him with some girl's legs tossed over his lap as he whispered into her ear, but I couldn't see Jackson or Dash.

I tried to make my way over to Lars, curious about how he was doing, when a voice stopped me. "Looking for your precious BFF?" I spun to find Byron leaning against the wall, his eyes bloodshot. "Try the last room at the end of the hall."

I started walking that way, partly because I finally knew where he was, and partly because I didn't want to be near Byron.

"Don't say I never gave you anything!"

KISS AND BREAK UP | 197

I ignored his last jab, and when I reached the end of the hall, I steeled myself, shaking my hands out. Dash was probably in there getting high with Jackson, and I needed to prepare some kind of speech. I could've kicked myself for not doing that on the way over here instead of daydreaming. I needed to have something to say that would make him listen, even if he was wasted.

Resolved to just outright blurting the truth, I pushed open the door, then quickly shut it behind me. When I looked into the dark, there was no drifting smoke and no cloying scent of marijuana. No, the scent in the room was one that had cement filling my stomach and caused my next breath to cut straight through the middle of my heart.

Two figures were moving on the bed, and unable to do anything, let alone alert them to my presence, I just watched as Kayla pushed back the duvet and released a moan that I swore I'd hear for years to come.

I must have made some kind of sound that alerted them to my presence because she looked over at me, a sinister smile curling her mouth as Dash's body moved over hers, the bed creaking, and the sheets shifting.

A rough curse left him, and he rolled off her. "You're not done," she said.

"Can't," he said, his voice like gravel. "Too fucked up."

Kayla's face pinched as if she was offended. "Well, I guess now's a good a time as any to tell you we've got company."

My body thawed, my hand reaching blindly for the door handle behind me as Dash said, dark and dry, "Like I fucking care. Wait, do they have a smoke?"

"Why don't you ask her yourself?" Kayla's breasts bounced as she rolled and stood from the bed, naked. "Got a smoke, Peggy?"

Dash sat up so fast, he swayed, but I was already out of there.

I raced down the hall, missing a step as I all but threw myself down them. A guy caught me, and I mumbled my thanks, then raced down the rest of them with my vision blurred and my heart left bleeding on the floor above my head.

How could he? And with Kayla?

Outside on the drive, I slowed to a walk as her warnings came back to hit me square in the core of who I was. I hadn't believed she'd be able to hurt me. With the exception of Byron, I hadn't believed I had anything she'd wanted. I hadn't been worried about Dash because I never once thought he would touch her.

I'd been wrong.

"Going so soon?" Dash's casually cold voice entered the smog.

I tossed a glance over my shoulder, noticing he'd found a fix of nicotine, then let a sour laugh fly free.

"What?" he asked, hot on my heels as I bypassed a group of girls who were smoking and watching us. "You just got here. You can't leave yet."

"And what would I see next if I stay, Dash? You having sex with someone else?"

His laughter was bitter and lacked any remorse. "I didn't finish, so probably."

We'd left the driveway, and I was halfway to my car when I spun around and shoved him. "You hate me that much?" He didn't even move.

"Yeah," he said through his teeth, blowing smoke into my face. "I do."

"I guess the feeling's mutual now then, so I'll see you in some other lifetime." I turned for my car, swiping at my cheeks.

He snatched my wrist, pushing me up against someone's car as he loomed over me, his chest pressing into mine. "It fucking hurts, doesn't it? You couldn't admit it, but I see it now. It's written all over your face. You care more than you should, and it fucking kills you."

"Fuck you." I tried not to choke on the words.

"You already have, Freckles," he said through another bitter laugh. "Six ways from Sunday, you've fucked me, and I've yet to find anything satisfying about it."

"Let go." I tried to pull the hand he had pinned to the cool metal behind my head free.

"Why'd you even come here?" When I didn't answer, his voice rose to a growl, his eyes aglow with fury. "Why, huh? Tell me."

"To try talking to you, to apologize, but it doesn't matter now."

His brows gathered, and the tension in his jaw slowly loosened. "It doesn't?"

"No," I said, and I took the opportunity to push him off me. "It doesn't matter that I wanted to tell you I love you too because you've gone and wrecked it." I stalked toward my car.

Just as I reached it, he grabbed me from behind, arms tight around my waist as he rasped into my ear. "You love me?"

I tried to pry his arms off me, digging my nails into his skin. "It doesn't matter anymore. Let fucking go."

"No." His teeth grabbed hold of my earlobe, and he released it as he murmured, "I'd say we're even now, then."

I didn't want to do it, but I had enough despair coursing through me that I let go of what I should and shouldn't do and did what I had to. I reached behind me and felt his entire body still as I wrapped my hand around his junk. A groan thundered into my ear. I ignored the shiver that took hold and squeezed.

"Son of a whore," he bellowed, his arms unfolding as luminous cussing drifted into the night.

I yanked open the car door, diving inside as he remained bent over, cupping himself.

When he looked over at me, a crazed glint in his eyes, I flipped him off, then peeled away.

TWENTY-EIGHT

Dash

I remained on the grass in front of someone's house until the pain in my balls eased enough to let me breathe properly.

Except I still couldn't breathe. Though that was thanks to a different kind of pain.

Pain that mingled with excruciating joy, the likes of which shouldn't even coexist.

I wanted to tell you I love you too.

The admission followed me back inside, repeating obsessively as girls tapped my arms, and some guys tried to nab my attention. I went upstairs, flopping down onto the space beside Lars, who was looking like he was about to start flying, he was so damn high.

"Was that Peggy I saw run outta here?" he slurred.

"Uh-huh," I said, kicking my feet up onto the glass coffee table as I tried to rack my brain into thinking properly. My boots made a jarring sound as they met the glass, but I didn't care. She loved me. Peggy said she was in love with me.

After she saw me fucking some other chick.

A groan heated my palm as I swiped it down my face and slumped further into the couch. Fuck. *What the fuck have I just done?*

I wasn't certain she'd forgive me for this. I knew her, and she'd forgive me for a lot of things, but the choked timbre to her voice and the hurt glaring at me in her eyes, I knew I was screwed.

But she had to. She'd hurt me first, and worse than that, she'd done it right after I'd told her I'd fallen for her. Mere hours, if we're getting technical. And I was all about technicalities right about now.

She decided to tell me after I'd messed up. There was a difference. So fuck it, I was going to get high and send this night down the barrel straight to hell.

Jackson stalked through the gathering of people hanging in the living room, his eyes searching, then fixing on us before he approached quickly. He kicked my feet off the coffee table then took a seat, his expression grim. "Do none of you assholes answer your phones?"

Lars didn't say a thing, just stared through thin slits that once resembled eyes.

I took a drag of my blunt, then chased it with a sip of Jack. "Don't even know where it is." That was true, though I was certain I'd left it in the room somewhere after unsuccessfully fucking Kayla.

I cringed, taking another large, burning sip of whiskey. I couldn't even say I hadn't been thinking. Oh, I'd been thinking all right. With my dick and my bruised heart and ego. Probably not in that order, but that was neither here nor there. I'd fucked up, but I hadn't known she felt that way about me, and after what she'd done at homecoming, I was struggling to believe she was even telling me the truth.

She probably just missed me.

All I'd wanted was revenge. Sweet, mind-numbing revenge in the form of an escape.

So fuck Peggy. She'd destroyed me. It was only fair I do what I want.

All my thoughts were blown to dust when Jackson leaned forward. "Willa told me some stuff last night."

"That your dick is worth your parents divorcing after they find out you've been screwing each other?" Lars burped, laughing.

Well, well. I was tempted to ask Lars how he'd found out, but I just snickered instead. "Nice."

Jackson's head shook, and he looked like he wanted to smack our heads together. "Shut the fuck up. And no, she told me that things got heated between Peggy and Byron, but she stopped it."

"Heated?"

Jackson scratched at his cheek. "They were making out, and he was touching her, but she told him to stop."

Everything turned red. I jolted to my feet, then swayed.

Jackson pushed me back down on the couch. "Sit down. You can't do shit without getting expelled, and he's not even here. I saw him leave about ten minutes ago."

"Like I give a fuck if I get expelled."

Jackson sighed. "Apparently, she was all messed up over you, didn't know how she felt and didn't know what to do, so she slammed the brakes on and bit the hell out of his lip."

I said nothing, my vision still spotting.

"You see the cut on his lip?" I frowned, remembering it and the way people had called Peggy a savage. "She bit him to make him get off her, then Willa and Daphne stopped the limo."

As Jackson kept talking, I remembered where I'd been while this was happening between her and Byron. Inside the dark warehouse feeling like I'd been stood up, like the sorry son of a bitch I was.

She'd had to bite him to make him stop.

I should've tried harder. I shouldn't have left her with him to go drink my feelings away. I should've pushed even more. I was Dash Thane, and I didn't stop until I'd gotten what I'd wanted.

But this time, I couldn't handle the challenge, so I'd stepped back, hoping that for once in my life, I wouldn't have to demand I be given something. Something that couldn't be bought or handed to me.

Standing, I set loose a string of curses so foul that Jackson stared at me as if he was waiting for me to explode. "I'll kill him next time. I'll—" Jackson pushed me back onto the couch, and I stood back up, getting in his face. "Quit doing that, asshole."

His green eyes flared. "She was his girlfriend, and you fucked around, playing games instead of being straight with her."

"I was straight with her." But then I'd bailed, leaving her confused, like a coward. I blinked, stepping back and scraping a hand over my hair.

"Where's Peggy?" Kayla asked, wrapping her arm around mine.

I shook her off. "Get gone before I throw your ass out the window."

She gasped, then laughed. "You're such an asshole."

"Hey, Kayla," Lars said, a lift to his lips as he sank back into the couch cushions.

She stopped, flipping her hair over her shoulder as she fluttered her lashes at him.

"Word is that your boy just left with Annabeth."

Her brows pulled. "What?" A laugh tittered out of her, then her expression fell. "No way."

"Left about fifteen minutes ago," Jackson said.

Kayla's lips cracked and her shoulders visibly shook as she raised a hand to her forehead. "You're lying." Yet her tone lacked conviction.

I didn't know if he had, and I didn't care. So long as he was nowhere near me right now.

"The hell would we lie about something like that?" Lars

flicked a hand at her. "Never mind, believe it or don't, just fuck off before we catch something."

Her face contorted in outrage, but she didn't hang around, and neither did I.

After stumbling to the room to find my phone, I made it to the stairs before Jackson grabbed my shoulder and hauled me back. "I swear to God, you keep manhandling me, and I'll—"

"You'll what?" he asked, a look in his eye that said he could do with an outlet. "If you want out, I'll take you home. You're wasted. You're not going anywhere else."

I needed to see her, and this shithead was intent on stopping me.

Peggy. Fuck me. I wanted to throw myself down the stairs, guilt a pulsing beat in every vein in my body. It repulsed me to know she'd been mauled by that dog, but now I'd broken her too.

Lars joined us as we filed downstairs, Raven nowhere to be seen.

"Take me to Peggy's," I said as we climbed into his truck.

"No." The truck roared to life, the headlights illuminating a bunch of girls dancing in the street.

"Yes," I said, my head falling to the glass as it spun in hazy waves.

Jackson said nothing, and I tried to lift my head, but I'd over-done it, and all too soon, blackness took hold.

Lars and Jackson had hauled me out of the car and left me on the porch. Lars needed help getting back to the truck, so Jackson rang the doorbell and left me there.

Couldn't exactly blame him, but it did take my dad a

206 | ELLA FIELDS

considerable effort to help me inside.

Showered and lying face down on my bed, I replayed the events of the previous night over and over. It never got any easier to relive. I was a masochist of the worst degree.

But if I was going to feel like shit in every possible way, I was going to make sure I did it right.

Church slithered along my body, then his paws started kneading my back. I wasn't wearing a shirt, so his nails were a bit of an issue, but he was one of the only things I loved, so I'd put up with it. Not like I didn't deserve a bit of pain anyway.

"Knock, knock." Dad opened my door.

I didn't even bother looking at him and grunted. "Usually people knock, rather than say, knock, knock."

"I wouldn't get smart with me, drunkard." He paused, and I heard him take a slurp of coffee. I'd kill for some coffee, but I wasn't sure my stomach could handle anything. "Now, I was eighteen once ..."

I groaned. "Not this shit again."

"Shut your mouth. I was eighteen once, and I remember with not a lot of clarity how much shit one can get into. However, this needs to stop, Dash. Get control of yourself."

"I haven't lost control of a damn thing."

"Partying every weekend, getting suspended from school for beating someone up, and let's not even get started on the lack of respect you have for me and your mother."

I coughed, my chest rattling. "Mainly just Mother Dearest."

He made a growling sound, and I cringed. *Too far.* "Fine, fine." I waved an arm. "I'll be better, do better, whatever."

Dad remained there, his judgment and the unspoken words he was keeping tucked away hanging heavy in the stale air of my room. After a minute, he sighed. "You have today to be hungover, then I want you up and out of the house. No video games tomorrow."

That had me rolling over. Church protested, his nails scoring into my back. I hissed. "What? What does playing a few games have anything to do with?"

"You have brand-new bikes in the garage and acres of land behind the house to ride them on. Get out and do that, or I don't know …" He threw around the hand that wasn't wrapped around his mug. "Clean up this shit-sty of a room."

"That's what Franny is for," I said to his retreating back.

"Franny said she doesn't want to enter your dungeon anymore. Occupational hazards."

"Occupational what?" I glanced around at the junk lining the floor. It wasn't too bad. Just food wrappers, clothes, textbooks, gaming consoles and cords, and some empty glasses and bowls. I harrumphed, then flopped back down on the bed to bask in my misery.

Today, I would mope.

Tomorrow, I would mope too, but I would do it while trying to win my best friend back.

TWENTY-NINE

Peggy

"Peggy." Mom tapped at the door. "I need to head into town for a bit."

I rolled my head off my pillow enough to mumble, "Awesome."

A pause, then, "Are you sure you're okay?"

"I'll be fine."

Mom waited a beat. "Okay. Call me if you need anything. Hopefully, I won't be long."

I felt like reminding her that I was eighteen and I was quite capable of being left home alone, broken heart or not. That wouldn't fly, and it wasn't fair to take how I was feeling out on her, but I was beginning not to care.

It cost too much to care, when all I could see were two figures moving in a bed, and hear the sound of Kayla's moaning. In a continuous loop, it all circled and recycled. I couldn't shut it off. So I tried to sleep instead, but even behind tear-swollen lids, everything chased me and demanded I look.

Look at what you've done.

Look at what we'd gone and done.

A few kisses had changed everything. Or maybe it would've changed anyway. Who knew. I suppose we might never know. But it shouldn't have happened the way it did. If we were always destined to wind up walking this path with each other, I didn't think it was meant to be like this. Anything but this splitting ache that wouldn't remove its teeth from my heart.

Thudding at the window had me rolling over, and I blinked, wiping my mouth as a shadow appeared behind the curtains.

"Pegs."

My heart plummeted, then bounced.

He rattled the window. "Let me in, Freckles, or I'll blow this cardboard box down."

"Go home, Dash."

"See? A box. I shouldn't have been able to hear that, but I did." He paused. "Or maybe I just imagined it, but whatever. Let me in."

I ignored him but watched as his palms slid down the glass trying to find enough purchase to lift the locked window.

"Fine. You've left me no choice."

I frowned at the words, then my heart boomed as he wedged something beneath the old wood, paint chipping and falling as he tried to jimmy the window open.

"Oh, my freaking God." I threw the covers off and, clad in only an extra-long T-shirt, panties, and my hair a mess atop my head, I raced down the hall to open the front door.

As if this was his plan, he was already there, a blinding grin on his face as he stepped inside, making me stumble back a step. "You look like hell."

"Are you serious right now?" I shut the door, not to keep him in, but to keep anything that might be said away from any neighbors walking by.

He tipped a shoulder, then walked into the living room, leaning against the back of the couch with his ankles crossed. "I'm here to grovel."

My bleary eyes widened as I laughed. "Who actually says that? Instead of just doing it?"

His smirk was going to have my nails clawing at his face

if he didn't wipe it off. "Clearly, I do. Want me to get on my knees? I haven't put my mouth on you yet, but if you sidle on over here, I'd be more than happy to service you." His eyes journeyed down my thighs, his teeth pinching his full bottom lip even as his fists and jaw clenched. "To rid any and all remnants of the scum who touched you."

Saliva thickened over my tongue, and my throat swelled. "You're such a dick."

I went to the door, about to open it, when he said, "Okay, okay. That was probably too soon. I'm sorry, okay? Like insanely fucking sorry."

I stopped moving, my body tensing all over.

"I'm self-centered, but we know that." His footsteps neared, boots heavy on the wood floor. His voice became a soft plea. "I didn't know you were so confused, Peggy. I didn't think you even liked the guy. But even so, I know I went about this all wrong. I've fucked it all up, and I'm sorry."

My lungs froze, air puffing out of me on a dry exhale. "You'd have known if you'd have listened to me at all these past weeks. I told you I liked him. I told you what we were doing was scaring me."

"Again, I fucked up. But the thought of you letting him touch you like that," he said on a harsh exhale, "it tore out my damn heart."

"Funny, I didn't realize you even had one."

"I deserve that."

I swallowed, my eyes burning as I turned to his tortured expression. He looked like hell, too, but the best kind. His blue eyes were more vivid over the pillows cushioning them, and the careful mess he made of his hair was flattened in ten different ways. His white shirt was crinkled, as were his jeans, and his boots unlaced.

Heat coalesced at the same time hate and hurt wrapped tight around my heart. It didn't seem fair that standing before me, I was able to finally appreciate everything he was as more than just a friend but also be too wrecked to even want it. "How'd you come to this miraculous realization anyway?"

"That doesn't matter." I frowned, because it did, and he took a few steps closer. "I wish I'd made sense of what I was feeling before all this happened. I wish I'd swallowed my pride before I let it get the better of me. I wish I was capable of thinking before I act. I wish for so many things, but wishing is pointless because here I am, unable to make any of them come true." My tongue felt too thick to talk, so I didn't. "Freckles, I'm done with wishing. I only want to make this right."

My eyes closed. They reopened as his hand met my face, his thumb brushing over my skin as he stepped even closer and peered down at me. "I love you. I've always loved you. And I don't know when exactly that love changed, or why it had me acting like more of a dickhead than normal, but I know it wasn't recent. I know I'd be lying if I tried to say it was all brand new." His throat bobbed. "Because it's not new. What's new is that I can finally recognize what I feel and admit it."

I felt my heart beating through every limb, every vein, and every breath as I absorbed what he'd just said. "You ..." I couldn't even talk, my vocal cords had become cotton candy—flimsy, unreliable, and too damn soft.

Dash nodded, his thumb reaching my bottom lip and grazing beneath it, eyes tracking the connection. "Yeah, no more bullshit. I've always said what I mean and mean what I say." His lips twitched. "Until it came to admitting how I felt about you. Which says something in and of itself, yeah?"

My lashes drooped to his lip, where a tiny cut still resided from his brawl with Byron. I wanted so badly to absolve him of all that'd happened, but as I stared at that lip, I couldn't stop myself from thinking about Kayla. "You knew you loved me, yet you were okay with having sex with someone else?"

His lips tightened, and his thumb ceased moving. "There's not a lot I can say besides I'm sor—"

"You're sorry, yes, we've established that. But Dash"—I laughed, backing up and losing his touch—"I couldn't go any further with Byron because it made me sick. Because I was beginning to think that maybe I was in love with you, too."

"Peggy, fuck." His hands balled at his sides. "I want this. Us. More than anything else in the world. And if we could just start over, you know I'd never do that—"

"But I wouldn't be able to forget." I squared my shoulders, infusing enough steel to straighten my spine and strengthen my voice. "I can't forget what it felt like to see you in that bed with her, of all people."

He came toward me, but I backed away. He stopped, pinching the bridge of his nose. "I-I don't even know what to say. I was fucked up, and I fucked up, but I'm not the type to wait around for someone to decide they finally want me, Peggy." A harsh laugh erupted. "I'm the type who'll fuck someone else to help me forget someone else. And we weren't together. I never thought we'd speak again."

Tears dripped, and I flicked them away, my heart squeezing. "While that may be true, it's all too big a mess now. So there's really no point in having this conversation."

"There is," he ground out through a tight jaw. "There is because we're us. We couldn't live without each other even if we didn't fall for each other, and now we definitely can't."

"You didn't feel that way forty-eight hours ago," I had to remind him.

He tossed his arms out. "Because I hated your fucking guts

forty-eight hours ago. You destroyed me, Peggy. If I'm being honest, knowing you were making out with him, knowing he touched your cunt in that limo is *still* destroying me."

I flinched. "See?" Emotion smeared my voice, tainting my vision. "Just go. We're wasting our time and only making this worse."

"No time with you is wasted even when we're breaking."

My fingers curled, nails striking my palms. "I don't want to break anymore. I want you to leave."

"Over Kayla? Come on," he said. "We're more than this bullshit."

How he so easily discarded the pain that he'd caused from his actions had something dark and all-consuming cracking open inside me. "Don't you dare belittle how I feel." I was seething, my teeth clacking. "But you would because that's what you do. You're Dash Thane, right? The boy who ignores how others feel and does and says whatever he wants, and forever gets away with it."

His nostrils flared. "That's not fucking true."

"It is. *It is* fucking true. But not this time." I marched to the door, flinging it open. "Get out."

He didn't move. "This is a mistake. We've both made enough mistakes. Can we please not make anymore and, instead, find a way to move past this?" His eyes were begging, but his words were far from enough.

My laughter cracked and ebbed in the air around us. "Go, Dash. Now."

"No, just listen to me," he growled.

"Why should I when all you do is downplay what you've done? The way you hurt me?"

"Because I love you."

"Well, I don't want your damn love. Not now. Not tomorrow.

Not in ten years."

Shock painted his features a paler hue. "You don't mean that."

I picked up the oriental vase from behind me, one of the only items Mom took from Dad's place, and threw it at him. I missed. On purpose. But it was enough. It made his feet stumble to the door, and I pushed him the rest of the way out.

"Peggy!" He pounded on the door when I slammed and locked it. "Peggy, don't fucking do this."

"It's already done. And it never should've started," I yelled through the wood. "Go home before I call the cops."

He didn't move for at least five minutes. I felt him there, like a smothering blanket in the heat of summer, while I sat on the floor with my back against the door and cried.

I stayed in bed the rest of the day, my tears drying on the pillow until I had enough energy for new ones to dampen it again.

I'd wanted this. I'd wanted to know what it was like to fall for someone and experience all the things the girls at school experienced. Even if I'd gotten hurt. But those who hadn't had their heart broken were nothing but foolish dreamers to think they could handle it. And had I known just how completely love could ruin me, I never would've set out to find it.

For what I found loomed closer to home than I ever saw coming, which only made it all the more devastating.

Mom had given me space, and I'd been grateful, but she'd apparently thought she'd given me enough when she entered my room later that night and curled up behind me.

She didn't touch me, and she didn't pry. She just waited, offering comfort with her presence.

And though I tried, I tried so hard not to set every torn piece of me free, I had to. It needed out. It needed to find a safe place to land. I couldn't keep it trapped within or else I feared I'd never leave my room again.

She didn't say anything as I spoke, but I knew she was listening, and as I choked out everything that'd happened with me and Dash, I wanted to cry harder as I heard it all out loud. "I don't know what to do now," I whispered when I'd finished. "What am I supposed to do now?"

Mom spoke then, her hand coming to rest on my hip. "You continue to feel, and you continue to do what feels right."

I was surprised yet relieved she wasn't telling me to forgive him. "How could he do that, though?"

Mom shifted closer. "There's no excusing it. He did it, and it's done. But I do believe he's sorry, that he regrets it, and that he loves you."

I scoffed, wiping my eyes with my sheet. "He's a conceited brat."

She laughed. "True. But he's a conceited brat who would do anything for you. To the point of ruining himself." A yawn escaped her. "However, that doesn't mean he gets to use that, what you did when you didn't know how you even felt, as an excuse to hurt you."

I thought about that. Turned and twisted it over as I sat up and drank the glass of water Mom had brought in with her. The cool liquid slid down my dry throat, and I tried to picture what life would be like moving forward without Dash. It seemed incomprehensible—undoable—to continue being me without him there. But I had to. He'd left me no choice.

"I don't want to go to school tomorrow." I set the glass down, then slipped back beneath the covers.

Mom pulled them over herself, her eyes closing. "I'll give

you one free pass for a broken heart, but it's up to you how you use it." After a moment, she added, "I would've given you two, but you broke my vase, so no dice."

I smiled, and the movement on my lips felt foreign but nice. I could only hope I'd remember how to keep doing it.

THIRTY

Peggy

I opted not to use my free pass and dragged my weary self to school.

The news of Lars, the poor bad boy scholarship student, being Annika's baby's daddy spread like wildfire. It became the only thing on people's lips if they weren't eating, and when I saw Daphne by our lockers Monday morning, I knew she was trying to hide just how much it was hurting her.

"You okay?" I asked. "Sorry, that was stupid."

"It's fine." Her brows scrunched, a layer of concealer heavy beneath her eyes. "You look like shit."

Before I could say anything, she was pulling me toward the girls' bathrooms, Willa tagging behind.

A few juniors lingered, applying lipstick and straightening their knee-high socks. With one hiss from Daphne, they collected their things and made themselves scarce.

"You didn't need to do that," I said, watching the door close behind them.

"I did. What happened Friday night?" Daphne opened her bag, plucking out her makeup bag and rifling through it.

I looked at Willa, who shrugged and came forward with a hairbrush. My eyes widened as she launched to her toes to reach for my tangled hair.

"With Dash?" I scowled. "Ow."

"Sorry," Willa said. "Knots galore."

Daphne started brushing foundation over my face. I didn't

typically wear it, but I didn't protest when she said, "You're so blotchy it looks like you have eczema. So shut up and let me work." My mouth snapped shut, and she groaned. "I didn't mean shut up about Dash. What happened? Lars and Annika's baby news might be a hot topic, but that doesn't mean people don't know about Kayla and Dash."

I contained my sigh being that Daphne's face was inches from mine. "Of course."

"It's Kayla, so naturally, she wants the attention on her." Daphne pulled back, inspecting my face, then nodded and grabbed her powder.

I closed my eyes as she brushed it everywhere. "I walked in on them."

Willa gasped, the brush getting stuck in my hair.

"Jesus, Willa." I rubbed at my scalp.

"Sorry. That's … no wonder you look like shit. Why didn't you call us?"

"I was busy being miserable."

Daphne snapped the lid shut, then turned and grabbed her mascara. "He's such a fucking idiot."

"Biggest asshole," Willa added.

"I went there to apologize, to try to explain, and then I found that?" I felt tears gathering, but I pushed them back as hard as I could while Daphne finished coating my lashes. "Then, somehow, he found out exactly what happened in the limo and came to my place."

Willa's touch vanished. She moved to her bag, grabbing an elastic. "That was me."

Daphne's gaze snapped to her as she capped her mascara. "You told Jackson?"

Willa offered me the elastic. I took it, glaring at her.

She bit her lip. "I'm sorry. But I knew he wouldn't talk to

you. Jackson was going out with them that night, and I thought it might help if he knew the details."

Daphne's button nose crinkled. "Your heart was in the right place, but still, that's shitty, Willa."

Willa nodded, and I flipped my head forward, scooping my hair into a small ponytail and tying it up. I knew her intentions weren't to betray my trust, but rather, she'd wanted to help in some way, so even though it irked me, I chose to let it go. "Don't worry about it. But I'm sorry to say it won't make a difference now that he's gone and slept with Kayla."

Daphne put her makeup bag away and checked her own makeup right as the bell sounded. "Try to ignore her smug smile. She's just gloating."

"He didn't even orgasm." I don't know why I said that. It was petty, but hell if I cared about being petty or not anymore.

Willa laughed. "Oh, my God. Really?"

I nodded, smoothing some of the foundation caked near my eye. Daphne's skin tone was a shade darker than mine, but the bad match didn't look terrible and was a vast improvement from how I'd arrived at school.

Daphne snorted. "I can't believe you watched."

"I couldn't move," I said. "Like a bad wreck or something, I could only stare like an ogling moron." I blew out a breath. "And now, I'll pay for it forever."

Willa pouted, then rubbed my arm.

Daphne sighed, then flicked her hair. "His loss, and I bet he's already feeling it."

I wasn't sure if she was referring to Dash or Lars. I shouldered my bag, following them out and down the hall to our lockers where we quickly dumped our stuff and headed to class.

Lunch came and went before I realized I'd been bracing myself for a storm that wasn't coming. Dash hadn't shown, and no one seemed to think anything of it. Perhaps they thought he was still suspended, but I knew he should've been back by today.

Lars and Jackson stalked through the cafeteria, the former about to stop at our table, when he stumbled, swaying into Jackson, who cursed and glanced around. "Get it together, man."

"Daph," Lars said, or slurred.

I wondered if he was drunk and eyed him. The untucked shirt, absent tie, and haphazard hair. Then I looked at his blood-shot eyes. He was something; that was certain.

"Go eat something, Lars." Daphne took a sip of her water through her straw. "You look like hell."

"I am in hell. We need to talk." The whole cafeteria seemed to be holding their breath as he wobbled closer, his hands slapping onto the table as he leaned over Daphne.

She appeared content to ignore him, but I knew she didn't really want to. Her feet shifted beneath the table, and her shoulders tensed. "Go," she said.

"Oh, fuck you. You don't want me now, is that it?"

Daphne kept her eyes down.

"Huh?" Lars bellowed. "At least look at me when you lie through your ten-thousand-dollar teeth."

Daphne braced her hands on the table, about to get up.

"Mr. Bradby. Head to the principal's office. Now."

Lars's hands slipped off the table as he threw his head back, a quiet, rasped laugh falling past his lips. "You've got to be shitting me. Why?"

Mr. Denkins just arched a bushy brow as he gestured to the doors.

Lars groaned, and Jackson thumped him on the back. "Get it over with."

We watched in silence as they left, and then all at once, mouths started moving.

Including mine. "He's high?"

"When is he not?" Daphne said.

"I didn't think they got high at school." I folded the wrapper over my lunch. My appetite still hadn't entirely returned.

Willa chewed her pasta, then swallowed. "They don't. Well, not always."

I licked my lips, watching as Daphne tried to act like the past few minutes didn't happen. "You are allowed to be upset, you know," I finally said.

Daphne rolled her eyes. "I am, dummy. I'm just not letting him see that."

"Why?" Willa asked. "He clearly still wants you."

Daphne slammed her water bottle down on the table. "He's knocked up another girl. I'm not going to become an extra on some teenage parenting special."

I knew she didn't mean that. The glass filming over her eyes betrayed her bitter words.

Willa wrapped an arm around her shoulders, and Daphne closed her eyes, collecting herself. "Just because she's having his baby doesn't mean they need to be together. My parents are proof of that."

"I know. But I don't want to be in the way of some poor kid's parents potentially being able to raise he or she together." Daphne grabbed her bag, checking her phone. "You never know, this is high school. Annika might not be so intolerable five years from now, and I won't be the reason they look at each other and wonder what if somewhere down the line."

With that, she got up, heading for the doors with eyes following the swish of her hips.

Willa and I glanced at one another. "Should we follow?"

I shook my head. "I think she needs a minute. She knows we've got her."

Willa finished eating, and I wished we'd sat outside. He wasn't here, but I couldn't help but look for him in every empty chair.

Especially during the last class of the day, where he was supposed to sit next to me. It was beginning to drive me mad. I didn't want to look for him. I didn't want anything to do with him. Ever. Again.

But why wasn't he here?

Outside, I raced to my locker and swapped out my books, grabbing my keys as I made a beeline for the glass doors that led to freedom. The freedom to feel without everyone trying to dissect you like some science experiment. The freedom to be angry instead of keeping it carefully veiled, lest you be known as the heartbroken fool who was slightly deranged.

"He made this groaning sound." Kayla's voice caught my feet, stopping them in their tracks at the bottom of the steps outside. "It was yum like you wouldn't believe. And he's as big as the rumors suggest."

The curtain covering my anger dropped, and I glared at her. "Seriously?"

Kayla tilted her head, blinking like a doll. "I'm sorry, are you talking to me?"

"I'm not sure. Were you the one just talking about having sex with a guy who couldn't even blow his load with you?" At her gasp, I grinned, malicious satisfaction curling deep. "Oh, yep. That was you, right?"

"You're just jealous it wasn't you."

I couldn't stop the words from fleeing my lips if I'd tried. "Uh-huh. That's why he was able to come down my throat within a minute of my mouth being on him." I nodded. "I'm so damn jealous."

Her cheeks flamed, her lips flattening, and I laughed, flipping her off before cutting through the students that'd paused to listen and heading to my car.

I took my broken heart pass on Tuesday and bummed around the house, alternating from crying, eating, gaming, and more eating. My appetite had returned, but I wasn't proud of the choices I made.

I drizzled more chocolate topping into my tub of cherry ice cream, then scooped a massive heaping into my mouth as I restarted the game. Dash hadn't been online, and I was keeping the hell off social media.

Nothing made an already angry heart angrier faster than people boasting about their best selves.

"Mother trucker," I spewed, coughing as I swallowed the ice cream before it'd melted enough. I threw the controller down, then picked up the tub as the game unexpectedly updated.

The door opened and closed, and Mom's heels clipped over the wood as she probably dumped her bag in the kitchen, then she headed this way. "You've used your free pass."

"And I'm using it wisely," I said around another glob of creamy goodness.

Her lips twisted as she spied the chocolate sauce on my dresser. "Just don't get any of that on the sheets. I washed them yesterday."

I waved her off, checking the TV screen and groaning when I saw the update still hadn't completed.

"Okay, well, I'll order in some pizza so you can make the most of it." She left, and I would've fist pumped the air at the thought of garlic pizza, but I probably wouldn't be able to fit it in.

A pounding on the front door had Mom's heels stopping, and I set my ice-cream tub down, about to restart the game, finally, when a high-pitched voice had my whole body stilling.

I moved to my bedroom door so I could hear better.

"He hasn't been here," I heard Mom say.

"You're lying; he's always here. It's like his second home or something." May made a sniffing sound, and I could picture her nose in the air as she peered down it at our tiny foyer. "I just want to know if he's okay."

Mom repeated herself. "He isn't here, and he hasn't been for a few days."

May was quiet a moment. "Well, where's Peggy? Does she know?"

"What's wrong? He hasn't been home?" Mom asked.

May huffed. "If he had, I wouldn't be subjecting myself to this."

A short burst of laughter from Mom. "Goodbye, May."

"Wait," May said in a rush. "He hasn't been home since Sunday morning. It's not like him to be gone for longer than a night. His fucking cat gets anxious."

Church did get anxious. He'd usually only eat when Dash was home. Still, I couldn't make myself move. *Where had he gone?*

"Have you notified the police?" Mom asked.

May didn't sound like she liked the sound of that. "No, Mikael said he's just throwing a tantrum, and that we'd only make an unnecessary fuss by acknowledging it." It was like May to make a fuss but not like this.

"Yet you're worried," Mom said.

May said nothing for a long moment. "Let me know if you see him." Belatedly, she tacked on, "Please."

Mom must have nodded because then the door shut, and I walked down the hall to peer through the living room curtains as May pulled away from the curb in her pearl white Mercedes.

"You haven't heard from him?" Mom prodded behind me. "At all?"

I let the curtain fall. "No. Nothing."

"Yeah, girl! Shake it."

I swung my hips faster, the black dress I'd stolen from Mom's closet swishing around my hips, flashing a little too much thigh.

I didn't care. I didn't care about anything as I kept swigging from the bottle of vodka in my hand, and dancing over the sand.

"Fuck off, Tenterson," Daphne said, kicking sand at him.

He raised his hands as he backed up. "Hey, she's dancing of her own accord. I'm just here to watch."

As were the other five guys creeping closer with drinks in hand. The music coming from the tiny speaker was loud enough to surround half the bay, and I was surprised any of us could hear a thing, let alone talk.

I didn't want to talk. I just wanted to forget, and it'd occurred to me late Wednesday night when I'd found a half-emptied bottle of wine on the counter that Mom and Phil had shared, that alcohol was probably good for that.

I'd finished it, blamed its disappearance on Phil when he'd left for work the next morning after spending the night, and then made plans to get my hands on more. A hangover was worth it. Anything was worth being able to shut out the memories that kept me from sleeping. From smiling.

He'd taken enough from me, and I wouldn't let him take any more.

"Whoa, baby. I never knew she had hips, let alone knew how to shake 'em," a masculine voiced called.

My hips slowing, I narrowed my eyes at the voice, then crooked a finger. He'd do. There was something to be said about seeking distraction with another human being, and I felt that rush as Danny approached. Felt it sweep through me like a drug wrapped in promise.

Maybe I couldn't do what Dash had done to me, but I didn't need to go that far to aid in my quest of distraction and forgetting.

His hands hit my waist, and his breath stank of beer as he lowered his head, his hands squeezing. "You smell good for a drunken dancer," he said.

"And if I didn't?" I purred, unsure if I was successful but not caring.

The timbre to his voice changed, became rougher, as he rushed out, "I probably wouldn't care. Just looking at you is making me hard."

Game, set, and match. I grabbed his face, my body and lips swaying into his, and then he was pulled away. "Hey, what the fuck?"

"Go prey on someone who's not trashed out of their minds," Raven said, shoving Danny away when he made to move back to me.

Danny looked at me, and I winked, taking another drink from the glass bottle in my hand. It burned going down, but it was a nice match to the one residing in my chest. "Come find me later, Peggy."

I probably wouldn't, but I smiled anyway and ignored the glare Raven was sending me. "Pegs," he said, plucking the bottle from my hand. He turned to Daphne, but she was ready, hands on her hips and her arched brow daring him to say something to her.

He turned to me. "What are you doing?"

"What's it look like?" I said, laughing as I tried to yank the bottle back from him.

He tucked it behind his back. "It looks like you're drunk as hell and acting nothing like you usually would."

I jumped, trying to reach it when he raised it over his head. "Dang it, you're too tall. Just give it back; it's not funny anymore."

"It won't be funny when you wake up tomorrow."

My hands met my hips. "I'm having fun. Is that not allowed?"

Daphne crossed the sand. "Come on, Pegs. You are getting too drunk, and I'm bored. Let's just head home."

"No," I snapped, backing up a step. "You can go, but I'm staying."

Mom didn't even know I was here, but I was eighteen, for Christ's sake. I could go to a party if I wanted to.

Raven sighed, then pulled out his phone. "What are you doing?"

He paused with it halfway to his ear. "Calling in reinforcements."

"Like who?" *Please don't say Dash. Please don't say Dash.* I didn't know where he was. No one did, but I wouldn't put it past him to finally answer his phone at the most inconvenient of times.

But then I stopped. "You know what? Go right ahead."

Daphne trailed me as I moved up the grassy sand, grabbing my flip-flops. "Are you calling an Uber?"

"I'll walk."

Raven caught up, then walked on ahead, and I wasn't sure how he'd gotten to the top of the grassy knoll so fast. "Let's go, ladies. It's getting late."

"Ugh. We don't need an escort."

Daphne pressed her phone to her ear. "You take her home.

I'm not walking."

Raven smirked but waited for me to catch up.

"I'll text you tomorrow."

In answer, I flipped Daphne off for aiding the end to my fun and shoved my sandy feet into my flip-flops.

"If you say his name, I'll punch you in the stomach," I warned Raven as we headed down the street.

We crossed it, then skirted through an alleyway to the adjacent street. "Wasn't going to say anything. Haven't heard from him in almost a week anyway."

A week? I'd almost said it out loud but stopped myself. *Don't ask, don't ask.* "Where the hell is he?" I fisted my hands. "Never mind, I don't want to know."

"Sure, you don't." He sighed, reaching into his pocket to check his phone. "And none of us know. But we'll find him if he keeps hiding."

I didn't want to talk about him. A dark cloud funneled through me, polluting my insides at the thought of him partying it up somewhere. Dash moped, but he was good at doing it in style. "You were at the party?"

"Nah, but one of the guys who lives down the street from me was, and he messaged me over Facebook, saying you were there, then asked where Dash was."

"We're not a two for one," I said, realizing too late I'd fallen into talking about him yet again.

"Uh-huh." Raven slowed as we reached my street. "I'll see you on Monday. How about you stay indoors until then, yeah?"

I flipped him off too, and he chuckled, watching as I scuffed my feet over two lawns and driveways until I'd reached mine.

Quietly, I moved around the house to my bedroom window, ignoring the pang that decided to pay me a visit when I imagined Dash doing just this, and shimmied it up. It creaked, and then

Mom's head flew out of it, her eyes struggling to blink open.

I shrieked and stumbled back, landing in the garden bed. "Were you sleeping by my window?"

"You bet your dress-stealing ass I was," she said, groggy. "Get in here and use the damn door, for Pete's sake."

I bit my lips, a little petrified as I took my time rounding the house. The moon popped in the midnight sky, the trees that lined the creek behind our house lacing it in shadows. I'd waited until she fell asleep to sneak out, certain it was a sure bet. I'd forgotten who I had for a mother.

She opened the door, locking it behind me. "Have you been drinking?"

"Yes." There was no point in lying. "I wanted to forget for a little while."

A sigh left her, then a yawn. "I'm pretty pissed right now, Peggy, and not in the fun way like you." She tightened her fluffy robe. "But we'll fight tomorrow. I'm too damn tired right now."

Relief flooded, and I skipped down the hall to my room. "Sounds good to me."

"How much trouble are you in?" Willa asked the next day as we scrapped over the phone. I'd been grounded, so they couldn't come over for our scrapbooking date, but I was too hungover to do anything but gaze at the ceiling fan anyway. "Grounded for life."

"Shut up," Daphne said, then paused. "Wait, seriously?"

The image of Mom's red face, and the cussing she'd spewed this morning over breakfast, made my head pound harder. "I think so. But I'll probably go out next weekend."

They were quiet a beat.

"Why?" Willa asked.

"Because it's fun. Because I'm eighteen. Because I should be doing this stuff." I stifled a yawn. "And because it helps, okay?"

That last part had Daphne saying, "True that. But don't overdo it again. There's flirty drunk and then there's too much of a hot mess drunk."

I winced, not having a great deal of memory of what I'd done but remembering enough. "I was the latter?"

"Mm-hmm."

"That's a tad embarrassing." I'd need to make sure I stayed a bit classier next time. "So have either of you finished the history assignment?"

"I did last week," Willa chirped.

Of course, she had.

"Nope, I'm starting it tonight. Let me guess, you've done at least half?" Daphne asked me.

"Actually, no." I peeked over at where my laptop sat under a heap of clothes and books on my desk. "Maybe I'll start it later." Or maybe I'd take another shower and another nap to avoid having to face Mom again.

"Did Jackson go to the party last night?" Willa asked, sounding cautious.

"God, Willa. I already know," Daphne said, exasperated. "Everyone knows."

Willa made a choking sound, then coughed. "Shit. I just got lemonade up my nose."

"How does that even happen?" Daphne asked.

"Because you made me choke."

I smirked at the ceiling, my feet swaying as I lifted my legs. I decided to put her out of her misery. "I didn't see him."

"Neither," Daphne said.

"Weird," Willa said. "He wasn't home last night."

"Are you guys like serious or something?"

Daphne snorted. "What Peggy meant to ask was is your secret relationship the real deal, or are you just messing around because it's hot and taboo."

I guffawed. "That is so not what I said."

"But we want to know, right?" Daphne laughed. "Come on, Willa. Just tell us."

She was quiet a minute. "I'm still trying to process the fact everyone knows."

"Well, process quicker. I need to charge my phone soon."

"Bitch," Willa joked. "We've been official for a while." Her voice quietened. "Not that it matters."

"How long is a while?"

I loved how Daphne interrogated. Well, at times like this. It meant I didn't have to scrounge up the courage to ask things.

"Few months, maybe. But it's been going on longer than that." I heard a door closing before she continued. "We just didn't know what to do."

"You're not blood related. What's the big deal besides your parents?"

"Um, our parents." She sighed. "Not to mention, we have the same surname. It's not exactly normal."

"It isn't," I said before I could stop myself. "I mean, I get it, but like Daphne said, you're not actually related so it's not that bad."

"We have pictures together of us crawling. We gave up our pacifiers at the same time. Our parents used to try to pass us off as twins." She groaned. "They'd never, *ever* be okay with it."

"Well, duh," Daphne said. "But you've only got like eight months until school is out, and then you guys will be getting ready to leave for college."

My eyes widened. "Oh, please tell me you're applying for

the same colleges."

"Look who's excited now," Daphne said.

"Shut up," I snarked. "I need the excitement. Don't judge."

Willa laughed. "It's okay. And yeah, we've applied for some together."

We wrapped up talking about Jackson when Willa heard a noise outside her room and started whispering. My eyes were beginning to grow heavy, so I hung up, mumbling something about seeing them on Monday before I fell asleep with my phone hanging from my fingertips.

THIRTY-ONE

Dash

The Silver Bridge hotel wasn't the finest establishment in the area, but it did let me pay cash, so I booked a room, ordered a shit ton of food, and began my new life as a binge-eating, heartbroken, daytime TV watching champion.

Well, I don't want your damn love. Not now. Not tomorrow. Not in ten years.

Those words had shattered me where I'd stood, and I'd left most of me behind when she'd shoved me out the door. It was easier that way. To breathe, to eat, to sleep without the constant turbulence those broken pieces would shake alive.

Making my own new place in the world, where there were no memories of Peggy and no constant reminders of what I'd ruined, was the best idea I could've had, quite frankly.

And so that was why I was pissed when my scumbag friends somehow tracked me down.

The phone barked, and I picked it up, confused that it was ringing. I put it down to possibly owing the front desk some money, seeing as I'd only paid for a week. It was now Monday, and I needed to haul my ass to an atm.

"There's someone here asking for you—hey!"

"Dash, what room number?" came Jackson's voice.

After I'd gotten over my shock, I smirked. "Take a wild guess." Then I hung up, leaving the phone off the cradle.

It took him five minutes, which was kind of sad, really, but he eventually found me. Three thuds smacked on the door. I took my time getting up. "I don't want none of your beef sausage, Larry James. I've already told you, I'm straight."

"What the fuck?" Great, Lars was here too.

"No, I'm not down to fuck. Females. I like females." I drew the words out, straight-faced. "But I have this friend back home who might like your number. He goes by the name interfering ass—"

"Dash, shut the fuck up and open the door."

I sighed, unlatching the chain, then returned to my sanctuary on the bed.

"Wow, nice digs," Raven said, and I scowled, not realizing he'd joined the Dash-has-gone-missing express. "I'm digging the fungus over there."

"So's your mom."

Lars chuckled. "Can't be too messed up if he's making cracks about your mom."

"Room 66?" Jackson drawled. "You're missing a six."

I kicked my feet up, uncaring I was only wearing a T-shirt and briefs. Their fault for intruding. "We have imaginations for a reason, stickler."

"Nice thighs. You work them quads, baby?" Raven waggled his brows.

I fought the temptation to tug at my briefs. "I already told you, Larry. I'm fucking straight."

Raven played for both teams and gave zero fucks what anyone thought about it.

It didn't bother me, so long as he didn't go making out with any dudes all up in my space.

Raven sighed, perching on the edge of the forty-year-old laminate desk. "I knew a Larry once."

"Who cares? Can we just grab him and leave?" Jackson peered around. "This place is fucking depressing." He sniffed, then raised his shirt to his nose, mumbling behind the cotton. "And it smells like moldy feet."

"Lay off my sanctuary. It's been my trusty companion this past week." I opened a bag of Doritos, popping one into my mouth and crunching. "Unlike you shit-stains."

Jackson guffawed. "How the fuck were we supposed to know you were holed up in some musty ass hotel like a beaten down, wounded pussy?"

Lars nodded, stealing my bag of chips. "And let's not forget the world doesn't revolve around you, asshole. We all have our own problems."

I scowled as he shoved a handful of my chips inside his mouth, then smirked. "How is the new wife?"

"She's not my wife," he said, coughing and spraying orange crumbs all over the floor.

"Fucking gross." Raven laughed.

Lars flipped him off.

"She's not … yet." I tucked my arms behind my head. "You'll need to put a ring on that eventually."

"Easy, Dash," Jackson warned. He might have made himself out to be the softhearted one out of all of us, but he was the most conniving, by far. The only difference between us was that he thought things through a little better, rather than acting on impulse.

A trait I wished I'd had. I'd give him that much but nothing else. I didn't have anything left to give anyway. "Why?" I glared at Lars. "Fight me."

He rolled his eyes, and I laughed. "Another time. I've got places to be. Can we jet?"

"Sure you can. I'll see you guys never."

"Who gets your bikes?" Raven asked, his eyes glinting. "If you're not coming back, someone needs to use them."

"Lars because he's the broke one and he'll be even poorer soon."

Jackson coughed, trying to smother his laughter.

"Thanks, man." Lars nodded.

"You're welcome. Now feel free to leave whenever." I reached for the remote. "I've gotta find out if Maria ends up marrying Stephan or if Giovanni breaks up the wedding."

"You're kidding." Jackson turned to watch the tiny TV come to life.

Raven jumped onto the bed, kicking his Vans covered feet to the mustard duvet. "I'm down."

We fist bumped, then I yanked a fresh bag of chips from the nightstand and ignored the glares from the other two silent sentinels in the room.

"What have you told your parents?" Lars asked.

I sighed, hitting pause. "That I'm in mourning, and I'll be home when I'm not." So probably never.

"Mourning?" Raven asked.

"Over what could've been." I felt like adding *duh* but refrained.

Lars's brows rose. "They're okay with that?"

"Not exactly. Dad thinks I'm joking. Mom's just glad to know I'm alive."

Jackson laughed again, then threw his hands into the air. "Come on, he's fine, and clearly content to be a high school dropout who lives in a mite-infested hotel. Let's bail."

Lars followed him to the door, but Raven looked torn. "I can't believe you've just been allowed to stay here."

I couldn't either, but I had a feeling I only had a few more days before my dad found me and hauled me home. I planned to make the most of it before that happened.

Lars rapped the doorjamb, wincing as some of the paint flaked off it. "Look, we know you fucked it all up with Peggy." I waited, tense and ready to launch the remote at his head. "But lying around here isn't going to make her forgive you."

She'd never forgive me, but I was hoping she'd at least miss me. Maybe come and find me to make sure I was alive, then she'd hopefully melt and let me kiss the life from her. That was getting a bit sappy, but I didn't care. I'd do sappy for Peggy. I'd do sappy, and it'd be as easy as breathing for Peggy.

"Nice chat. Bye now."

Raven stretched his arms over his head as he stood. "You're seriously not coming?"

"No, and if I felt so inclined, which I don't, my own car is in the lot, which I'm guessing is how you found me." I chomped down on some more chips, hitting play.

"You're a miserable sonovabitch."

"We already know this, Jack, Jack. No need to waste your words."

They left, the door shutting behind them.

The silence that lingered in their sudden absence bit sharply. For someone who enjoyed being alone, I was surprised by how much I actually didn't mind having them here.

Peggy's really fucked me up, I mused, digging out some more chips.

The door reopened, and Jackson stuck his head back inside. "Oh yeah, forgot to tell you. Peggy seems to have a new penchant for dancing half naked on the beach while drinking vodka and letting assholes rub all up on her."

"Bullshit," I wheezed, unable to fathom it. My chip fell from my hand as he whipped out his phone and crossed the room, shoving a video in my face.

It was Peggy all right, wearing some black scrap of material and swaying her body into Danny Vestin.

"Mother of a sorry fucker." I launched off the bed, racing around the room to collect my things.

THIRTY-TWO

Peggy

Monday was a bust.

I'd arrived late on purpose to avoid any gossip-mongers staring their fill after the little show I'd put on last Friday night.

I needn't have worried. Not only because they were all still too caught up in Annika and Lars's flakey presence, but because I'd actually done something fun, even if slightly stupid. I shouldn't be embarrassed for doing the things most girls in our year would do if and when they partied. Dancing and drinking, however sloppily.

Ugh.

After fluffing my hair and applying an apple-scented gloss, I grabbed my bag and headed for the door.

"Oh good, you're up. Take the trash out, please."

I stopped and looked over my shoulder at Mom, who was in her robe on the couch with her Kindle in her lap and dusk pink mug in hand. "Not working today?"

"I've got my period, and my daughter's recent proclivity to engage in reckless behavior has me in need of a mental health day." Her eyes darted up at me, and she sipped her coffee, loudly.

"Such a librarian," I muttered, dumping my bag and dragging myself to the kitchen to empty the trash.

"Such a teenager," Mom said, and I cracked a smile despite not wanting to.

"Anything else before I'm late for school?" I tried to keep the sass from my voice, but well, it was Tuesday, and I didn't feel like trying much of anything.

"That'll be all," she said, and I grabbed my bag. "For now."

I half rolled my eyes, then waved over my head as I passed by the living room to the front door and grabbed my keys.

Inside my car, I turned the music up, needing something to drown out my thoughts. When left to their own devices, they chose to torture me with the same images on repeat until I could hardly see.

I parked next to Daphne's little Merc, then flipped down the visor to check my hair. I'd straightened it this morning, and without the bouncing curls, the strands hung just past my shoulders. I'd also lined my eyes with a hint of eyeliner and went to town with mascara. A layer of concealer muted the freckles that dusted my nose and upper cheeks.

"No curls today?" Willa asked, jumping down from Jackson's truck when he pulled in a few spots over.

He gave her a smile that reddened her cheeks, and with his bag over his shoulder, stalked over to the building that was starting to feel like a prison cell.

"I had some extra time," I said, closing the door and locking it before pocketing my keys. We waited for Daphne to finish tying up her hair into a high ponytail, then we crossed the lot and joined the cluster of students heading up the wide concrete steps.

My skin prickled as we weaved between bodies smothered in expensive perfume, aftershave, cologne, and hairspray. Our lockers were within sight when I had the urge to turn around and discover why my stomach had begun squirming.

I ignored it, unlocking my locker and sorting through my books. "Shit," I hissed when I saw my history book. "I haven't finished the assignment."

"It's due today," Willa said, closing the door and tucking her things against her chest.

I knew that, and I knew I had to do it. I'd been distracted at every turn, my brain unwilling to function as it usually did.

"Who cares," Daphne said. "You've never been late to hand one in before, so he'll give you another day without it costing you."

I still didn't like it. This was senior year, and if there was any year, any semester, to take seriously while applying for college, it was this one.

Almost rubbing my eyes out of frustration, I remembered how much eye makeup I'd put on, and dropped my hands. They hit my sides with a slap as Danny stopped by us, his grin digging into his cheek. "Sup, drunken dancer. Better see you out this weekend."

It was all I could do to smile, and even that felt insincere.

"Oh, fuck," Daphne exhaled.

"What?" I turned to her, then followed her gaze to the middle of the hall.

"Damn it all to hell," Danny said. "When did he get back?"

"Better run along," came Lars's voice.

Daphne looked at me, her eyes panicked, then darted down the hall to class.

Lars's grin dropped as he watched her disappear, and he wiped a hand over his mouth. Danny was long gone, and it took me longer than anyone else to realize why.

Unlaced boots drifted toward us, and my eyes caught the low hanging pants, then his untucked shirt, and the haphazardly looped tie.

No.

A chill swept through me as his arctic eyes zeroed in on me, his jaw hardened and covered in enough whiskers to surely get him written up. His hair stood every which way on his head, the golden strands not even moving as he neared.

He was back.

About to make a run for it, I almost slammed into Lars's chest. He caught me, steadying me and nodded at Dash over my head.

I didn't want to turn around. I didn't want to see him. Bile was simmering, threatening to make a churning mess out of my stomach.

"Freckles."

I pulled away from Lars, bumping into Dash with tears filming my eyes before I raced down the hall.

I should've known he'd catch me. He darted in front of me, bringing me to a stop. His eyes were bright, clear, and hovering over my face with a calculated gleam.

"You can run, Freckles, but I can run faster."

My brows gathered, and so did the fury slowly tensing every one of my limbs. "Move." I tried to step around him, but he met me step for step.

"I'm not going anywhere until I've stared at you for as long as I can."

I clicked my tongue. "The bell is about to ring."

He tipped a shoulder. "So I'll stare at you until it does."

We both stared then, he with that annoying twitch to his lips, and me with a thousand and one things I wanted to scream at him playing on mine.

Students moved by, some stopping to look at us while the others continued their conversation as though we didn't exist.

The bell rang. I raised a brow when he didn't move. "Well?"

He inched closer, his finger lifting to my hair. "While this looks sexy as fuck, I miss your curls. Your freckles. I miss you." I stood suspended, my chest heaving, as he lowered his head, his

lips drifting over my cheek. "And you need to go the other way."
With a sneaky peck to my cheek, he staggered back, grinning
before leaving me there.

"Freaking asshole," I muttered, turning on my heel with my
cheeks burning and my heart pounding.

I sat through class seething, emotion a constant lump in my
throat, making it hard to concentrate. He had some nerve, putting himself right in front of me as if he hadn't crushed me beyond repair.

People were still hung up on Lars and Annika, the latter
wasn't at school today, but they weren't so hung up they hadn't
noticed Dash's reappearance.

"I heard he got suspended and his dad sent him to military
camp for two weeks," someone said between classes.

"You're an idiot. Who goes to military camp for two weeks?"

And even worse from the cheer squad, "He met some chick
online, then ran off and stayed in a hotel with her."

"No way," Selina breathed.

Annabeth nodded. "So way. Fucking Tinder, taking all the
decent guys."

I munched down on my lips at hearing that. Dash Thane
was so far from decent, even he would laugh at the word.

He was a selfish, conniving, egotistical scumbag.

There was nothing to romanticize about that, but they
didn't care. Whatever got their stupid hearts beating faster was
apparently called decent.

I knew there was little to no truth behind most of the whispering, but regardless, the fact he was gone and just decided he'd
come back had my hackles raised.

I spent lunch in the library, frantically finishing my assignment before history that afternoon. Even there, in the silence permeating the room, I couldn't escape him. He filled my head, clenched every muscle, and shortened my breath. But I had to ignore it. Him.

I barely had my paper done before it was time to get back to class, but it was better than nothing.

The halls were almost empty as I scurried down them, my boots feeling heavier than usual. Mr. Andrews was about to shut the door when he saw me approaching. His moustache bounced to one side, and I offered a weak smile in apology as I skirted by him and to the back of the room.

And then I discovered an asshole in my seat.

"Saved it for you. Thought you might like it warmed."

I dumped my stuff on the table where he was supposed to sit and did my best to ignore him.

"Okay, before we get started, papers are due on my desk on your way out."

A few groans littered the air, and we all flipped our textbooks open as Mr. Andrews started circling the fact sheet on the board.

Something landed on my table. A wadded piece of paper. I ignored it, keeping my eyes trained on the board and my pen twirling between my fingers. As if I didn't care. As if his presence was nothing to me. As if he didn't even exist.

As if.

Another bit of paper landed on my lap, and when Mr. Andrews got busy opening his laptop and searching for something, I gave in, opening the one that'd rolled into the pleats of my skirt.

Forgive me?

I withheld a bout of disbelieving laughter and shook my head.

Another piece landed by my hand. I licked my teeth, trying to ignore it, but the temptation to peek at his piss-poor efforts had me opening that too.

Okay, so maybe not today. But one day?

I tossed it back, hitting him in the forehead. He laughed, and the teacher lifted his head, glaring at Dash. "Mr. Thane. Back for one day and already finding something amusing?"

Dash stretched his arms over his head, his shirt rising. "I was just thinking of a joke my girl told me the other day." He waved his hand. "Carry on."

I swallowed as I caught a flash of his hip bone and pushed my eyes to my table.

His girl?

Mr. Andrews narrowed his eyes, then shook his head. "Unless you wish to share next time, try to control yourself."

Dash grunted. "Noted."

As the lesson continued, my table became covered in tiny balls of paper. I wasn't sure if he'd pre-ripped them or if he'd become a professional silent paper ripper while he was gone, but no one seemed to notice. Not even the ones that'd missed the table and landed by my feet.

I love you.

I want you and only you.

Let's taco-bout how much of a fuck-head I am.

We can make out after?

I really fucking miss you.

The last one stilled my hands and the air filling my lungs.

With my throat thickening, I scrunched them all back up and slipped them inside my pencil case. On my way out, I left my half-assed paper on the teacher's desk, then hurried to my locker.

I needed out of there, away from him, and to remember what he'd done.

That was hard to do when I could feel him on my heels, stalking silently behind me.

Kayla threw me back into the abyss, stepping out from her clique of friends to waggle her fingers at him. "Dash, baby. Where've you been?"

He said nothing, and I didn't know if he'd stopped to talk to her. I kept walking until I'd reached my locker and swapped out my books. I grabbed my bag, slinging it over my shoulder and closing the door.

Byron stood there, his face and eyes hard. "You're with him? Or Danny? Which one is it?"

Legs quaking, I took a step back. "What?"

He shook his head, looking around before lowering his voice to barely a whispered growl. "This is bullshit, Peggy." He collected himself, taking a deep breath. "We never even said we were done."

"No," I said as I took hold of all the hurt and embarrassment that'd clung to me since that night. I held it close, using it as fuel. "I'm pretty sure I made myself clear, though."

"If you need your ears checked, I'll happily rip one off and inspect it for you." Dash loomed at my back, and I wasn't sure how long he'd been there, but judging by the whites of Byron's eyes, I didn't think it'd been long. "Just saying."

"Have a nice vacation?" Byron drawled with a hard glance at me, then he sneered at Dash. "You're lucky I didn't press charges."

Dash hissed between his teeth. "And you're lucky I didn't get the chance to kill you."

Byron took a step closer. "I'd love to see you try again—"

I cut Byron off. "Enough."

"Quit being so butt hurt. I'm sure Daddy will pay to fix your butchered nose if you ask nicely."

Byron's nostrils flared. Dash pressed closer to my back, and Byron tracked the movement, teeth gritting. "She know you fucked Kayla?"

Dash growled, and I backed up, effectively forcing him back a step.

Byron laughed. "She's a shit lay, isn't she? But hey, beats fucking nothing."

While I might not have liked Kayla, I hated the way he so easily trashed someone he'd once called his girlfriend. If he could say that about someone he used to care about, then who knew what kind of hurtful things he'd have said about me that weren't even true.

"You're the smelliest piece of shit, Woods."

Byron shrugged, moving backward as he smiled. "Guess that's why I almost had your girl. Like calls to like."

"I'm not his …" I snapped my mouth shut. It was pointless to argue that with Byron. Besides, I wanted nothing to do with him. The sooner he walked away, the better.

"Whatever, Peggy. You're not so different after all, are you? Fooling around with this scum while we dated. I hope karma eats your fat ass."

I gaped at him.

Dash was already moving before I could stop him, and Byron laughed, raising his hands. "Have you squeezed it yet? It's fucking delicious. I highly recommend."

Dash grabbed him by the shirt and threw him into the row of lockers, all the while Byron kept his hands raised, the smile on his face goading.

"If you so much as even blink—"

Raven pulled him off him, and Byron shook out his shoulders, chuckling. "Do you wanna get expelled? Fucking idiot."

Mrs. Truncheon rounded the corner as Dash glared at Byron's back.

I exhaled, relieved, as she continued down the hall, coffee cup in hand.

"You let that shit bag squeeze your ass?" Dash strode over, his eye twitching.

"Not that it's any of your damn business, but no." I smiled at Raven, then headed outside.

Willa and Daphne were standing by Daphne's car, talking, and Jackson was up ahead, almost at his truck.

Dash caught up to me, his arm brushing mine. "Can I come over? We need to talk."

"No." Rain started to sprinkle from the sky, and I cursed, quickening my pace to keep my hair from frizzing.

"Freckles," he pleaded.

I turned on him. "Don't call me that ever again. And quit following me." He went to protest, but I beat him to it. "It's done, okay? We took a risk, and it didn't pay off. We fucked it all up, and now there's no going back."

With his eyes misting, he said, "You don't mean that."

"I do. With every part of me, I mean it when I say I'll never be able to forgive you." I drew in a sharp breath, almost croaking my next words. "So do us both a favor and quit this insanity. Find someone else, get over it, and do what you do best."

"And what's that?"

"Whore around. You couldn't commit if you tried, and everyone knows it. All you care about is yourself, and your weak efforts to try to prove otherwise are just a waste of time."

His eyes dropped to the ground, and he cleared his throat.

A boulder of guilt trampled me, but I couldn't take my words back. I didn't want to. They needed to be said.

Willa, Daphne, and Jackson all just stared as I climbed inside my car. The door was almost shut when Dash grabbed it, leaning over it to glare at me. "You're wrong. I've been committed to you since before we even knew what the word meant. Sex has nothing to do with this. I'd happily only fuck you for the rest of my life, because what I do best?" I blinked away a tear as he smiled a grim, dimple-less smile and went to shut the door. "That would be loving you."

THIRTY-THREE

Peggy

On Wednesday, I found a note in my locker.

I'm the biggest idiot alive.

Thursday too.

I don't deserve you, but that doesn't stop me from wanting you forever.

On Friday, I didn't even look at it before tossing it into a trash can on the way to class.

I'd ignored Dash, his every advance, his every heated look or silent plea, and I felt good about it. Confident that with time, I could shake him and the sorrow that lined my heart. One day, it would simply be scar tissue. One day, it wouldn't feel like I'd pummeled it with a meat tenderizer. One day, maybe I could look at him again without yearning for something he'd destroyed.

That night, I waited until Mom had left for her date with Phil. She was staying at his place, and I was supposed to be grounded, but I was going out. I'd messaged Daphne and Willa, asking them to come to Wade's with me, but they'd declined.

Willa was hanging out with Jackson at home while their parents were out of town, and Daphne, well, I didn't know what she was doing. But I bet it wasn't watching reruns of *Gilmore Girls* like she'd said.

I didn't drive. As reckless as I was feeling, I wasn't so blind that I'd do something that foolish. I was going out to forget, and that meant drinking, so there was no way I was staying at Wade's or leaving my car there.

After donning a tight denim skirt, ripped over one thigh, I tugged on a gray sweater with the Rolling Stones printed on it, then stole a pair of Mom's black Manolos. I looked casual but dressed up enough to seem like I didn't care what anyone thought. Perfect.

The Uber driver dropped me off in the middle of the street, and she whistled. "Banging party, kid."

I handed her a twenty. "Let's hope so."

Pulling down my skirt after I'd stepped out of the car, I glanced around the dark street teeming with teenagers. The stars were fading behind dark globs of clouds, and the moon was but a slice of silver in the sky. There were more cars and more people here than I'd seen since the first time I'd attended one of Wade's parties, but I tried not to let that throw me off.

It didn't matter who was here. All that mattered was that I was, and I was going to have some fun.

The drinks were easy to find, and find them I did. I nabbed a whole bottle of Johnnie Walker and drained as much as I could without making my makeup run. My hand dug into my hair as I started swinging my hips to the sultry R&B bass that was thundering through the house. Following the music into the living room, I waved at some people who offered me a smile and ignored the curious glances from others.

I started slow, drinking and bopping around as people sprawled over the couches and danced over the coffee tables and jumped up and down on the floor.

A guy with venom tainted eyes had his hand wrapped tight around the neck of a bottle of Jack, and I squinted at him, trying to place whether I'd seen him before or not.

I hadn't. Wade must have invited the whole town, and that was why there were so many people.

I kept drinking, and his head tilted as he watched me down the burning liquid. It soon caught fire and spread through my limbs. The sigh that left me had my eyes shutting as I slouched back into the wall.

When I opened them, the guy from the couch was there, leaning against the wall next to me. "Name?"

"Does it matter?" I licked my lips. He had nice eyes. Dark, depthless, and framed in a thick layer of black lashes that matched his cropped hair and the stubble peppering his jaw and thick neck.

His thin lips met, then opened as he smiled, flashing me a glimpse of his teeth. "I suppose it doesn't."

I could hardly hear him, and I'd lost interest in dancing. I crooked a finger at him to follow me, knowing he would. I was probably a sure thing to him, and that was precisely what I wanted him to think. We moved to the stairs, and the sight of Raven talking to a caramel-skinned guy who sometimes rode with them had my ankle almost rolling.

He looked up, his brows rising and my name on his lips.

Not wanting to cause any alarm, I waved, smiling easily, then continued up the stairs.

"Know him?" the guy trailing me asked as we neared the top.

I grabbed the railing as a group of guys raced by, throwing themselves down the stairs and leaving us in a dust of laughter. "Raven? Yeah. You?"

He shook his head. "New to town. I haven't seen you at school."

"I go to Magnolia Cove Prep." I took another swig of

whiskey as we meandered by a couple of girls making out in the hall, then headed toward the upstairs living room.

The guy said nothing, and sick of calling him *guy*, I gave up the lame attempt at remaining mysterious. "I'm Peggy."

His shirt pulled taut at his arms as he swung them and surveyed the half full room before looking at me. A smile bloomed as he said, "Todd."

We sat on the floor by a long-arched window, and I listened as he told me about where he'd grown up and how he'd had to move here due to his mom's job transfer. She was a nurse, and he was hoping to head to medical school after college.

"What about you?"

I'd kept drinking as he'd talked, my head spinning as I stared at plastic cups getting kicked around on the marble floor in front of us. I hadn't wanted to know about his life, but as he spoke, I found his deep voice a nice fit for the numbing taking place inside my head.

"Me?" I asked, my head swaying a little too far to the left.

He frowned at the bottle between my legs. "You've had a fair bit of that."

"It's good." I took another sip, then offered it to him. He declined by lifting his own bottle. "And I want to get into computer science. Design some games."

He laughed. "Whoa, that's awesome."

"Yup." I popped the word. "Can we make out now?"

Once again, he laughed, then coughed. "Oh, wait. You're serious?"

I nodded, licking my lips as I tried to build the excitement by staring at his. I could kiss him. I wanted to. I planned to kiss a lot of boys before I ever let another one close enough to ruin me so completely again.

Setting his drink down, he glanced around the room, and I

did too, but from our vantage, all I saw were legs and more trash rolling around on the floor.

Warm skin met my skin, turning my face, and then his forehead was almost touching mine, the scent of alcohol heavy on our breaths. "Are you going to remember kissing me tomorrow?"

My lids felt heavy when I blinked. "It depends how well you do it."

Eyes blazed and then closed as his mouth melded to mine. He took the challenge seriously, his lips firm and coaxing mine into action.

A growl rippled around us, and the fact I'd evoked that sound from him already had my hand reaching for his face. Until another set of hands pulled me from the floor, and I clued in.

Todd hadn't made that noise. It'd come from the furious cussing wall of man who was slinging me over his shoulder.

"Dash!" I screamed, ramming my fists into his leather clad back as he hollered at Todd.

"Do you have a death wish, motherfucker?"

"She didn't say she had a boyfriend." A pause, then, "I wouldn't hold her like that too long. She's had a lot to drink."

Dash's grip on my thighs only tightened, and I feared it'd bruise if he didn't let me go.

My stomach sloshed, and my head swam. "Don't tell me what to do, or I'll rip out your idiot tongue and feed it to your ass." Then we were bouncing downstairs as I continued to scream.

No one stopped him. No one even tried to help me. They all parted like the Red Sea, and it wasn't until I was thrown into the back seat of his car and the doors shut that he said a word to me.

"It's like you want me to wind up in prison." The engine started as I slapped my hands around on the door, trying to open it. "Locked. You're not getting out of this car until I let you out, so quit it."

"Argh." I flopped back onto the seat as he sped down the street. The world was upside down, streetlights and rooftops dancing by the windows. "What are you even doing?" I shouted the words.

"Taking your ass home." His tone was more curt than usual, and I heard leather creak as though he was clenching the wheel too tight.

"I didn't want to be rescued. I was having fun." I forced myself to sit up, realizing that was a bad idea when everything took its time to take shape before my blurred eyes. "Who the hell do you think you are?"

"Yours, but apparently, it's taking some time for you to get the memo."

"Maybe because you fucked someone else."

Another growl followed his hand slapping the wheel. "We weren't together, and you'd flayed me right open too, Peggy. Do we need to go over how once again? Because even though just thinking about it kills me, I've got no place else to be."

"He was my boyfriend."

"He was never your boyfriend."

I leaned forward, hissing at him. "He was too, yet I still wouldn't have sex with him."

"Enough." Dash's throat corded. "This isn't a game anymore, Peggy. It never was."

"It's nothing anymore, Dash. Get over it already and leave me alone."

He parked in front of my house. "If it's nothing, then why are you so intent on getting drunk and making out with other guys?"

"Because I can, and because I hate you, and because I want to forget all about you."

He undid his seat belt, turning to me with raised brows.

I groaned, launching myself at the door that still wouldn't open. "Let me out."

Dash sighed, then unlocked the doors, and I almost fell to the grass. He rounded the car, locking it and hoisting me into the air.

"Jesus. Just put me down."

"No." He marched over the grass, stopping to grab the spare key from its hiding place behind a broken piece of wood on the exterior of the house, then unlocked the door.

After setting me on my bed, he walked back out of my room. I thought he'd left when I heard the front door close until his footsteps traveled back over the ancient floor.

"You can leave now," I said, kicking off Mom's heels.

Dash grabbed them, leaving the room again to take them to hers while I stripped out of my skirt.

He returned as I was pulling the duvet back, a bottle of water in hand. Holding it out to me, he took a sweep of my bare legs, breathed out a loud exhale, then left the room again.

"The hell are you doing now? You better be leaving!"

"Not leaving," he said, returning with a bag of chips and splitting it open.

Shucking off his boots, he watched as I got settled and took slow sips of water, then set the chips next to me on the nightstand. "You should eat something to help soak up all that Johnnie."

I put the bottle down and frowned as he took his jacket off. "And you should go home."

He climbed over my legs, lying down over the duvet and curling onto his side. "Already am."

Those words had me sputtering, they were a fist colliding with my chest, and I yelled, "No, you're not. You wrecked me.

You ruined me. You destroyed me. You're not home. You're not anything to do with me. I can't …" I drew in breath after breath, unable to get enough air as the world turned an array of bright colors. "Where did you even go?"

"Shh." He pulled me down to the bed and rubbed my arm. "Settle down, or you'll be sick. I stayed at some shit-star hotel for a week and watched soapy as fuck TV." Seeing my narrowed eyes, he added, "On my own."

"Seriously?"

"Seriously."

My heart wouldn't stop galloping. "I hate you."

"I know." He sounded defeated, but I knew better.

"I despise you."

"I know."

"Was it worth it?"

"No," he said. "Fuck no."

The burning in my eyes couldn't be extinguished, so I let the agony roll free.

Dash watched, his own gleaming and causing my tears to fall faster.

"Please don't cry, Freckles." I'd never heard or seen him so vulnerable. "Please," he whispered.

"It's your f-fault," I stammered.

"I know." His breath blew warm over my face as he sighed. "I know."

The pounding started near my temple, and as it grew, morphing into a giant ball of pain inside my skull, it forced my eyes open.

Sunlight crested the bed, its soft rays indicating it'd not long began its ascent into the sky. The glow fell over the bed, and I shut my eyes, my mouth dry and coated in a layer of film that would probably take three rounds of brushing to clear.

They were heavy, but I forced my lids open again, taking in the sharp angles of the man lying beside me. His hand was close to mine, and the hairs dusting it matched that of his lashes, a dark brown that drew attention to his arctic eyes.

The depths beyond were frightening. Though the temptation to test the frigid waters called to me, I'd never felt it so acutely as I had this past month. Now I knew better.

You could get lost in a face like his—the high cheekbones, the feathered arches of his brows, and the masculine jaw. The dimple and his smile were an extra dose of unnecessary charm.

But it was his eyes. They wouldn't just cause you to lose your way; they would haunt you until you lay trapped beneath their intensity.

Even asleep, all he was couldn't be gentled. He was a slumbering beast veiled behind an angelic face.

His voice caught me before his eyes did. "I'm so hard right now, I could probably hump your mattress and come."

My head thrashed as I attempted to roll my eyes. "Good morning to you too."

One bright blue eye blinked open, and the groggy smile that illuminated his face had my breath stalling, a harsh puff of air leaving my nose. "Fuck, I love waking up next to you."

I rolled to my back, closing my eyes against the brawl taking place inside my head. "You should go before Mom gets home."

"Not so fast, Freckles."

"Stop calling me that."

He huffed, his voice rough from sleep. "Like you can ever stop me."

I said nothing, wishing he'd leave and wishing he'd stay and tell me this had all been one messed-up nightmare.

"Do you remember kissing that guy last night?"

"Of course, I do." I didn't care that it would probably hurt him to say that. I wanted to hurt him. "He was sweet, and he—"

"Okay, claws in." He yawned. "I'm not going to lie, it felt like I'd swallowed a bouquet of knives when I saw that."

Ignoring the nausea his words ignited, I tried to think back to how he'd even known I was there. An image of Raven popped into my head. God. *Duh.*

"What do you want me to say, Dash?"

"Well, that you were at least thinking of me. I'm pissed, Peggy, but I'm trying with everything I've got here."

"Trying?" I sighed, not in the mood to fight with him.

"Trying to ignore it long enough to focus on the long-term goal."

I barked out a disgusted laugh. "Long term. And what is that?"

His voice roughened. "Your lips on mine for eternity, and no one else's ever."

Flutters filled my chest cavity, taking flight. I tried to squash them. "I'm not sorry." I wasn't.

"I know you're not. That's why I'm still here. I know you only did it because you're fucked up over me."

"Your ego knows no bounds." I pushed the sheets off, wanting away from him.

"Call it what you like, but we both know it's true, Peggy Sue."

I adjusted my panties, which were stuck between my ass cheeks, knowing he was watching, and smirked at my opened drawer as I plucked out a fresh pair.

"You're going to fucking kill me."

"Nope, I'm going to shower. Be gone when I get out."

I washed my hair, taking my time under the hot spray to

make sure I erased every bad decision I'd made the night before. After brushing my teeth and rinsing my mouth, fog trailed me to my room, and my stomach dropped as I saw Dash with his hand around himself.

"What are you doing?"

He grunted. "What's it look like?"

I threw my damp towel at him. "Stop it."

He caught it with his free hand, then groaned as his eyes skirted over my body. "Thanks. Now lose the other towel."

My stomach flipped, and my lips parted. "No."

He smiled at the soft tone of my voice. "No?"

I couldn't take my eyes off his length. Entranced, I stood there, feeling myself grow wet as he pumped himself faster, squeezing and groaning while he looked at me.

He'd taken his shirt off, his jeans and briefs bunched at the tops of his thighs. "Dash."

"Come here."

I did. Lord help me, I couldn't stop myself from closing and locking the door, then moving to the bed.

"There's my girl."

His words wrapped around me like a warm embrace, sending lava through every vein and directly between my legs. Grabbing my hand, he removed the other from his length and took my face with it. "Now let me kiss away the memory of every asshole who's dared to put his lips on yours."

I fell over him, my lips ravenous as I gripped his cheeks, then sank my fingers into his hair, my legs sliding over to straddle him.

His tongue was hot, and I tasted mint. "Did you brush your teeth?"

"Stole some mouthwash," he said, ragged, then bit my lip. Air hit my skin as he tugged on the towel I'd wrapped around myself. "Holy hell, I think I'm about to blow."

I started rocking into him, rationale dissipating with the promise of pleasure and everything I wanted but couldn't have lying right beneath me.

"I can feel you," he whispered, his hand digging into the back of my head as the other one palmed my breast. "So hot and wet over my dick."

I whimpered, shockwaves of bliss exploding as my hips moved faster and his tongue moved from my mouth to my neck, licking before his teeth scraped at my skin, then pulled. I gasped, and he soothed the sting with his lips. "Shit, it's like I'm fucking thirteen again. Gonna come."

My hand held his head to my neck, my eyes mashed shut as I chased the magic coursing through me. "Me too."

A deep throated groan was my only warning before I felt warmth coat my stomach, my panties, and his teeth clamped onto my skin.

It sent me over, and his fingers found the dip of my spine, tracing the curve as I swayed over him, riding it out, our heavy breathing the only sound other than the birds outside my bedroom window.

I fell on top of him, and he laughed as his spunk stuck to both of us. I didn't care. I didn't even care that I couldn't be with him. Right now, I was at peace. And that peace, accompanied by his hands outlining every dip and line of my back, became enough to have my heavy, swollen eyes fluttering closed.

THIRTY-FOUR

Dash

Time moved slowly yet way too fast as I listened to the sound of Peggy's quiet breaths and felt them heating my skin.

Her face had nuzzled into my neck, and even though I could feel my own sperm sticking to my stomach and hers, I wouldn't have moved for anything.

Her skin was silken, fine hairs rising with each sweep of my fingers. I couldn't believe I could do this. That I was doing this. That she was sprawled over me, entrusting me to hold her as she dreamed.

It felt like a dream. Like some type of foreign landscape I'd only ever dared to imagine before, but never thought I could bring to fruition.

My eyes drifted closed as I tried to soak in every damn thing about these stretched minutes in time. For even though I hoped that when she woke up, she'd forgive me and we could do this every day, I wasn't sure if she would.

Seeing that guy pawing at her face the night before, watching her kiss him as I'd shoved my way through the partygoers to get to her was akin to walking over hot coals.

I was ready to pound his head into the wall, but I had to check myself. I was there for her, and bloodying up some loser wasn't part of the plan. I'd done that already, and it'd done us no good. The plan started and ended with her. And I was still trying to end it by begging and hoping for a new beginning.

I knew why she kissed him, and though I'd wanted to slap her ass and growl obscenities at her for stabbing me repeatedly in the chest, I couldn't. She was kissing him because of what I'd done to her, and she'd continue to act like someone she wasn't until it stopped hurting.

I hoped like hell that after last night and after she'd rubbed her clit over my shaft until her breaths whistled out of her, that some of that pain had dispersed.

My eyes flashed open as the front door did. I glanced over at the bedroom door, seeing it was locked, and released a relieved sigh.

Peony's footsteps clipped over the shitty wood floors, the creaking causing Peggy to stir.

I dragged my fingers over the curve of her spine, obsessed with touching it, with being able to touch her, and she settled again.

Her hair was damp, tickling my face as the scent of melon and some kind of flower wafted into my nose. I'd guessed her scent must have been related to her shampoo, given she wasn't usually one for perfume. Now it was confirmed. I fought the idea to take it home to sniff. Too far up the creep scale. But still, I pondered it.

Yeah, I did whip my dick out while she was showering, but I had to. It was that or go and beat one out in my car, and I'd much rather get busted by her than the neighbors.

Perhaps I'd taken my time. Perhaps it all happened exactly as it should've. She'd never know, and even if she did, I wasn't fucking sorry.

"Peggy?" Peony called.

Shit.

The door rattled. "Peg? You up?" Another rattle. "Why is your door locked? We've spoken about this. It's dangerous."

Well, all in like a dolphin. My hands tightened around Peggy when I felt her harsh inhale. "She's asleep," I said, my voice rougher than I wanted it to be.

The door stopped rattling. "Dash?"

"The one and only."

There was a long pause, then, "Did you sleep over?"

I'd done it time and time before, but judging by the careful tone of her voice, I knew Peggy had told her how our friendship had changed.

Peggy sat up, her eyes blinking repeatedly and her tits right in front of my face. "Yeah," I finally said.

Another stretch of silence, and I didn't give a shit who was on the other side of her door, I had two perfect globes bouncing within reach of my hands and mouth. I chose the mouth, being that my hands had already had their turn.

"Tell her I'd like a word when she wakes up."

"No prob." I sat up, and Peggy's startled expression morphed into a cut off shriek as I slapped a hand over her mouth and used the other to hold her down on me as my mouth got acquainted with her dusky nipple.

"Dash." She pushed at my shoulders but gave up as my tongue laved at the hardened peak. Her thighs tightened around me, and her hands relaxed over my shoulders. "Stop," she panted.

I did, but only after dragging my teeth over my handiwork, earning me a knee quiver and a quiet moan. I laid back down, watching her chest heave as I tucked my hands behind my head. Her creamy skin glistened where my mouth had been, and she grabbed my chin, moving my gaze to hers. "My face is here."

"To be fair, I've spent all my life staring at your face and zero time staring at your tits. Let me try to even the score a little." I licked my lips, then grabbed her hand from my chin, biting her fingers.

She hissed, then giggled, then she was rolling off the bed.

"Wait, what?" I tried to grab her, but she was already standing and throwing a clean army green T-shirt on that hit her mid-thigh.

"You need to go," she said, grabbing a brush and dragging it through her hair.

"Says the woman with my cum on her stomach."

She dropped the brush, then lifted her shirt, giving me a nice view of her gray, stained panties. "Ugh." Reaching for the wipes on her desk, she tugged one out, wiping her stomach before tossing it in the trash.

"Yeah, don't worry about me."

"I'm not." But then she tossed the packet at me. I read the label. Vanilla scented makeup remover wipes. I shrugged. They'd do. "So are we going to have breakfast with your mom and tell her all is good?" I tested as I smeared a wipe over my pubes and lower stomach.

Peggy stilled, a hair elastic dangling from her fingers.

Her face was clean, bare of any makeup, and my chest clenched. With her curls framing her freckle dusted face, she looked like my Peggy once again. "You're fucking stunning, Freckles."

Her shoulders drooped, her determined gray eyes softening. "You still need to go."

"I'm not going until we've talked this shit out."

"There's nothing to talk about," she said, tying her hair atop her head. "Maybe, eventually, we can go back to being friends. But today's not that day, okay?"

My heart was about to collapse. "Pegs."

"No." She sighed, then bit her lip as her gaze shuttered. "It's … I don't want to. I'm sorry."

"What about this morning?" I sat up, confused and growing angry.

"What about it? You hook up with girls all the time and walk away. This should be no different."

My heart caved in, and a weightless laugh flew past my dry lips. "Okay, sure."

Getting up, I snatched my shirt and boots, pulling them on as she watched me.

"I didn't mean—"

"You did mean it, and it's true, but you're forgetting something important here," I said into her face as I crowded her against the desk.

Her hands flung out, searching for stability among the mess that cluttered the white surface. Her eyes begged, pleaded for me to keep my mouth shut. But I'd kept my mouth shut for far too fucking long when it came to her.

"You're forgetting that I could never walk away from you. So yeah," I said, pressing my forehead to hers as I let my fingers find the curves of her hips. "I'll go. But I love you, and I know you love me too, which means there's no walking away from this."

I kissed her nose, felt her trembling exhale on my mouth and inhaled it, then took it with me as I grabbed my jacket, unlocked the door, and left her room.

Peony was in the shower, for which I was grateful, because each step I took drained every reserve I had. There was no way I could manage facing her too.

I'd just walked in the door when my phone beeped. Dad rounded the corner, clad in sweatpants and a gray wifebeater, coffee and phone in hand. "Where've you been? You're grounded."

"Peggy got wasted and needed rescuing."

Dad's brows met, creases furrowing his forehead. "What happened?"

I looked at a text from Jackson.

Emergency skate park meet.

Locking the screen, I slipped my phone away. "Like I said, she got drunk."

"That's not like her." He slurped his coffee, and I tried not to cringe.

"Tell me about it." I went to move by him. "Hopefully, there won't be another repeat unless I'm with her."

I made it halfway down the hall before he spoke again. "You're still grounded."

"There's another emergency."

"With whom?"

I closed my eyes and counted to ten. "I don't know. All I know is it's an emergency."

"If you come home stinking of weed, I'll confiscate your Xbox and phone."

Church came prancing down the hall, his folded ears twitching as he met my leg and started curling himself around it. "Not to sound like I don't like having you here and all—"

Dad snorted. "Let's not waste time with lies."

"Fine. Why are you home so much all of a sudden?"

At that moment, Mom's heels clapped down the stairs, heading this way.

Dad actually smiled at her as she used our hallway like her own personal runway. I looked back at her and found a mirrored smile. A real one. Teeth and all.

Ew.

"Okay, so this is fun, but I have places to be."

"You're grounded," Mom said, breezing by me to latch her arm around Dad's waist.

"What is this? Gang warfare?"

Mom rolled her eyes, then inspected her nails. "So dramatic."

Dad hummed, taking another sip of coffee. "Wonder where he gets that from?"

Mom and I both glared at him.

He chuckled, then jerked his head. "Go on then. Be home by four. We're going to dinner."

"Okay." I stopped. "Say what?"

Mom's red lips pursed as she fiddled with the waist of Dad's sweatpants. "You heard him. Dinner. Where we eat food. Together."

I blinked, then started backing away before they suggested a trip to Disneyland.

I'd been before, but it was Peggy's mom and dad who'd taken us, not long before they'd split.

"Four, Dash," Dad reiterated.

I waved over my head. "What-the fuck-ever."

Raven and Lars were already there, Raven's remote-control car doing three sixties in the bowl.

"Didn't know it was an official car date," Raven said.

I grunted, sliding under the railing with my own. "Couldn't be fucked to ride."

"What's with the dazed look?"

"My parents."

Lars raised a brow.

I set my car down, turning on the remote. "Call me crazy, but I think they might actually dig each other."

Lars scoffed. "They are married."

"Yeah, but Dad's been home more, and I haven't seen Emanuel since the start of school."

Raven lit a cigarette. "Guess maybe they're tired of messing around."

I made my little Mazda RX-7 leap over the smaller jump, cringing as it hit the ground too hard and the bumper scraped over the concrete. Hitting the brake, I shook my head, baffled. "The world is changing. I don't do well with too much change." I'd do better if I had a certain curly haired blonde still at my beck and call, but I'd make it happen. No other alternative existed for us. We would be us again but even better. Dash and Peggy 2.0.

If she thought I could be friend zoned again, I'd kiss the stupid right out of her.

"Tell me about it," Jackson said, jumping over the rail with a bottle of Jack.

"You fuck." I leaned forward, pulling a squashed as hell pack of cigarettes from my back pocket. Sliding one between my teeth, I talked around it. "Bringing something to drink when I can't fucking have any."

He cracked the top as I lit my smoke with Raven's lighter. "I'm not sharing anyway."

Jackson sat over the lip, legs hanging. I frowned at his tense posture and the way his shoulders were curving inward as though he'd been battling something for too long and was now defeated.

"Why can't you drink?" Rave asked, taking his lighter back.

"Daddy Dearest said not to, and I rather like my Xbox and phone." I blew out a long stream of smoke, my eyes closing as the nicotine worked its magic. "Need them to stalk Peggy, or I wouldn't care so much about their sudden attempts at parenting."

"Enough about your shit." Jackson downed a long chug of

whiskey, then swiped a hand over his mouth. "Got actual problems here."

We all looked at him, waiting. "Well?" I asked when he did nothing but stare down into the bowl.

He took another sip, not even wincing as he swallowed. "Our parents found out."

"Fuck," Lars spewed.

Raven's mouth hung open.

I pursed my lips. "And?"

Jackson shook his head, glaring at me, then sighed. "And Willa's moving to her dad's."

"They caught you?" Lars asked.

I laughed through a haze of smoke. "No shit, Sherlock."

"No," Jackson said, and my cigarette almost fell from my mouth. "Someone tipped them off."

THIRTY-FIVE

Peggy

I can feel you. So hot and wet ...

Growing flustered, I removed myself from bed. From the memories tied to it and the temptation to touch myself as I let them blaze through my head.

After dressing, I scarfed down a banana while Mom made coffee. She'd been quiet yesterday after our talk on Saturday, which pretty much consisted of one question.

Did Dash and I have sex?

Mortified couldn't even begin to cover how I'd felt as I'd stood before her with my hair still mussed from his rough hands. I'd said no and told her that he'd just stayed over. Her brows had lifted, and the twist to her lips stayed as she surveyed my face. Whatever she saw there must've been enough for her to leave it alone because she didn't push. She'd merely said not to lock the door again.

"I'm missing a sock," I said around a mouthful, sick of the silence.

"Oh? Why don't you try looking for it?"

I snapped my eyes at her, swallowing the mush in my mouth. "What have I done now?"

Blowing on her coffee, she leaned back against the green counter. "Something's not adding up."

I waited for her to elaborate, tossing the banana peel into the trash.

"You and Dash. How did he end up coming over when you

supposedly hate him?"

I forced my eyes to roll. "Because it's Dash. He does whatever he wants."

"Not always with you. He's pushed, but he's also respected your boundaries." She paused, bobbing her head. "Well, sometimes."

I then regretted telling her so much about what'd happened between us. Sighing, I walked over to the table, checking I had my chem book in my bag, and then zipped it shut after slipping my lunch inside. "I caved a little." There, that was definitely true.

Mom hummed over the rim of her mug.

I took the opportunity to bail while I could and smacked a kiss on her cheek. "I'll see you later."

"Straight home," she hollered as I shoved my feet into my boots at the door.

"Aye, aye, captain." The screen door slapped shut behind me.

I parked beside Daphne, ignoring the black on black Range Rover that was stalking into the lot behind me and the fizzing exploding inside my stomach.

Blowing out a stuttering exhale, I checked my hastily applied mascara, fluffed my curls, and grabbed my bag.

"You look different." Daphne sipped from a takeout cup against her car.

Slamming the door, I locked my car as a nervous laugh escaped. "What?"

Her eyes roamed my wrinkled blouse and skirt, and the socks peeking above the tops of my scuffed Docs. She shrugged, taking another sip. "You heard me."

I was saved from answering her random assessment by the one person I was hoping to avoid. "Beautiful morning, ladies."

Daphne's brow lifted. "If you say so, Thane."

Dash swaggered closer. And closer. And he wouldn't … he did. His arm wrapped around my shoulders, and he pressed a loud kiss to my head. "Missed you, Frecks."

I pushed him off, my cheeks aflame as I grabbed Daphne's hand and dragged her over the lawn. "Ew, it's damp. Use the sidewalk, my heels will sink."

We moved to the walkway, and she groaned at the dirt caking her black heels. "Ugh, Peggy."

"Move it," I hissed, glancing over my shoulder at Dash who was walking lazily toward us, devilish grin in place.

"What is going on?" Daphne picked up the pace.

"He interrupted my make-out session with some guy at Wade's on Friday, threw me over his shoulder like some gorilla asshole, and then carried me to his car is what's going on."

Daphne cackled, and some of the guys on the lacrosse team stopped and stared as she threw her head back. "Oh, God. Shut up. Did he really?"

"Really." I sighed.

We climbed the steps. "And then? Come on, it didn't end there."

"I was drunk as hell, so he took me home." She said nothing, and when I glanced at her, almost running into someone's backpack, she spun her hand in a *keep going* gesture. "And we did nothing."

"Bullshit." She laughed. "I know you did. You have that look that says you got laid or close to it."

I almost tripped as we neared our lockers. "I do not."

"Do too," she chirped, unlocking hers.

"Fine." I shoved my bag in and plucked out my English book. "We did something the next morning." She slammed her locker, leaning close with expectant eyes. "I can't say; it's kind of embarrassing."

"We humped each other like pre-teens," Dash said from behind me.

I squeaked, spinning around to slap him in the chest. "Fuck off, Dash."

He mock gasped. "Language, Peggy Sue. That's no way to speak to the man who rubs you just right."

Daphne snorted out a burst of laughter behind me. "Later, lovebirds."

"We're not—"

Dash slid a hand over my mouth. "She sees through your lies."

I bit it, growling at him. "Would you stop? What is wrong with you?"

He crowded me back into the locker. "You're wrong for me. In all the right ways." He squeezed my cheeks between his fingers, pursing my lips and quickly smacking his against them. "I'll see you at lunch, lady love."

My face was on fire as he swaggered down the hall to his friends and left me there for everyone to gawk and snicker at.

Who the hell did he think he was?

I should've known. I was the one person who knew him best. Yet I'd forgotten the words I'd uttered just this morning.

Dash Thane did whatever he wanted.

I met up with Daphne at my locker before lunch, needing to grab mine from my bag.

"He's seriously not backing down." She examined her coral-colored nails.

"Tell me about it." I huffed, plucking out my lunch. Something fluttered to the ground, and I groaned, wanting to leave it there.

My heart wouldn't let me and neither would Daphne, who picked it up and held it out to me between two fingers. "What are you going to do?"

I opened the letter, my eyes skimming his messy words.

I'm such a prick.
And a dick.
And a fuckwit.

But I love you.
And I know you love me too.
That's why I wrote this shitty-ass poem for you.

Daphne fell into fits of laughter, and I slowly folded the paper closed, biting my lips as I tucked it inside my bag.

"You totally have to show your grandkids that."

"You're acting like we're some foregone conclusion." I slammed my locker, my chest a bubbling, bouncing, mess.

Daphne bit into her apple, chewing before she commented. "Because you're probably the only one who doesn't see that."

We pushed inside the cafeteria, heading for the back doors to sit outside. "He slept with Kayla. How am I the only one, besides her, who remembers that?"

"Because you love him, and it hurt you, but he was hurting at the time, and he's a dick even on the best of days." She took another bite, mumbling around it, "If you and Byron hadn't gotten a little freaky in the back of that limo, he wouldn't have been so crushed. He would've continued to fight for you, and you know it."

Guilt gripped me, and I blew some curls from my lips as the wind washed over us. "This is all so stupid and messed up."

"Love is always stupid and messed up."

I pointed at a table near the garden ledge, hoping Dash wouldn't bother looking for me. He always sat with his friends at lunch anyway. "Have you spoken to Lars?"

She tossed her apple into a trash can, taking a seat. "I don't want to talk about him."

"Fine. Have you heard from Willa?" I asked as I slid into the bench seat.

The weather had cooled, but not so much that I'd rather sit inside among the prying eyes and careless whispers. Where I was easy prey for Dash.

I'd thought too soon. "Oh, Peggy!"

"Shit." I fumbled and dropped my sandwich on the ground.

Daphne started choking on her water as Dash took a seat right next to me, straddling the bench. "Dropped your lunch? No problem. I bought you some mac and cheese."

Daphne was crying, fanning her eyes to keep her makeup in place.

My heart was racing, stumbling over nonexistent hurdles, and landing flat on its face. "Dash, please go." I didn't even look at him.

His knee bumped my thigh as he scooted even closer. So close that if a teacher walked out here, which they would soon, he'd be asked to move. "Not going to happen. Also, I heard you mention Willa." He unwrapped some utensils, stabbing the cheesy pasta with them and pushing one toward me.

Heat rose from it, and the smell just about had me salivating. I tried not to buy too much from the cafeteria even though Dad took care of anything to do with school. Mom liked to make my lunch. Ever since we'd moved out of Dad's, it was something she seemed to take pride in. But I couldn't say I didn't get excited on the days when I didn't bring any.

Swallowing my pride, I pulled the mac and cheese closer, stirring it before blowing and taking a bite. "Thanks," I grumbled.

"You're welcome." He began eating his own.

"What about Willa?" Daphne asked.

Dash swallowed his mouthful. "Right. Yeah, someone tattled on her and Jackson. I don't think she's coming back."

My fork dropped, and Dash caught it before it hit the table, setting it in the bowl. "She's not coming back?"

"Holy shit." Daphne blinked, wide eyes directed at the wooden table.

"Yep," he said, uncapping his water and taking a sip before offering it to me. I declined. "Apparently, she's been kicked out. Gone to live with her dad."

Her dad lived half an hour away on the outskirts of the cove, and I turned to Daphne, unsure of what to even say.

"She didn't tell us," Daphne said, her forehead creasing.

Dash waved his fork around. "I daresay she's had more pressing matters to address, like, oh, I dunno, moving out of the house she's grown up in."

Daphne thinned her eyes at Dash, who just kept eating.

He had a point, though, and so I tried not to feel butt hurt over it. "We need to call her."

Daphne nodded. "Emergency scrap date."

We finished eating in silence. Mainly because I was starving, but also because I didn't know what to say with Dash right there, and the shock sitting heavy between me and Daphne.

When Lars came to the table, Daphne stilled, then immediately packed her things and said she'd see me in geography.

"Jesus," Lars groaned, rubbing his chin. "She really hates me, huh?"

"You did get some other girl pregnant while you and her were starting to get serious," Dash said.

Lars almost growled. "It was before we started hooking up."

"Potato, potahto," Dash sang.

I spoke before the fists Lars was clenching on the table could do any damage. "Keep trying."

He blinked at me beneath dark lashes, his jaw relaxing. "Yeah? She say something to you?"

"I wouldn't tell you if she had." I packed up my lunch. "All I'm saying is that you should keep trying." I got up, taking it to the trash before heading to the door as the bell rang.

"Freckles," Dash said, exasperated. "Not even a goodbye? I bought you lunch."

"You shouldn't have expectations when you do nice things for others." I stalked between the tables inside the cafeteria, keeping my eyes trained on the doors ahead.

His hand snuck around my waist as soon as the doors shut behind us, and he pulled me into a tiny alcove behind a row of lockers. "Dash, no." I pushed at his chest as he pressed himself against me.

"Be mad, but just look at me while you're doing it." I scowled at him, and he chuckled, his thumb dancing over my cheek. "That's it." The humor faded from his expression, and his eyes took on a softer sheen. "Did you get my poem?"

A sound left me, half laughter, half breath. "Yes. Very romantic."

He grinned, then licked his lips, and I knew what he was about to do, so I ducked beneath the arm above my head and raced down the hall.

His laughter shadowed me. "Never forget that I can run faster, Freckles."

THIRTY-SIX

Peggy

I hadn't been online since Dash left my room on Saturday. Partly because I knew he'd probably be online, and partly because I had no motivation to play.

But after school the next day, and another round of Dash cornering me at every turn, I needed to switch off. He was everywhere—at school, in the parking lot, texting my phone with pathetic but kind of funny gifs, and worst of all, in my head.

I couldn't shake him. But at least online, I could ignore him. Maybe even just block him. Though that was likely to have him showing up at my house.

I shoved my homework aside, then shimmied on my stomach to my nightstand and nabbed the remote. While I waited for it to load, I checked my phone, hoping for a message from Willa. There'd been radio silence, and Daphne and I had wondered if maybe her parents had taken her phone.

I had to believe she'd get in touch or else I was going to find Jackson, who showed up at school today looking like he'd sunk to the bottom of a whiskey barrel and almost drowned.

The game loaded, and I went through the motions, deciding my weapons needed an upgrade. I picked the battle axe and some nunchucks. That'd do.

I lasted all of five minutes before someone shot me, and then a message popped up on screen. I knew he'd been online, but I'd just been happy he'd let me be. Until now.

F*ckoffandie666: Want me to kill them for you?

Don't respond, don't respond, don't re—

PegSue12: I'm good, thanks.

F*ckoffandie666: Yeah, you are. ;)

Ugh. My phone rang, and I switched the game off to answer it.

"I can't even. I know we can't party, but I need out. Movies?"

I pondered it, unsure. "I'm grounded."

Daphne groaned. "Just ask, maybe she'll be fine with it."

I told her I'd call her back. I could go for some popcorn and a different kind of distraction.

"Hey, what's up?" Mom asked.

Laughter rang sharp in the background. Familiar laughter.

"Where are you?"

She scoffed. "At a friend's. Why?"

I shook my head, jumping up off the bed to check my purse. I only had a twenty, which wouldn't be enough. "Daphne wants to go to the movies."

Mom laughed at something someone said. "Sure, just be home by nine."

I frowned, pulling the phone away from my ear and checking I'd indeed called my mom and not someone else. "Seriously?"

"Yeah, I'm kind of busy, 'kay? I'll see you later."

"Wait," I rushed out. "I need some money."

She sighed. "I won't be home for a while, so you'll have to come and get the card."

Dad gave us a credit card to use, but Mom tried to avoid using it, not wanting to take too much from him when they weren't even married anymore. She knew giving it to me would be a bad idea, but she did let me borrow it when I needed something and she was strapped for cash.

I grabbed my keys and purse, quickly giving myself a once-over in the mirror before nodding. "Okay. Where are you? Phil's?"

"No, I'm at May's." She hung up, and once again, I stared at my phone.

"May's." I mouthed the word over and over, unable to make sense of it as I drove to Dash's.

And damn it, he'd been online, which meant he was probably home. Which meant I'd need to sneak in, grab the card, and bail.

I called Daphne on the way over, and we went over the movie times, deciding on one in an hour.

"And tacos," she said before hanging up. "I need some freaking tacos."

I agreed, then hit end call on the steering wheel before driving through the looming opened gates.

Mom's secondhand car looked like an alien perched between two super models as its faded blue paint glimmered in the afternoon sun between Dash's Rover and May's Mercedes.

I moved up the curved stairway to the heavy oak doors and pushed one open. I didn't want to ring the doorbell and alert everyone to my presence. It was better if I just grabbed the card and made a run for it. Not to mention, I was supposed to be grounded. Whatever Mom was doing here had her forgetting about that.

I slipped off my boots. The house was huge, but I wouldn't put it past Dash to hear their thud on the expensive wooden floors. Tiptoeing down the hall, I stopped and caught myself. I was acting insane. Completely stupid. Who cares if he saw me?

I'd just leave anyway, like I'd planned to. I did have plans.

Squaring my shoulders, I wound down the ever-winding hall until I heard the sound of laughter in the family room closest to the kitchen.

I halted in the arched entry, trying to make sense of what I saw before me.

Mom and May were sitting together, side by side, a champagne bottle open on the glass coffee table and a bunch of photographs between them on the maroon chaise.

"He looks dashing," Mom said, holding a picture up to better survey it.

May laughed. "Oh, you used to always say that, thinking you were so damn funny."

"I am funny," Mom retorted, taking a sip of her champagne.

"Keep telling yourself that." May pursed her lips, flicking through a stack of what looked to be pictures of me and Dash from homecoming, judging by the flashes of bubblegum I glimpsed that matched my dress. My ruined dress.

I swallowed, then made my presence known by clearing my throat. "Uh, hi."

They glanced over, and May smiled. A real smile. Teeth and everything.

God. What was happening?

"Darling, come in. Look at these," she cooed, gesturing for me to join them by patting the empty space next to her.

I shifted closer but remained standing. "Oh wow," I forced out, staring at the photo of Dash and me. He was smiling against my head, and I was ducking mine, smiling at the ground. Before I knew what I was doing, I'd taken the photo, holding it close as my heart beat faltered.

We looked happy. Even when we were anything but. As if it were natural for us to find comfort among one another while the world continued to shift beneath our feet.

My eyes welled. A tremor flitted through my hand as I gave the photo back.

May waved me off, taking a sip from her flute. "Keep it. I've printed dozens."

Of course, she had.

I smiled in thanks, then cleared my throat again, trying to rid it of emotion as I rounded the coffee table to Mom, who was fishing in her purse for her wallet.

"Don't get too crazy," she warned. "What are you guys seeing?"

"Some romantic comedy."

Mom raised a brow. "You hate those."

"Daphne's idea." I sighed, slipping the card and photo inside the breast pocket of my blouse. "We're grabbing some tacos, so don't worry about dinner for me."

"Tacos?" May perked up. "I haven't had a taco in years. We should get some. Do they deliver?" she asked Mom, already googling on her phone.

Mom smiled at me with a look that said she'd explain later.

"Uber eats," I told May.

"Uber what now?" She furrowed her brows, her long nails tapping over her phone screen.

"A driver will pick up your order and bring it to you," Mom informed.

May's mouth gaped. "That is genius. Why haven't I heard of this before?"

I shook my head, smiling at the ground as I went to leave. "Well, have a good after—what are these?" A stack of applications laid on the glass coffee table. I must have missed them in my first quick assessment.

"Dash's college applications," May said. "Would you mind

checking them? He's been adamant he only applies for the schools you plan to apply for, so it's best to be sure."

My heart stopped as I picked them up and began sifting through the pages.

All three applications were for schools I'd told him I wanted to attend. One local to us, Gray Springs, and one in New York.

"Looks fine to me." I set them down in a messy heap and exited the room. "See you later, Mom."

May hummed. "Are they still fighting?"

I didn't catch Mom's response, too intent on getting out of there before the tears finally escaped.

Jumping into my boots, I raced for my car and stumbled slightly when I saw Dash leaning against the driver's side door. "Told you I'm faster."

He had one foot tucked behind the other and wore no shirt, his black sweatpants hanging low on his sharply defined hips. His stomach contracted as he pushed off my car, taking a slow step forward in his slippers. "Did you think you could come here, and I wouldn't know?"

"How did you know?" I asked, trying to blanket the emotion that'd almost split me in two mere seconds ago.

He huffed, scratching at the stubble growing in beneath his chin. "I feel it every time you enter a room, Freckles. Quit being foolish."

"I'm not the fool. You are."

"I've been the biggest kind of fool. The worst." His teeth dragged over his lip, and my breath plumed, rushing out of me as I stared. "Where are you going?"

"That's none of your business."

A brow lifted, and he crossed his arms over his chest, making the muscles in his arms appear even bigger. "Well, I've got no place to be. My girl keeps bailing on me, so I'll just wait right here until she opens her pretty mouth and tells me what she's up to."

"I'm not your girl."

"Then quit looking at my body like you want to lick it."

I coughed out a laugh, then dragged my eyes from his smooth looking skin. "You're so full of yourself."

"You can be full of me too, if you'd just forgive me."

My stomach heated. "You did not just say that."

His teeth flashed, lips curving into his right cheek. "I'll say it again for those hard of hearing." His voice rose to a shout. "You can be—"

I slammed against him, shoving my hand over his mouth. His tongue swiped over it, his eyes glittering blue jewels pressed between entrancing lashes. "Stop this, right now."

I realized my mistake when his arms circled me, holding me tight to his body. My hand dropped to his chest as I tried to push off him. "I'll ask one more time before I wrestle your keys from you. Where are you going that's so important you had to come and get your Dad's credit card?"

Damn him for knowing every fucking thing. "To the movies."

He tutted, his eye twitching as his hold tightened. My breasts squished into his warm chest, and all I could smell was that clean soapy scent mingling with the fading aftershave on his skin. "Over my dead body. With whom?"

Overheating. I was overheating, and I had to go. "Daphne."

He didn't release me. His hand drifted to my chin, tilting it for his mouth to lower over. "I think I'll come with you to make sure you're not lying."

Oh, my God. I had to end this because he would. I knew he would. "I saw your college applications."

A harsh breath vacated him, feathering my lips. "You did, did you?"

I nodded, and his hold loosened just enough for me to push off him but not enough for me to escape. Though I definitely could have if I wanted to. I suppose I didn't want to. "What did you do that for?"

His brows knitted. "Because it was always the plan."

I wasn't sure if he was referring to college or us. "But then we landed in a steaming pile of crap. You can't base your future off the decisions I make for mine."

"Like hell I can't," he said. "And I can study business at any old crummy college. Those plans are flexible, but the plans I have for you?" He shook his head. "Nowhere near the realm of flexible."

I gave up on holding them back, and he wiped at the tears leaking out. "What if—"

"What if what? We've fucked it all up already, and now we have one option." He kissed a lone tear near my eye, licking it as he whispered, "To go all in. I'm already there, waiting for you to let go and meet me in the deep end."

"I'm scared," I said, unsure where the admission had come from.

"Good." Dash's body felt impossibly warm against mine as if even his skin was trying to reassure me. "If love doesn't terrify you, you're not in love. And if you're not in love, then what are you, Peggy?" He didn't wait for me to answer that. He opened the door, then helped me inside. "I'll be tracking your phone, just FYI." After tapping the roof, he watched as I backed out.

I was still reeling from all he'd said. So much so, that his last comment didn't even bother me.

THIRTY-SEVEN

Peggy

ash continued with his usual antics for the remainder of the week, and I was tired. So damn tired of feeling like I was hanging from an unraveling thread. I needed to let go, but instead, I continued to wait for the snap.

If you're not in love, then what are you, Peggy?

I knew exactly what I was. I was terrified, and I was still bleeding, which only compounded that terror.

Letting go of it meant I had to forgive, move forward, and try to heal. I wasn't sure I was ready for it, but I wasn't sure I could keep hanging there, hoping to escape more heartbreak.

Holding a grudge close to your heart was easier. It was simpler, in some ways, than addressing the reason it was there, like a piece of cement blocking an artery, in the first place. He'd hurt me, but I'd hurt him first. This wasn't a game, and it wasn't fair to either of us, yet there was no real way to win or lose.

Willa finally called from a new number, saying she'd fill us in on Saturday.

When she showed up at my house, there were tears, hugs, and more tears as she tried to tell us what'd happened.

"Who told them?" I asked, the photo of Dash and me sitting atop sheets of paper that would blend well with my dress.

Willa scrubbed at her face, wearing no makeup yet still looking stunning with her naturally long, thick lashes and swollen, pink lips. Her eyes were red, but her complexion was clear. "I have no idea."

"We'll find out," Daphne said, stabbing the glue stick at her. "Mark my words. And when we do …" She dragged the glue stick in the air across her throat.

Willa cracked a smile, and I patted her hand. "So that's your new number?"

"Yeah," she said, staring down at her closed album, paper and shapes stealing out of the edges. "Dad got me a new phone even though Mom had warned him I wasn't allowed to have one."

Daphne harrumphed. "Not like she can say shit after kicking you out."

Willa smiled again. "That's exactly what Dad said."

"What did he say about you and Jackson?" Daphne asked.

She took her time answering, adjusting the collar of her light brown peasant dress. "He wasn't happy. But then again, he hates Mom, so I think even though he doesn't think it's okay, he's trying to be accepting of us to spite her."

I began cutting out the moon I'd stenciled onto the bubble-gum pink paper. "Are you and Jackson still together?"

"Yeah," she said, though her voice was unbearably soft. "But I don't know how it's going to work. I start at the public school on Monday, and Mom is probably tracking his phone."

I pushed aside the memory of Dash saying he was tracking mine, only to have more memories roll in. The carefree way he so easily kept touching me now, trying to kiss me when I least expected it, or even when I did.

"Public school." Daphne crinkled her nose, then checked herself when I glared.

"I met a nice guy from there at Wade's last weekend."

Willa frowned. "The one you kissed?"

I nodded. "His name is Todd. Say hi for me and tell him I'm sorry Dash is a dick."

Daphne huffed out a laugh. "Todd. Cute."

"He was cute, actually."

Willa stared down at her closed album, her lemonade still full in front of her. Setting the scissors down, I wiggled my chair closer and wrapped an arm around her. Her head fell to my shoulder while I rubbed her arm, and I heard her breath hitch. "We'll still see each other."

"Every damn weekend." Daphne moved closer, grabbing her hand and squeezing. "And you'll make some new friends. Just don't let them replace us, or I'll get stabby."

Willa hiccupped, laughing. "I don't want new friends. It's senior year; everyone already has friends."

"Including you," I said. "So if you don't make any more, that's fine too. You have us."

Daphne nodded. "You'll always have us."

After a few minutes, we returned to our work, and Willa settled, taking a sip of her drink. "So," she said, putting it down, "what have I missed with Dash?"

"Such good things." Daphne folded a sheet of paper in half, then began cutting along the creased line. "He's upped his game, but does little Miss Peggy Sue fold? No." She shook her head, laughing. "No, she has not."

I rolled my eyes as Willa got Daphne to explain all he'd done at school. I stared at the photograph of us on the table, wondering what he was doing, and longed, even if it was for just a second, for him to be in my room after the girls had left.

I missed him.

I'd missed him for far too long, and I had to wonder if missing him was the worst mistake I could make when to be with him would be as easy as inhaling my next breath. If only I could just forget what'd happened. "Maybe I don't need to forget," I said.

"Huh?" Willa said.

Daphne frowned. "You talking about what Dash did?"

I sighed. "Maybe I'll never forget, but does that mean I can't forgive him?"

Daphne started humming. "You know where I stand on this. He didn't knock someone up, so as far as I'm concerned, knock yourself out."

Willa slid her finger around the rim of her glass, then licked it. "It's going to hurt no matter what you do. But it might hurt less if you're happy instead of holding on to every reason not to be."

"Wow." I blinked. "That's kind of deep."

Daphne laughed. "But it's true."

I pondered that as she and Willa discussed the color scheme for her page.

And looking at Willa, who was doing her best to remain hopeful in a situation that would be crushing every drop of hope she collected, I decided Dash was right.

I was being foolish.

I just didn't know how to admit that to someone with an ego bigger than my house.

Mom hadn't divulged anything about her sudden reconnection with May.

That night, as she was lying on the couch searching through the channels while Phil cooked dinner, I decided to step outside my own problems and ask her about it.

"How'd you and May make up?"

Mom dropped the remote, rolling her head to face where I'd perched on the arm of the couch. "After she came here looking for Dash, I called her a few days later to see if there'd been any news."

"You did?" I couldn't mask my surprise.

She made an irritated sound. "I practically helped raise that boy, so of course, I wanted to know if he was okay. And well, I guess we just started talking instead of screaming and getting angry."

"Huh," I puffed out.

She nudged me with her slipper. "This about Dash? Or did you actually want to know."

"I actually did just want to know. But yeah." I inhaled deeply, my lips billowing as I set it free, and admitted, "Now I'm wondering about him too." It felt nice to be completely honest with her again.

Her smile said she agreed. "You guys still haven't made up?"

I shook my head, plucking at a loose thread in my gold and gray polka dotted pajama pants. "No."

"Because making up this time would mean things aren't exactly in friendship land anymore."

My eyes shot to her knowing ones. "Pretty much."

She kicked her legs up, moving over and patting the couch for me to sit down. "You're scared?" she asked when I'd taken a seat.

"Yes." I pulled my legs up to rest my chin on my knee. "I mean, it's already changed so much that I don't even know why I am, or how to take the next step."

Her fingers toyed with my curls. "It doesn't always need a big discussion or an elaborate gesture. Sometimes, you simply just take the step, and then another one, and another, until it feels right."

I stewed over that as we ate dinner, and then I dawdled back to my room and switched on the Xbox.

Dash wasn't online, but I waited, playing with Raven until I saw his username pop up.

PegSue12: If you can kill me, you can come over.

There was a pause before he responded.

F*ckoffandie666: Does that mean …?

PegSue12: I suppose you'll have to try to win to find out.

He didn't respond, but he played a mean game. I laughed as a bomb landed on my house and cursed him for destroying something that cost me thirty dollars to build.

I'd just escaped and was racing across the street to sneak into a building when he shot out of nowhere. I retaliated, bullets spraying and my axe flying, and then my stomach sank.

He was dead.

We both said nothing for the longest time, and as my heart threatened to explode with every beat, I typed out another message.

PegSue12: Come over anyway.

He logged off a second later, and I began flitting around my room. Nerves shot through me from head to toe, and I flapped my hands around my face, trying to think clearly.

Once I could, I hit the bathroom and brushed the remnants of mushroom ravioli from my mouth, then I tried to do something about my hair, but it was a lost cause.

"Pegs."

I turned and saw Mom leaning in my doorway, her head

tilted curiously. "What are you doing?"

I stilled my clammy hands. "I told Dash to come over." Then I panicked for a different reason. "Shit, I mean, crap. I forgot to ask you—"

She raised a hand. "That boy has never once asked permission to enter our home. But honey"—she raised a brow—"chill. And leave the door unlocked. I'll be in the living room."

I nodded even though she was gone, then jumped as my window flew up, and Dash flew in, the bed bouncing as I hurried to shut the door.

"That was quick."

"Longest ten minutes of my life." He kicked off his boots, and they landed in front of my desk. "Come here."

I blinked, kind of stunned by his confidence, but then again, it was Dash. I took my time moving to the bed. He hooked his hands behind my legs when I reached him, bringing me between his thighs, thumbs caressing through the flannelette.

"Are you diving in?" he asked, and the edge of vulnerability in his gaze, to the planes of his face, and saturating his voice threatened to send me under in an instant.

My pounding heart was bruising my chest and every breath I tried to take without giving in.

Unable to take anymore, I tipped his chin and lowered my lips to hover over his. "Yeah. You win."

"Freckles." A silent laugh hit my mouth before his lips whispered across mine. "We both win."

THIRTY-EIGHT

Seven months later
Dash

She was radiant, draped head to toe in moonlit silver that shimmered under the glow of the stars.

As I helped her out of the limousine I'd rented, my chest filled with something other than air. Warmth drenched each inhalation I took, furthering the heating of my heart and tightening each breath.

"You look like magic."

Peggy pressed a hand to the tiny tiara tucked in her hair. Not by some dumbass rigged prom committee, but by me. "After a whole night of dancing?"

"Especially after that." The driver closed the door, dipping his hat to me after I'd given him a generous tip, and then returned to his side of the car.

Slipping her hand inside mine, I picked up our overnight bag with the other and led her to the doors of the hotel. A few other students were checking in, but I didn't give a shit. Let the hypocrites assume what they wanted. They were here with partners for the same reason.

Yeah, we hadn't had sex. Over seven months together, and we'd still never done it. Though it didn't mean we were new to each other's bodies.

No fucking way.

I'd been willing to wait, even when she'd pushed, knowing this particular night would be the right time to rid the memories that sometimes soured her gray eyes whenever she caught sight of Woods or Kayla. But I'd gotten to know every delectable inch of her body in every other way I could, sometimes to the point of madness, as we explored late into the night.

We'd finish, we'd play a game, watch our movies, rip on each other, and then we'd start exploring all over again.

She was every fantasy brought to life. Not a day went by when I didn't catch myself staring at her, even for just a moment, without feeling like I'd been given a gift I probably didn't deserve. A gift handed to me before we could even mumble and trip over each other's names. A gift I almost lost in a mixture of bad decisions and unrecognized feelings.

"What are you thinking about?" Peggy asked once we'd checked in and stepped into the elevator.

An older couple stood to one side, a woman with stiff cheeks smiling at us knowingly.

I didn't return it, but Peggy did, while I flicked the button for the top floor. "You sure you want me to answer that while in the company of strangers?"

Peggy's cheeks bloomed beneath the light layer of makeup covering her freckles. It didn't cover them completely, and I planned to have her sweating enough that I could trace my tongue and fingers over them until the sun woke. "Keep your lips shut."

I tugged her close, bending to brush my nose over the side of her head. "Are you sure? I think you'll like what I was just thinking about."

Her hand tightened in mine, but she otherwise remained silent until the elevator dinged and the couple stepped out.

When the doors closed, she gazed up at me. "Scale of one to ten?"

I pretended to think hard about it. "Eleven."

She laughed, and I was about to shove her against the mirror and steal that laughter with my mouth when the doors reopened.

We exited and headed down the beige carpeted hall to one of the two penthouse suites. I didn't know who'd booked the other one, and I didn't care. I'd booked this four months ago, knowing the other spoiled brats at school wouldn't wait too long to snatch one for themselves.

Peggy slid the key card in, the door beeped, and we pushed inside.

Her hand left mine as she wandered to the window. I set our bags down, then tugged my black tuxedo jacket off and flung it over the chair in the foyer.

Her hands pressed against the glass, her breath fogging it as she gazed at downtown and all the trees, water, and houses below. "It's always felt so small."

"The Cove?" I asked, strolling closer as I undid my cufflinks.

"Yeah. But looking at it like this"—she stopped, her head turning, and a smile shaping her lips—"it's anything but. It's kind of beautiful."

"It is," I said, my eyes on her as I tossed the cufflinks. They hit the floor with a clatter, but I didn't care to see where they'd rolled.

Peggy's hands slid down the glass as mine landed on her hips, caressing, shifting the smooth material of her gown over her even smoother skin. "What do you think it'll be like?"

"What?" I asked her neck, moving her long curls aside to graze my lips over the curve of her neck.

A fluttering sound preceded her answer. "College. Being away from home."

My tongue pressed flat against her jumping pulse, and my

front flattened hers to the glass. "You already know the answer to that."

Her hum was more of a moan. "Enlighten me again."

I spun her around, my hands grabbing hers and raising them above her head against the window. Her eyes were on my mouth, and her chest was rising and falling faster with every breath.

With a lick of my lips, I lowered my forehead to hers and let our noses touch. "It'll be an adventure. The kind where I can take home with me."

Tugging her hands away from mine, she kicked her heels off before throwing her arms around my neck. "I hope you're going to do what I want you to."

Her words heated my skin, my heart, and my dick.

I pressed my hands to her ass, letting her feel how hard I was. "You've still been taking the pill?" Her mom had gotten her a prescription a month after we'd started dating. I'd brought a string of condoms with me, but fuck if I wanted to use them.

It was her and me for eternity. I wanted no barriers between us if we didn't need to use them. Besides, I'd never gone bareback before. I'd heard it was indescribable, but there was no one else I'd ever take that risk with.

Peggy owned all my greatest risks. She always would.

I didn't care that she'd bleed. I wanted it. My dick throbbed with how much I wanted to be the one to make that happen. To break her open, steal her innocence, and transform her into a woman made only for me.

When she sank her teeth into my neck, then kissed the sting, it seemed she agreed. "Yes. Every day. It's even in the bag."

After the shitstorm that was Daphne and Lars, it was fair to say Peggy was a little spooked on the whole young parenting deal. I couldn't blame her, even if most situations probably weren't as complicated as theirs.

Tugging up her dress, I lifted it over her head and kept my eyes trained on hers as the silken material slipped from my fingers and cascaded into a puddle on the floor behind her. Slowly, I let my eyes drop. She was wearing a strapless bra, white with a tiny bow in the center.

That tiny bow, the lace material cushioning her breasts, made air clog deep within my lungs.

I cleared my throat, my finger rising to brush over the bow before tracing where the ribbed edges of her bra met her milky skin. "Maybe I should go beat one out in the bathroom beforehand. We can make out after, and I'll get hard again."

Peggy laughed, then reached behind her and unclasped the bra, and my mouth dried as it dropped to the floor. The air-conditioned space tightened her nipples. I'd like to think it was from me too, but I didn't much care. My hands slid around them, thumbs ghosting over the tight knots, then I squeezed.

Her hands met mine, holding them to her tits as her thighs rubbed together. I glanced down and saw the matching white panties. "They need off too."

"You do it."

"Yes, ma'am." Before I did, I bent low and threw her over my shoulder, then traipsed through the open space living area, almost tripping over the dark rugs bedecking any space that seemed too empty, and kicked open the bedroom door.

Onto the king-size bed, she flopped, and only then, as she lay laughing in a sea of cream linen, did I grab the edges of her panties and pull.

I tossed them over my shoulder, and they landed on the flat screen hanging on the wall, which only made her laugh again.

As much as I wanted inside her, finally, the sound was too beautiful for me to cut short. So, skidding my fingers up her thighs, I prolonged it. "Dash," she squirmed, trying to smack my hands away.

They glided inside her thighs, and I grinned as she met my gaze right before I pushed them apart. Now, it was time to cut off her laughter.

My tongue feasted on her, tortured and loved her, knowing that she probably wouldn't gain much pleasure, if any at all, once my dick filled her for the first time.

My fingers unfolded her, flicking at that bud before sliding halfway inside and carefully twisting. I knew, no matter how much I prepped her, it was still going to hurt, so when her moans became croaked whispers, her thighs shaking continuously as my fingers and tongue kept her dancing on that heady edge, I let her come.

Her legs wrapped around my head, almost rocking it side to side as I tried to draw every molecule of bliss from her body. I wanted her wrung dry from pleasure, so wet and overused from it that she'd be as relaxed as possible.

Wrenching her thighs from my head, I pushed up and quickly tore off my shirt, then kicked off my pants and briefs. I didn't waste any time, knowing that if I did, she might creep inside her head and grow too tense. It wouldn't be because she was worried; it would be because no matter how much she wanted this, she knew it was going to hurt.

Her eyes were half shut, hands reaching for my skin as I climbed over her and pulled one of her legs up my back. When she felt me hard against her wet entrance, she shuddered, and her hand met my face. "It's okay."

I nodded, then kissed her thumb when it neared my mouth. With her leg around my back, I leaned on my elbow beside her head, and used my free hand to press inside her.

"Holy sweet mother of hell," I said, groaning as I eased in, trying to keep from ramming inside.

Her eyes remained on my face, and if it was hurting yet, she didn't let it show. Her fingers kept touching my lips, and her eyes were sated jewels, content to stare at me. "What does it feel like?"

"Tight," I said, my hips bobbing, wanting to rock faster, slam inside her, take, worship, rut until I could hardly see.

"Yeah?"

I nodded, my nostrils flaring as I kept butting up against that barrier. I wanted it gone. I needed it erased. I needed all the way in before my heart gave out. "Like melting velvet."

"Yeah?" She liked that, her lips lifting. But I could see the pain in her eyes now. "All in, Dash. Let go."

At those words, I paused, blinking down at her. I lowered over her body until our mouths were meeting and every inch of our skin could feel one another's electrified heartbeats. "Keep your eyes on me," I whispered.

Her mouth brushed mine. "Okay."

My hips pulled back, and the arm that wasn't keeping me from squashing her with my weight completely slid around her back to her shoulder, holding her to me as I plunged deep, and she choked on her next exhale.

I could've stayed lost in rapture for hours, but I climbed my way to the surface, and peppered her face with kisses while I carefully rocked in and out of her.

Her eyes stayed clamped shut, her nails scoring into my back. I kept kissing her, forcing her lips apart as my cock forced her walls to adjust. When her nails slipped from my skin, her hand moving back to my face and into my hair, I knew the worst of the pain was fading, and I gave myself permission to thrust a little faster.

Her breathing steadied, but she still struggled to meet my

tongue, and instead, she moaned lightly as I nibbled at and whispered how good she felt to her lips.

I'd never felt anything like it. Pure fucking nirvana. So wet, so hot, so tight, and combined with a young woman who made me see stars just by kissing her, I was fucking annihilating.

The mess I'd made of her started making itself known between our harsh breaths and rough moans, and I couldn't hold on one more second.

It was too much. She was too much. Too much of everything I'd never known I'd need. I was inside her. My best friend. And I never wanted to leave.

"Fucking, fuck." I came, shaking like a damn leaf and holding on to her for dear life as she stroked my back.

"Dash?" she asked after a moment.

"Hmm?" My head was spinning. I was pretty sure I was still half hard inside her. "Shit, sorry." I went to move, and her arms tightened around me.

"No, stay."

We laid there, just breathing and touching for the longest time. "Are you okay?"

"Perfect."

I huffed into her skin. "I'm squishing you, and I'm pretty sure I should clean you, maybe get you some Tylenol." I paused, rising to my elbows. "Shit, I knew I forgot something."

"Dash."

I swiped a hand through my hair, exasperated with myself. "I had it next to my bag and everything, but Church was trying to climb inside and—"

"Dash."

"And then I must have knocked it to the floor, then Mom was asking how long they'd get for phot—"

Peggy snapped, grabbing my cheeks. "Dash, shut up. I'll be

fine." I frowned, and she laughed. "I can't decide which I like best, your smile or your scowl."

"There's no need for competition. I can do both at once."

She laughed harder as I smiled and scowled, her pussy clasping tighter around my dick. Yep, I was ready to go again. When her laughter faded, she drew a line between my brows. "Do you think it'll always be this way?"

"It's been this way for eighteen years," I said. "Only, it just keeps getting better."

"Even after it gets worse?"

"Especially then." I kissed her nose. "We can have makeup sex now."

"Ass," she said.

"You love me."

"I do." A wistful smile attacked my heart. "Falling in love with you has been the hardest, most exhausting, exhilarating, and wondrous thing to ever happen to me." Her finger trailed over the bridge of my nose. "Because you made sure you happened to me, Dash. And I'm so damn glad you did."

Relief and a thousand violent feelings stampeded through me. My heart exploded, my arms encasing her head as I tucked my face beneath her chin and whispered on a hoarse breath, "Peggy Sue, I fucking love you."

"2.0," she said.

"Two point fucking 0."

THE END

Facebook page
m.facebook.com/authorellafields

Instagram
www.instagram.com/ellafieldsauthor

Website
www.ellafields.net

ALSO BY ELLA FIELDS

Frayed Silk

Cyanide

Corrode

Bloodstained Beauty

GRAY SPRINGS UNIVERSITY:

Suddenly Forbidden

Bittersweet Always

Pretty Venom

ABOUT THE AUTHOR

Ella Fields is a mother and wife who lives in Australia.

While her kids are in school, you might find her talking about her characters to her cat, Bert, and dog, Grub.

She's a notorious chocolate and notebook hoarder who enjoys creating hard-won happily ever afters.

ACKNOWLEDGEMENTS

My husband and my children. <3

Michelle, thank you for everything you do for me. From spreadsheets to beta reading to two hour long phone calls about everything else in-between. Boats for life.

Lucia, I cannot. You already know of the many ways you've helped me. I will find youuuu

Allie, thank you for loving Dash and Peggy so much, and for all your encouragement and feedback. By the time this book releases, I will have hugged you in real life! Say what?!

Giana, your enthusiasm for everything I do means so much to me. You're the truest of true and I love you.

To the rest of my dearest friends, I breathe easier because I have you in my corner and in my life. I love you so much I'd ask someone to hold my Frenchie for you.

Jenny, from editing4indies, book number eight. Insanity. So much love and thank you.

Emma, thank you for proofreading. You're amazing and so damn lovely.

Lauren, thank you for the always epic graphics and helping with a final proofread.

Nina and the team at Social Butterfly PR, you ladies are the epitome of teamwork. Thank you for everything you do.

Stacey, Champagne Book Design, the way you transform words into books astounds me every single time. Thank you.

Annette, you generous, beautiful, soul. Thank you for all you do.

Sarah, from Okay Creations, yet again you've left me speechless and so in love.

My early readers, street team, bloggers, and the members of my Tea Room, I cannot thank you enough for the endless support and love you've shown me. You're all incredible, and I'm full of indescribable gratitude for you all.

To you, if you've picked this up and finished it, thank you. Thank you for returning to read more words from me. If it's your first time, thank you for taking a chance on me.

Thank you, thank you, thank you. <3

Made in the USA
Lexington, KY
26 April 2019